FAITH

"*W*ith all due respect, this don't look like you, ma'am." The security guard at the ferry checkpoint gave her a crooked smile as he handed her driver's license back to her. As Faith took the well-worn card, she noticed the intense farmer's tan on the young man's muscled biceps.

"Yeah, I was trying something," she mumbled as she shoved the card back into her favorite Louis Vuitton purse. Nobody would notice her bag was from two seasons ago on Saint Rose Island anyway.

"They say blondes have more fun," he said in that syrupy southern drawl as he extended an arm to usher her onto the ferry. "But brunette suits you. You got that young Angelina Jolie thing going on."

"Thanks," she said quietly as she hurried to the far end of the platform. Faith dug her phone out of her purse. Two bars and 35 percent. She thumbed to Natalie's name. When her best friend picked up, it didn't sound like she and San Francisco were almost three thousand miles away.

"Nat, thank God," she said. Faith stumbled as the ferry left the dock. All around her, couples and families stuck to the railings and gazed into the distance. She was the only single rider and definitely the only one wearing a whit of black.

"Hey! Are you already there? How's island life? Is it all coming back to you now, like that Celine Dion song?" She could hear Natalie munching on something and phones ringing wildly in the background.

"Not quite yet, just got on the ferry," she said. "Actually, yeah," she said as she gazed onto the banks of the passing islands. "Kind of. I didn't realize I remembered this ferry ride until just now." She had a glimpse of herself at around four years old, clutching her dad's hand while a towheaded toddler pulled at her new dress.

The warm breeze ruffled her hair. Faith wobbled slightly in her Louboutin heels. It had been stupid to wear them. She'd thought battling the hills of San Francisco in four-inch stilettos had made her a pro, but she had nothing on the shaky wooden slats of a southern ferry.

"Oh! Any hotties on board?" Natalie said. "I picture it, like, full of cowboys and gentlemen who stand up when you approach a table."

"Cowboys?" Faith laughed. "It's Georgia, not Texas. And there aren't any grand plantation tables on the ferry for me to try out your approaching-the-table test."

"Well, let me know when you find out. So how is it? I swear, it's not even officially summer yet, and this place is already

Her cousins were grown, and the guys were still making ends meet at board shops and bars. The girls had been husband hunting before they'd even finished their bachelor degrees. When she'd escaped that lazy Southern California surf town after law school and gotten an offer in Silicon Valley, she'd thought her aunt would be proud of her. Instead, all she'd heard was that it was the perfect place to meet a man who could take care of her.

"It's the generation of perpetual boys. They're never growing up," Natalie said.

"I don't know, not according to my cousins. You know the one I babysat growing up? She's twenty-one and just got engaged."

"No shit!" Natalie said. "To who?"

"I don't know, some actor-model in his thirties. He's had a bunch of small parts on television, then some soap commercial or something."

"God, and she can barely drink legally. What a waste," Natalie said.

"Yeah, well. I guess when you're the archetypal California blonde, your expiration date starts looming at that age." Faith pulled her oversize Oliver Peoples sunglasses down her nose. "And my aunt, well, you know. Always comparing me to her perfect sorority sister daughters."

She caught the eye of another ferry worker who walked by, arms full of rope. "Ma'am," he said as he nodded at her with a boyish smile.

"Who was that?" Natalie asked. "Ma'am? Dear God, you really are in another universe."

"Someone who works here," Faith said. "I think they're being overly polite because I stick out here like a sore thumb." She could see a lush green island start to appear in the distance. A couple of pristine white houses faced the ocean.

"Whatever! I saw that spray tan before you left. You'll fit right in."

"I don't know," Faith said as she looked at the women on board. There was an obvious ease to them. Their honey-colored hair was highlighted by the sun and fell in natural waves. Nothing like the processed and perfected "beach waves" painstakingly added at blowout bars in San Francisco.

"Don't be so hard on yourself," Natalie said softly.

"I'm not," Faith said. She pushed the thought of her clan of bubbly blonde and laidback surfer cousins out of her head. *I can't believe I thought coming here would make me feel like I fit in.* "So your aunt didn't tell you anything about this place? That's so mysterious."

"No, not really, but I don't think she knows much," Faith said. "I mean, I don't know how much my mom visited Dad's family out here. And when Dad died seven years ago . . ."

She let her voice trail off. It was true what everyone said. It did get easier not to cry when she remembered the car accident. But that didn't mean it actually got easier.

"I'm sorry," Natalie said.

"No, it's okay." She took a deep, pranayama-guided breath and pulled herself together. "When he died, I don't think introducing me to my southern roots was really at the top of his priority list."

"Yeah, but to not even know you *had* a whole other family over there? Why all the secrecy?"

"Who knows?" Faith said. "Looking back on it, my dad wasn't really the most forthcoming person. But you know, I'm sure he thought he had plenty of time."

"Well, *I* can't believe that your firm let you have the whole freaking summer off! I'm so jealous."

"It's not totally off," Faith said. "I'm doing some remote consulting here."

"Yeah, yeah, nobody wants to hear it," Natalie teased. "Everybody in this town is a virtual worker except me."

Faith hadn't told Natalie just how burned out with corporate law she was. Who got burned out at twenty-six? But as she looked into the clear depths of the jewel-colored water, she knew this was what she needed.

"We're five minutes from docking at Saint Rose on the afternoon express from Fernandina Beach," said a deep, slow voice over an intercom that crackled. "Thank you for riding with us, and y'all have a blessed afternoon."

"Oh, sweet tea, I heard that," Natalie said. "I swear, if you don't have some bodice-ripping southern romance where you christen every room in some wicker-covered plantation home, I'm revoking your woman card."

Faith laughed. "I'll see what I can do. But you'll have to swap the bodice for a tailored suit." She tugged at the fitted black skirt. What had she been thinking, wearing work clothes to go to an island? From San Francisco to Atlanta and then Savannah, she'd felt confident. Poised. Now she felt like she was about to reenact *Hart of Dixie.*

"Ugh, you're killing me. I have to wear a suit; you don't! Go put on a bodice or a sundress or whatever it is you wear down there."

"I'm on it. I'll call or text once things get settled."

"Okay, bye. Love you," Natalie said.

When Faith hung up, the exhaustion really hit her. The ferry rocked to rest at the dock, and as she stepped off, the first security checker offered his arm to her. "Miss Jolie, ma'am," he said with a twinkle in his eye.

"Uh, thanks," she said.

Only one person stood with a sign. "Faith Capshaw" was handwritten in gorgeous print. "Miss Capshaw?" he asked. "I'm Lee, part of the team at Greystone Inn. Pleased to meet you, ma'am. Can I take your bag?"

"It's a purse," she said, suddenly embarrassed.

"Oh! My mistake. Y'all ready? Let's get your suitcase and hit the road. Gonna have to hustle if y'all wanna get there before dark."

"Uh, is this the car?" Faith asked as she eyed the gold cart.

Lee laughed as he hoisted her luggage into the matching gold trailer. His bronzed muscles flexed in the Georgia sun. "Technically a golf car, ma'am. It's part of the estate. Miss Capshaw," he said, holding the little door open for her.

As they whipped through the winding roads, Faith was in awe of the Spanish moss and massive oak trees. Every now and then they passed gorgeous and perfectly preserved white plantation homes. She could only see a couple clearly, with their wraparound porches and Adirondack chairs. Most were hidden down long tree-lined driveways and behind ornate wrought-iron gates.

"Have you worked at Greystone long?" she asked.

"'Bout fifteen years, ma'am," Lee said. "I live there, too." He glanced at her. "From what I hear, you used to spend a good amount o' time here."

"Really?" she asked. "Who told you that?"

He shrugged. "Island life. People talk," he said.

She picked at a cuticle, a terrible habit. Lee didn't seem like the type to offer up information, but she was desperate to find out more. "What do people say?"

"What? You mean 'bout you?"

"Yeah."

He shrugged again. "Not much. Just that you, your cousin, an' your daddy used to spend most summers here."

"A cousin?" she asked. "Which cousin? Maxine? Ashleigh? Was it a girl or boy? From California?"

"Don't know the names, ma'am," he said. "All I heard is that it was just you an' one other, though. Think it was another little girl."

Faith chewed at her lip. There was no way her aunt would have brought just one of her cousins.

"Do you like it?" she asked, probing for a conversation and changing the topic. "Working here, I mean."

"GI's a great place, ma'am," he said. "But I don't know how much I'd call it work."

"What do you mean?"

He laughed. "I mean, I've lived here most o' my life."

"In the inn?"

"Yes, ma'am."

Not much of a talker, huh? Faith wanted to ask. But she was reminded of what her yoga teacher always told them. "Silence can often say everything you need." She struggled to keep from asking questions just to fill the quiet. By the time they pulled up to a driveway with old oak trees lining the way to a two-story bright-white home, she had started to relax.

Lee hopped out, jaunted to her side to open her door, and grabbed her luggage. He nodded toward the front door, and Faith was aware of the harsh click of her heels on the wooden steps. She gave him a look. "Should be open, ma'am," he said, and nodded toward the big wooden front door.

When the door swung open, she walked into what could only be described as a grand foyer that led directly to a parlor. The dark wooden floors were obviously newly polished.

"I don't give a damn!" a low voice yelled.

"What the hell is wrong with you? Don't you—"

Faith wavered at the french doors as she took in the two men arguing. They looked similar, obviously brothers. Both with sandy-blond hair and piercing light eyes.

"Hi," Faith said. "I'm—"

"Faith Capshaw," one of them finished for her. The one with the curious eyes fired up with a blaze of something she

. The other one had nothing but

he took
e.

. Alex and Mr. Caleb Caldwell," Lee

nt. "I

ith a laugh. "Lee, what the hell? Since
.thern hospitality?"

ing

na taught me," he said, which seemed to

Lee

e
s

.ld say something more, a coiffed woman
ded through the set of doors on the oppo-
oom, hair a silvered blonde and cut short. It
. trousers and silk blouse perfectly. She shot
e and walked directly toward Faith.

, I'm so happy you're here," the woman said as
aith toward her.

.!" Faith said. "Are you . . . I'm sorry. Are we

man laughed and tossed her head back. "No, sweet-
'm sorry. I'm Mae Caldwell, mother of these two," she
.nd nodded to the men. "And second mother to Lee."

' Faith said. She heard the disappointment in her voice.
.at was I expecting? A whole new family?

ou must be tired. We'll get you set up upstairs, and I'll fix
ou some supper. I know you told me on the phone that
you're eager to see the land and house, but you can see it in
the morning. It's not far from here. Alex will take you,"
she said.

Faith looked toward the men, and the one with the icy gaze
rolled his eyes. *Great,* Faith thought.

"He's the best at flying the plane," Mae said as s[...]
Faith's elbow and led her toward a wide spiral staircas[...]

"Plane?" Faith asked.

"Well, you could take a boat, but it would take a while."

"Oh. I see," Faith said. She was clearly out of her eleme[...]
have had a long day. Perhaps I should just go to bed."

"Of course. Lee, will you show Faith to her room? I'm g[...]
to stay down here and talk to your brothers."

Brothers? Clearly Alex and Caleb are related, but how does [...]
factor into the situation? Was he adopted?

Faith smiled at Mae uncertainly as Lee led her upstairs. Sh[...]
heard Mae head down the hall, but she still felt a pair of eye[...]
as they bored into her. When she glanced behind her, she saw[...]
Alex. He watched her with something like hatred in his eyes.

She quickly looked away. *What did I do? Why is he so angry?*

Lee saw the look on her face as they reached the landing, and
he looked toward Alex. "Don't mind him, ma'am. It's nothing
personal," he said quietly. "I've known Alex his whole life. We
were best friends when we were kids."

Were? So what happened?

She followed Lee down the long hallway. Large wooden fans
provided a cool breeze. "What's wrong?" she asked. "With
him, I mean."

"Alex, he just doesn't really like outsiders. 'Specially women.
Don't you worry, though. Mama Mae keeps him in line.
Keeps us all in line," he said with a wink.

Faith tried to shrug it off as she stepped into the room. Lee placed her luggage on the king-size four-poster bed and left her with a little bow. The warm walnut floors matched the wood of the bed and curtain rods. She tried to take it all in, but the white bedding looked too delicious.

She was asleep as soon as her head hit the pillow.

2

ALEX

*A*s always, Alex was up as soon as the pitch-black sky started to lighten. He'd always let the sun dictate his mornings. Just before dawn was the only time the heat and humidity were absent from a Saint Rose summer. He pulled on his jersey, Nike shorts, and Brooks shoes before sneaking downstairs for his morning run. Immediately, he was on autopilot. His body had memorized the loop of half the island years ago.

By the second mile, he'd lost himself in memories and thoughts. When he'd left the island at twenty, he swore he'd never come back. He was turning thirty this year. *How the hell have I already been sucked back here for almost four years?*

Like always, a crystal-clear picture of his wife filled his mind. *Late wife*, he reminded himself.

He hated that word. It was almost as bad as "widower." Even more, he hated the way people looked at him when they found out or were reminded. That combination of pity and sorrow. *And what am I supposed to say, anyway? Oh, thanks, but don't worry about it. She was a cheating bitch?*

Alex shook his head, willed Rebecca out of his mind. *Ex-wife,* he repeated to himself. *Ex-wife.*

Of course, she'd never had the chance to become his ex-wife. How was it fair that she got the late wife title, made him a widower before he was even thirty?

If I could go back to that night . . .

"Stop it," Alex told himself aloud. His voice sounded thunderous in the otherwise quiet. Before dawn, the island was most still. The crickets had retired for the night and the neighbors' roosters weren't awake yet. He concentrated on his breathing as he rounded the familiar oak tree at the start of the Harris property, the one with the branches that looked like they were praying.

Why'd she get the easy way out? The night of the accident, he'd finally bundled up the nerve to tell her he wanted a divorce. *I should have stopped her. I knew she'd been drinking.*

"She wasn't drunk," he told the darkness that had started to turn to pink.

"Just barely over the limit," was what the sheriff had told him. "Point oh nine."

He remembered the raised silver brow of the sheriff perfectly but not his name. But the coroner? With her, he remembered everything. First name, last name, and how her buttoned-up shirt clashed with her bright-red hair. "Fetal alcohol syndrome can be caused at the first trimester, you know," she'd told him.

"Fatal what?" he'd asked, dazed.

"*Fetal* alcohol syndrome? Oh, you didn't . . . your wife, she was . . ."

"Was what?" Alex had demanded as he pulled and played with his wedding ring in the cold waiting room.

"She was pregnant. Not far along at all, about ten weeks. I'm so sorry."

"Fuck you," Alex said as he came to the end of his run. He was covered in sweat. The first time he'd run more than a couple of miles had been the night he'd found out. It had been intuitive. He'd gotten home from the coroner's, put on his gym shoes, and had just run until his legs felt like they'd give out.

The next morning, he'd dumped the bacon—Rebecca's favorite brand—right into the trash. By the time he'd purged the refrigerator, pantry, and cupboards of anything that wasn't purely healthy, there was barely anything left. In nearly four years, he'd transformed his body into a flawless temple fueled by high protein and good fats, accompanied by a rigid running regimen and a lifting schedule in the afternoons he never deviated from.

Rebecca would be proud, he thought as he grabbed a towel in the mudroom and wiped down his chest. She'd given him hell for his aversion to the gym, his unhealthy diet, all throughout their marriage. "You're taking yourself right to an early grave," she'd always chided. "And leaving me where?"

"Look who's talking," he said as he opened the fridge to retrieve the bottle of whey protein shake he'd made last night.

The kitchen was quiet, but it wouldn't be for long. Soon enough, his mama would be awake and whipping up a full breakfast to showcase that southern hospitality. Given that girl who'd arrived, there was no doubt his mama would go all-out.

"Y'all be hospitable to her, now," Mama had said when she'd told him, Caleb, and Lee about her.

"Hospitable?" Alex had nearly barked. "The inn's been in our family since 1852! And she just expects to show up, and—"

"That's enough," his mama had said, quieting him with a single finger in the air. "Do as I say."

"Yes, ma'am," he'd said. Alex had left the room before he was tempted to argue more.

The sun had started to creep over the horizon. He shot upstairs and jumped in the shower to rinse off quickly before heading downstairs to fix his breakfast. Otherwise, he'd never have the kitchen to himself.

Alone in the kitchen, he scrambled some egg whites mixed with spinach and hunkered down at the round table in the nook. By the time he'd finished his plate, he could hear his mama in the kitchen whisking pancake batter together.

"Mornin', Mama," he said as he rinsed his plate.

"Good mornin', baby," she said. "Y'all sleep well?"

"Well enough," he said, his usual reply to their morning pleasantries. His mama's makeup was already on and flawless, an A-line navy dress beneath her spotless white apron. She'd given up long ago on convincing him to "dress proper" for meals. "Why don't you let the cook do that?" he asked as he watched her manage breakfast with finesse.

"I like to cook when I can," she said as she turned on a second burner. "Wouldn't hurt you to learn to cook a little, either," she added pointedly.

"Mama, don't start," he said. "I never hear you telling Caleb he needs to learn to cook."

"Caleb? Honey, I'll die a happy woman if your brother ever even learns to operate the toaster. Besides, he's the baby of the family," she said with a sigh. "You know what they say 'bout them."

"Too busy sailing the high seas and chasing sirens to learn what a frying pan is?" Alex asked.

His mama swatted at him. "Don't you be talking about your brother like that. He can't help he's a ladies' man."

"Yeah, that's what he is," Alex said.

"Hush, now. Can you get those melons Lee picked up from the stand, baby? They're in the spare pantry."

He was happy to have an excuse to escape the conversation, though he hated being reminded of Lee. He looked so *old*. When he'd left the island ten years ago, Lee had already signed on for a life of helping to run the inn. How he did that while still being the island's game warden, Alex didn't know. What he did know was that he saw that spark between his best friend—*former* best friend—and Rebecca the first time he'd brought her to Saint Rose. It was the primary reason it had also been the last time.

In four years, Alex and Lee had managed to speak no more than a handful of words to each other.

"Here you go, Mama," he said, setting down the ripe melons on the butcher-block countertop.

"Thank you. Oh, and the berries, too? I'm sorry, it just

slipped my mind that Matt picked a whole bushel of them the other day. Out on the back porch," she said as she started to whip homemade cream.

Alex sighed and went to the back porch. *Matt and his perpetual need to impress. As if Yale Law School and two Ironmans aren't enough.* He could barely remember Matt from childhood. He'd always just been the weird cousin whose room was lined with trophies. When Mama had told them that Matt was moving in with them when they were teenagers, he'd immediately tried to argue.

"He's your cousin, Alex," Mama had said. "And his parents just died," she added in a whisper, as if Matt were already there. "Show a little empathy, please."

He picked up the bags of berries. Already, the morning heat had started to settle over the estate. *At least that fancy degree's been good for something*, he thought as he surveyed the land. It was Matt who got Greystone on the historic registry, which came with the option to apply for grants to update it.

When he got back to the kitchen, his brother, Lee, and Matt hovered around the Keurig. Caleb and Lee were in their usual casual clothes. Matt, as always, looked like he'd spent just as much time getting ready as Mama.

"No," Mama said as Caleb tried to steal one of the few golden pancakes. "And we'll be taking breakfast in the formal dining room today."

"Why so fancy?" Caleb asked as he poured creamer into his favorite mug.

"Her highness," Alex said as he nodded upstairs.

"Alex," Mama said, a warning in her tone. "And just so you

know, we'll be waiting to all eat together, too. Y'all can have some toast if you're peckish."

"*Mama*," Alex said but was cut off by Matt's immediate, "Yes, ma'am."

"This girl's causing nothing but headaches," Alex grumbled under his breath.

"Beg your pardon?" Mama asked with a raised brow. "You say somethin'?"

"No, ma'am," he said as he watched Caleb examine the settings on the toaster like it was a spaceship. "Medium's usually pretty safe, Captain," he said.

"Thanks, man," Caleb said. He gave him a lopsided grin.

"And Alex, don't think you're skipping breakfast with the family this morning," Mama said. "I don't care if you already ate. I'll make some of that bland egg white nonsense if that's what it takes. You're not going to be rude."

"Yes, ma'am," he said sullenly.

When the girl finally came downstairs, she was dressed in what Alex could only consider hiking clothes. The light khaki shorts hugged her hips, and he could tell the seemingly plain white T-shirt was expensive.

"Mmm, smells great!" she said. Her long brown hair was knotted up on top of her head. "What is it?" she asked.

He tried not to look at her as Mama ushered her toward the formal dining room and ticked off the lavish breakfast she'd made. That was his policy for women. *Don't look, and definitely don't touch.* After all, he'd had enough women in the past few years to last a lifetime. When he really needed a warm body, there was always Erica. That widow out in

Savannah knew where he was coming from. No talking, just fucking, and that suited both of them.

Still, as he sat down to breakfast with Matt on one side and Mama on the other, he couldn't help but notice how hot Faith was. Those lips were incredible. It was the kind of pout women paid thousands of dollars for. The kind Rebecca tried in vain to copy with lip-plumping gloss and overdrawing her lips.

"Sugar, Faith? Cream?" Mama asked her.

"Oh no. Thank you. I like it black," Faith said. When she parted those full lips to smile, Alex had to look down.

It had taken all his willpower not to let his eyes linger on her ass when she'd gone into the dining room. She wasn't just hot. She was stupid hot. The kind of sexiness that only a big city could produce.

Across the table from him, Faith responded warmly to Caleb's flirtations. But there was a wall up in front of her that was nearly palpable. "You a teacher?" Caleb asked her.

"No," Faith said with a laugh. "Why do you ask? Do I look like a teacher?"

Not like any teacher I ever had, Alex thought.

"I don't know," Caleb said as he eyed her. "But I ask because you got the summer off."

"Oh. Well no, not really," Faith said. "I'm an attorney, but I'm working remotely for a few weeks."

"I am, too," Matt piped up.

Alex knew it came off as being interested, but what Matt really wanted to see was if she was any competition.

"What field?"

"Corporate law," Faith said. She wrinkled her nose. "Sounds boring, I know," she told the rest of the table.

"Not at all," Matt said. "I'm in estates, mostly. Not much demand for corporate law round here," he said with a practiced smile.

Faith laughed again. "Yes, I suppose not."

"Corporate law is fascinating, though. I took a few additional electives on it. At Yale. That's quite impressive that you found a firm in San Francisco. So early out of law school, I mean."

"Why do you think it's so early?" she asked, dredging a triangle of pancake in syrup.

"Well, I just assumed," Matt said. "Because you're so young."

Faith giggled. "Twenty-six, but thank you," she said.

What in the hell? Is Matt flirting? He scowled in Matt's general direction. Caleb, he was used to, but this was a first. Women. They always do this. Turn men into animals who only seek out pleasure.

"So what are your plans for today?" Matt asked her.

"Actually," Mama said as she finished the last slice of melon. "Alex is going to take Faith up. Show her our little island."

"Oh," Matt said, dejected.

"Yeah, I'm really excited," Faith said. "I've never been in anything but a commercial plane before."

"Well, are you ready to go or not?" Alex snapped at her.

She fumbled, caught off guard. "Oh! Sure, yeah. Let me just—"

"Alex," Mama said firmly. "Watch yourself."

"Meet me down at the landing strip in thirty minutes, then," he said. "May I be excused?" he asked Mama.

3

FAITH

What's his problem?

Faith watched him storm out the door. Mae just shook her head and gave Faith an apologetic smile.

"It's nothing personal," Caleb said as Faith's brow knitted. "He's just like that. Sometimes."

Nothing personal. Caleb was the second person to tell her that.

"I can take you by boat, if you want," Caleb offered. He had an infectious grin, she had to give him that. But the whole player vibe was a turnoff. She'd met plenty of guys like that back in California. Most of them were in suits and ties, of course. No, maybe it was her cousins and their surfboards that Caleb more closely resembled.

"No, thank you, though," she said. In her head, she calculated how much time would be saved if she just sucked it up and sat in awkward silence with Alex in the plane for a few minutes. "I'm fine going by air."

I made it through law school, I can make it through this, she told herself as she stood up.

Faith picked up her plate to take it to the kitchen, but Mae stopped her. "No, dear, don't you worry about that. Jessie will clean up."

"Jessie?" Faith asked. *How many people live here?*

"Yes, she takes care of the lion's share of cleaning round here. With my help, of course," Mae said. "She also does a spot of cooking from time to time when Gwen is too busy."

"Gwen's the cook," Lee told her as he scooped another pancake onto his plate.

"Oh." *They have servants? How many?* She really was in a strange new land.

"Y'all better get going," Mae said. "And don't you fret about Alex. He's moody, that's all."

"Yeah, the kind of mood that lasts four years," Caleb said quietly.

"Caleb," Mae said, a warning.

"Sorry, ma'am," he said.

"So where's the landing?"

"I can show you—"

"Caleb, sit back down," Mae said. "Faith is perfectly capable of walking the few feet to the strip herself. It's just the first trail to the right from the front drive. It'll soon turn to asphalt. Five-minute walk, you can't miss it."

"Thank you. Ma'am." Faith added as she tested the word out. It felt foreign in her mouth, but nobody seemed to notice.

"Just call me Mama Mae, dear. Or Mama, if you're comfortable."

Faith left the thick cloth napkin beside her plate and headed out of the house. The lawn stretched for what seemed to be miles, a rich green like she'd never seen before. In the distance, she caught sight of horse stables. A young man was leading two mares, one brown and one white, toward a fenced-in area.

The morning sun was warm, the early humidity adding a sheen to her skin. Before she'd left California, Natalie had told her, "Southern women don't sweat, they glow."

Faith retied her hair as she made her way along the trail. She pulled a ball cap out of her waistband and pulled her hair through the gap in the back. A small prop plane whirred ahead of her, and Alex stood with his back to the trail.

Suddenly, a bundle of nerves exploded in her stomach. Faith ducked behind one of the oaks to calm herself.

Except for the scowl that seemed permanently etched onto his face, Alex was incredibly fucking fine. There was no denying it. He was a touch taller than Caleb, probably just over six feet. The mop of dirty blond hair, the scruff of a beard, and those cold blue eyes were undeniable.

It didn't hurt that below the tight T-shirt and worn jeans, his body was sculpted like some kind of God's.

Alex turned quickly. His eyes caught hers, and his face went black. She felt redness creep across her face, the shame of getting caught. Without a word, he climbed into the plane, and the idling engine roared to life.

Faith's heart pounded mercilessly against her chest. She felt like she was a kid who'd been caught passing notes in study hall.

Alex stared at her and lifted his hand in frustration. *You coming or not?* he seemed to ask.

Faith hustled toward the plane and climbed into the passenger side—thankful for the growl of the engine to drown out the sound of her heart.

He gestured roughly to the seatbelts, and before she'd even clipped them into place, they were taking off down the short runway. It was unlike anything she'd experienced before, worlds apart from the demanding commercial flights she was used to. Faith sucked in her breath as she felt the wheels lift off the pavement. In seconds, they were soaring above the greenery.

The massive estate looked like a miniature. The wilderness below, wild and thorny, was also beautiful. *Like a rose*, Faith thought. Just past the rising forest, the land sloped down toward white sandy beaches. Thick, tall trees framed the paradise below.

"That's Smuggler's Cove, there," Alex said and pointed to a natural cul-de-sac.

His voice still carried that southern drawl, but it wasn't nearly as thick as his mom's, Caleb's, or anyone else's who lived at the inn. She was still trying to figure out exactly how they were all related. "Why's that?" she asked, eager to keep the conversation afloat, especially if it had nothing to do with how she had crept up on him.

"Why do you think?" Alex asked pointedly. He sighed. "Pirates used to bring all kinds of goods ashore there. Over there," he said, and pointed to another white plantation home, "that one's yours."

"Mine," she repeated as she gazed down at the property. From above, it looked like all the others. "Can we go down?" she asked.

He nodded and started to angle the plane toward an open field.

As they descended, a strong memory from what must have been twenty years ago hit her hard. She remembered being in a similar plane, pressed against her father's leg, and peering over him toward the islands below. *They'd seemed a lot farther away then,* she thought. And there was that little blonde girl again, her sticky fingers gripped between Faith's. She shook her head to clear the memories.

As soon as they landed and Alex killed the engine, she knew this estate was nothing like Greystone. *But maybe it can be,* she told herself. The grass was overgrown and wild with clovers. It was just a short hike toward the house, but Alex kept a fast clip just ahead of her.

It was still early, but the heat had already started to get to her. "Hey!" she called to him. "Can you slow down?"

Alex turned briefly. "There's only one house here," he said. "You know where you're going. 'Sides, I thought you'd been here before?"

"I . . . I don't remember much," she said. "Just glimpses, you know? I must have been five, six, or seven at the most the last time I was here. Mostly I just remember from a few old photos."

He looked almost sorry for a second.

Think of the upside, she told herself. The property was relatively far inland, which was good news since she'd read that rising tides had washed away some small houses and shacks used for fishing.

As they approached the house, muscle memory took over. She somehow remembered where there was an old stump that was hidden in the tall grass. She remembered tea parties with imaginary china while her little cousin pretended the Mad Hatter was in attendance, the scratchy weeds that flicked at her legs, and how bizarrely enormous the spiders had seemed at the time.

Faith remembered the two of them as they raced toward the grand estate when the triangle dinner bell rang. The boom of her father's voice in the kitchen.

As she approached the house now, it seemed like something out of a nightmare—and half the size of that she remembered. Of course, she'd forgotten the house entirely until she'd received the call from that estate agent. As soon as he mentioned Saint Rose and described the house and island, though, these nagging little memories started to pop up to surprise her.

Faith knew she shouldn't feel emotional about a house she'd forgotten about for two decades, but she couldn't help it. Now that it had returned to her, she realized it carried precious memories: her father, though he'd been so sad at that time, and the little blonde cousin whose name continued to evade her but even so seemed so much warmer than the cousins she'd grown up with in California.

It stung to see the house in such disrepair. Alex reached up to a nook on the porch and fished out a key. The wraparound was covered in dust and natural debris. "It could use some sprucing up," she said as she looked around. One of the windows was boarded up, and the paint peeled away in numerous locations.

"It's been sitting here unused for a lot of years," he told her as he unlocked the front door. "Think you'd be in better shape? After you. *Ma'am*," he said as he held the door open for her.

Faith wrinkled her nose as she stepped into what must have once been a fantastic foyer. In fact, she could somewhat remember the grandiosity. The Persian rugs and the twinkling chandelier. Now, it was covered in layers of dust that made the floors look dull. Overhead, there was exposed wiring, but the gorgeous chandelier she remembered was long gone. Faith coughed as she started to explore the first floor.

Room by room, she took the house in. It has "good bones," a realtor or flipper would say. But that probably didn't do her much good on an isolated island like this. *What am I supposed to do with this? Fix it up and then . . . what?* She'd only briefly looked at the price of real estate on the island because there was absolutely nothing for sale. When she'd emailed one realtor in Savannah, they'd told her, "People on the island tend to stay there. Properties are generally passed down generations."

Faith traced her finger along the intricate molding pattern of the wainscoting. "I have no idea what to do with it," she told Alex. "This is weird, but it's like a bad print of what I remember. You know? Like I feel protective of it, though I barely remember it."

He shrugged. "Maybe it should be a wilderness refuge. There are a lot of small land and sea animals that are only found on the Georgia coast."

She looked up, surprised, but Alex gazed fixedly out one of the windows. Or attempted to, anyway. The glass was so old it had turned cloudy. "Really? I didn't know that," she said.

"I'm not surprised. Look, it's up to you. I was just giving my opinion." He turned and walked out of the room. Judging by the built-ins, it used to be a library. *Why is he so touchy about everything? Apparently even Georgia wildlife.*

Faith found him in the kitchen, where he examined the carpentry. "Can we go back now?" she asked. Being in the house, on that island, had started to flood her mind with scattered memories. She had flashes and glimpses of the past but without enough glue to piece it all together.

He looked at her, wordless, and started heading back to the front door.

"I guess that's a yes," she muttered under her breath.

Alex locked up and started to walk back to the plane. *Did I say something wrong? Maybe he has some kind of connection to this place.* "Thank you for taking me," she said. Faith had to half jog, half walk to keep pace with him. "I . . . I have a lot to think about."

Alex didn't say anything. She could swear he somehow walked even faster.

Faith looked around the property. It would be nice to restore the house. Fix it up. After all, she had the money now . . .

Halfway to the plane, she gave up on keeping up with him. Instead, she let him barrel on ahead. He was brusque and harsh, but she knew he wouldn't just leave her there. Well, maybe he would, but his mom certainly wouldn't allow it.

She fell back and watched his ass all the way back to the

plane. *What a waste*, she thought. *With that attitude, there's no way he's getting laid. Why in the world does he clearly spend all that time honing his body?*

Faith felt herself flush again. *I'm the one who needs to get laid*, she thought. Running around this island, checking out the rear end of a total asshole who couldn't even drum up a little common decency.

"Y'all coming?" Alex called to her.

I wish, she wanted to say, but she bit her tongue. "Yeah, yeah," she said.

It really was too bad he was such a stick-in-the-mud. If he weren't, he'd be just her type.

4

ALEX

*H*e fell into his bed, exhausted and unable to remember the last time he'd gone to bed well after nightfall. Alex didn't want to think about how tough his morning run would be. However, stressing about workouts was still better than thinking about that girl for one more minute.

He'd been on edge the entire time they were together. The minutes with her had absolutely dragged. No matter what he had tried, none of his usual tricks worked. There was just something about her. Every part of her screamed sensuality, and it was a feeling he wasn't comfortable with. As soon as they'd landed back at Greystone, he couldn't wait to get away from her. It had been a nightmare to force himself not to burst into a full run back to the inn.

Alex had thought that once they reached the inn, it would be easy to avoid her. That hadn't been the case. Caleb had pounced as soon as they'd stepped through the door.

"Y'all have a good time?" Caleb had asked. He stretched out the drawl like he always did around Yankees.

"Yes!" Faith had said with a smile. "It wasn't what I expected. But it has a lot of potential."

"You a real estate tycoon, ma'am?" Caleb had teased her.

When she giggled, that smile and those lips lit up the room. "That hadn't been in the plan, but you never know."

"How 'bout I show you around the property?" Caleb asked.

"Sure. Just let me go put on some more sunblock."

Caleb gave Alex a wink as she squeezed between them toward the staircase. They'd both watched, unabashedly, as she ascended. With every sway of her hips, Alex willed the shorts to ride up higher, even as he chastised himself internally for such a thought.

"Goddamn," Caleb whispered to him. "You ever seen anything like that?"

"Not round here, maybe," Alex said. "But that's not sayin' much."

"Right," Caleb said with a laugh. He elbowed him in the ribs. "If they were all made like that on the mainland, you never would have come back here. Sorry, man," Caleb corrected himself.

Alex could see guilt for Rebecca all over his face. He didn't say anything. Instead, he went into the family room with its picture windows overlooking the property. He heard Faith trot down the stairs, and Caleb let out an appreciative whistle. The door slammed behind them. Through the window, he watched Caleb offer an elbow while Faith laughed and swatted him away playfully.

With a growl, Alex stomped to the kitchen, where Gwen was prepping. "Hiya, baby," she said. Gwen had been part of the home, largely the kitchen, ever since he could remember. "You hungry? Want me to make you something?"

"No. Thanks, though," he said. "I'm just going to make a sandwich."

Gwen wrinkled her nose. "With that expensive 'bread' you get shipped here?" she said. She shook her head. "You know, we have bread here."

"This is low carb, high protein," Alex said.

"Bread's not s'posed to be low carb or high protein."

Alex piled the sandwich high with the chicken cuts they sourced from the farm on the other side of the island. On a whim, he made a second sandwich and wrapped them both in tinfoil.

"You goin' somewhere?" Gwen asked.

"Fishing."

Alex packed up the gear, grabbed a hat, and headed for the pier. Fishing in the abandoned location was the one thing besides running that relaxed him. Without reception, without a watch, hours felt like minutes. By the time the sun started to set, he had no bites but was sure the tension Faith stirred up had to have subsided.

Damn, he thought as he made the short trek back to the inn. *I didn't think about Rebecca once.*

But as soon as he walked in the door, Faith was the first thing he saw. She'd changed into a familiar-looking white sundress spotted with tiny rosebuds. He couldn't put his finger on it, and then he realized it was one of Mama's vintage dresses.

Alex knew it from photographs. With that simple change, the last traces of proper corporate lawyer faded away.

Her eyes widened as Caleb crowed, "Look what the cat dragged in. Fishless to boot," he added as he scanned for any catches.

"Like you're one to talk," Alex told him. He couldn't remember the last time Caleb had gone fishing.

"You fish," Faith said. It was a statement, not a question.

"Can't call yourself a local unless you do, ma'am," he answered as he moved past them to put the gear away. Lee jumped out of his path, as always, while Matt hovered in the corner and took in how the dress hugged every one of her curves. Not that he could blame him.

In the storage room, he heard murmuring and the clinking of iced tea in glasses while he hung up the gear. She'd seemed so surprised at his suggestion of a wildlife preserve. *Isn't that what Californians do? Sit around and talk about saving the environment? What does she think I am, some kind of yokel who doesn't know there is a great big world out there?*

When he reappeared in the great room, his mama was in the center, where she led the conversations as always. "Alex! So glad you could join us. You missed dinner," she said pointedly. "I called."

"I was at the pier," he said.

She sniffed but didn't say anything more about his absence. "Well, at least join us for some sweet tea. Sweeten it with some gin for you?" she asked as she moved toward the cocktail table. The pitcher of golden iced tea was slick with condensation, eager to be poured into one of the cut-crystal glasses she made sure Jessie always kept perfectly polished.

"With, please," he said.

Alex watched Caleb fawn over Faith. He circled her like a shark and mercilessly sized her up. Either Faith didn't notice or didn't care. He was certain it was the latter. For all her sense of wonder and enchantment of the island, he knew you couldn't make it as a corporate attorney in San Francisco without being tough. *She probably uses that faux naivety to her advantage like they all do*, he thought as a cold glass was pressed into his hand.

"I made it strong," his mama whispered to him through gritted teeth. "Maybe it'll help loosen you up."

As much as he wanted to down the drink and get the hell out of there, he couldn't tear his eyes away from Faith. *What is her game, anyway? Why leave what had to be a hellishly competitive environment to spend the summer hanging around an island and looking at a decrepit old house?*

Faith leaned forward to set her glass down on a handmade carved-stone side table, giving him a view directly down the dress. He glimpsed her lacy white bra and deep cleavage and felt himself start to stiffen.

Fuck. Maybe I should text Erica soon and get this out of my system. Alex took a long swallow and finished the spiked sweet tea.

"Thirsty," Caleb commented and gave him a knowing grin.

"More like tired," he said. "Mama, you mind if I'm excused? I need to hit the hay, I'm beat."

"Well, if that's what you need," she said carefully with an arched brow.

"Thanks. Night, y'all," he called to the room in general. He was met with a sea of replies, though it was Faith's that stuck in his head. That seductive, low growl she had.

Alex made his way upstairs and clicked the heavy wooden door shut. He flipped on the fan and pulled his shirt over his head. Like expected, as soon as he closed his eyes his mind's eye was filled with that cleavage shot Faith had unknowingly given him.

He moaned, pulled one of the pillows over his face, and commanded Faith to leave his head.

Soon enough, she was gone—replaced by Rebecca in that tight black-velvet dress of hers that had always been his favorite.

She sat on the familiar tufted gray couch while tears of mascara ran down her face. "I can't believe you did that! You went through my phone?" She blubbered. "That's fucked up, Alex."

"*That's* fucked up? You think that's the fucked up part of the situation?" he said. She looked tiny curled up on that couch with a nearly empty glass of wine in her hand. He was aware of how he must seem as he loomed over her. Dangerous, like a predator.

"Yes!" she said. "I trusted you—"

"No," he said as he cut her off. "You don't get to say that. I trusted you. And not that it matters, I didn't 'go through' your phone. I was trying to use your phone, the one you were too stupid to even lock, to call your goddamned sister and wish her happy birthday because mine died! Jesus, Rebecca, you couldn't even delete the texts? You really think I'm stupid, don't you?"

"I didn't know you'd be going through my phone!" she yelled. A fresh torrent of tears threatened to fall.

"Fuck this. We're not getting anywhere," he said. "Just tell me who he is! And 'Mary'? You saved his name as Mary? What kind of idiot do you think I am?"

Rebecca started to choke on her tears while Alex sat down in the matching chair and dropped his head into his hands. He was too angry to fight anymore.

He heard the jingle of keys, looked up, and saw Rebecca stomping barefoot to the door. "Where the hell do you think you're going?" he yelled after her, but she slammed the door.

He only waited a minute before he jumped up to follow her. Surely she was going to his house—whoever it was she was fucking. *You gotta find her*, he told himself.

He didn't have to go far. Her little Nissan was flipped at the end of the road, lights still on. Alex knew she was dead before he even got to her. His own headlights lit up her mangled arm, which stuck out from below the crumpled metal.

Alex bolted upright in bed, covered in sweat. *Jesus. Even after all this time.* Some nights he knew he was remembering, dreaming, but he still couldn't stop it. *If I'd just stopped her. If I'd followed her right away—*

The clock told him it was three in the morning, but he didn't care. He needed to run. Alex jumped out of bed, grabbed some socks out of the drawer, and bounded downstairs. No lights needed to be turned on; he knew every nook and cranny of the inn.

As soon as he started to round the house toward the trail out back, he heard a boat engine running. *Fishing? At this time of night?* Unfamiliar men's voices erupted nearby in hushed tones. Alex slowed, pressed himself against the house, and peered around a corner. A trio of masked men approached the inn like they owned it. They didn't even try to be careful.

What the hell? However, it didn't seem to be the house they were after. They went directly to the cross Mama had erected in the front yard alongside the flagpole. One of the men tossed a bucketful of liquid onto the old hewn wood, while another lit and threw a lighter.

"Hey!" Alex called out instinctively. Any trace of fear was gone.

One of the men turned toward him and fired a pistol aimlessly.

"Fuck," he cried as he jumped back behind the house and covered his head.

The shot rang in his ear, but he heard the thud of their feet as they departed. Caleb, Lee, and Matt's voices burst through the front door. "What the fuck?" Caleb cried. Alex rounded the corner and saw their faces lit up by the flames.

"Alex!" Matt yelled.

"It's okay, they're gone," Alex said.

"What the hell is this—"

"Look at this," Lee said as Caleb ran for the house. He picked up a piece of plywood beside the fire. Written in crude Sharpie was, "Go Home Upity Bitch."

"Nice spelling," Matt commented. He stepped aside to let Caleb douse the flames.

Alex felt eyes on him. He looked up and saw his mama and

Faith as they peered through the windows. Both appeared worried, with his mama's hair wrapped in a silk scarf and Faith with her long hair in a loose braid that hung across her faded Pepperdine T-shirt.

Uppity bitch. Obviously the warning was for Faith, but why? She stared at the cross, confused and horrified.

What the hell is this all about?

5

FAITH

*A*s Faith stood beside Mae in the middle of the night and watched the men put out the flames, Mae rubbed her arm. "It's probably just teenagers," Mae said reassuringly.

Faith wasn't convinced. "I don't know," she said. "It's not like Greystone is the most opportunistic location."

"Don't worry, honey," Mae said. "Maybe you, you know, made an impression on someone while you were traveling. Don't take this the wrong way, but you don't exactly look like a local."

Faith pulled a face. She knew that was true, but so what? Since when did teenagers go on cross-burning rampages because someone was wearing a suit instead of cargo shorts?

"You should go back to bed, dear. Try to get some more sleep."

The look in Mae's eyes was one of pure motherly love. Faith's throat tightened at the sight. She couldn't remember her mother, of course, and her dad's way of showing affection had always been stunted. *Is this what it feels like to have a mom?* "No, I'm okay," Faith told her. "I don't think I could sleep much anyway. Besides, it'll be light soon."

"At least try. Trust me," Mae said.

Faith spent thirty minutes tossing in bed before she gave up. Outside, she could hear the running water and low voices of the guys as they put out the last of the flames. *What time is it in California?* Faith checked her phone. Nearly two in the morning, but it was Saturday. Natalie would probably be buzzed and lined up for pizza somewhere.

You up? she texted her. Immediately, she saw ellipses appear.

Not for much longer. WYD? Natalie replied.

Faith debated how much to tell her, if anything. Typing out, *NM, just watching a burning cross with a threat for me to get put out* looked insane and horrifying. Besides, surely it wouldn't be as crazy come morning. Faith settled for, *Nothing, miss you.*

As Natalie talked about the night's events, from getting kicked off the bar she'd been dancing on to seeing a recent fling at a club who ignored her, life back in California suddenly seemed tame compared to Saint Rose. *What time is it there?* Natalie asked.

Close to 5.

In the morning?

Couldn't sleep, Faith replied. Outside, she heard someone put the hose away. She itched to tell Natalie. Maybe someone from the real world could make her see it wasn't so wild. *Want to know something weird?*

Always.

Middle of the night, some guys came and burned this cross in the front yard. And left a sign that said, "Go home, uppity bitch."

Wait, what? Was it for you?

Seems like it.

Hold on, I'm calling u.

No, don't. Can't talk now, people are asleep.

But WTF, Faith? That's straight up some KKK shit. I knew it was Georgia, but WTF?

Idk, Faith replied. *Maybe it wasn't a big deal after all.*

You need to get out of there, Natalie said. *How long does it take to get an estate in order anyway?*

It wasn't like Faith hadn't thought about it. After all, it wouldn't look strange if she left early. She could blame work and nobody would know. Still, she'd never backed down from a challenge, and that's exactly what the night had been. *Working on it,* she finally replied.

I'm worried about you. How did checking out the prop go?

Was weird, too, Faith said. *I'd totally forgotten about that place, but as soon as we landed, all these little jigsaw pieces started to come back to me.*

Landed?

Took a little plane. One of the guys here flies.

Ohhhhh. There be men on the island, huh? Now I'm really worried about you. Or them.

Faith grinned. *Don't be. He's a total moody douche.*

Ew. Anyone there know your fam? I mean the nonbitchy side?

Natalie really did know everything about her. *Not much,* she replied. *But I keep thinking about this little girl I used to play with here. One person said I used to play with a cousin here but didn't know her name.*

Weird. You need me to come out there? I have two years of vacay saved up.

No! It's fine, really. Go to bed.

By the time she'd reassured Natalie that she would be fine, there was no denying it was dawn. Mae had been right, she should have tried to actually sleep. Today she was supposed to be taking a day trip to Savannah, and the thought of running errands all day was daunting. It would definitely be a multiple-cups-of-coffee kind of day.

Downstairs, she could hear someone turning on the stove while pans were pulled from cupboards. Faith dragged herself out of bed and to the shower. As she was standing in the clawfoot tub with the white curtain encircling her, sunlight poured through the windows. When she turned off the water, birds sang outside. *Maybe I was overreacting,* she thought. *And telling Natalie when she was drunk at two in the morning? Not exactly the best person to provide some assurance.*

By the time Faith had blown out her hair and applied her SPF-infused makeup, she could hear Mae talking to some of the guys in the kitchen.

"Smells good!" Faith said as she entered the kitchen. Her silky maxi dress and wedge shoes made her feel a little more like she belonged.

"Tastes even better, ma'am," Lee said. His espresso-colored eyes lit up when he saw her. She knew the expression. Lee was cute with his mop of nearly black hair. He stood out from Matt, Caleb, and Alex with their all-American looks, dishwater blond locks, and light eyes. Maybe in another life Lee would have piqued her interest by now. But there was something about him that gave her pause.

"Faith, honey, go on and sit down. Gwen and I will—"

"Oh, actually? I was planning on going into Savannah today and do some exploring. I think the ferry leaves soon, so I don't want to miss it."

"Alone?" Mae asked. She stopped stirring the batter in the yellow Pyrex bowl she held.

"Well, yeah . . ."

"Nonsense, I won't hear of it. Especially not after, well, you know. Caleb!"

"Yeah, Mama?" Caleb replied from the doorway. Faith jumped at his voice.

"Faith needs to go into Savannah today. Take her? Y'all can take the Land Rover on the mainland."

"Oh," Caleb said slowly. The disappointment in his voice was palpable. "I would. Really, Faith, I'd love to. But remember, Mama, we got guests coming today? I still need to prep the boat, and—"

"It's fine," Faith said as she cut him off. "Really, I'll be okay."

"Now, just wait a minute," Mae said. As if on cue, Alex tried to sneak through the foyer and outside. "Alex! Come here a minute."

"Yeah?" he asked sullenly as he poked his head into the kitchen.

"Faith is going to Savannah today and needs some company."

"Mama, I—"

"That wasn't a question. Y'all get going, and take her wherever she wants to go."

Alex shot her a look, and Faith shrugged her shoulders. *What would Natalie do?* She stuck out her lips and tried to look pitiful. Maybe these southern men needed a little damsel in distress to make them agreeable. "Fine," he said begrudgingly.

"Oh, yay! Thank you," she said.

"But we're taking the Mustang."

Faith wasn't surprised that the drive to the ferry and the short crossing was spent largely in silence. What surprised her was how quickly she'd become accustomed to his moods. She sneaked glances at him as they leaned against the railing. The perpetual five o'clock shadow couldn't hide the hard lines of his jaw. His white shirtsleeves were rolled up to reveal tanned, muscled forearms. She knew he wasn't the type to load up his hair with product, but the salty air had mussed it up perfectly.

"Y'all coming back from a honeymoon?" Faith jumped at the question. A middle-aged couple, sunburned and smiling, stood beside them.

"Honeymoon? Uh, no—"

"Oh, I'm sorry, sweetie," the woman said with a thick Georgia accent. "It's just, that's what most couples go to Saint Rose for."

"We're not a couple," Alex said gruffly. It was the first time he'd spoken since they'd hopped on board.

"Oh well. Y'all enjoy yourselves," the woman said. Faith watched them inch away out of the corner of her eyes.

The same crew worked the ferry. The young boys rained smiles down on Faith as they passed by. "Already headed back home, ma'am?" one asked.

"No, just a day trip to Savannah," she said.

"Good to hear, good to hear. Saint Rose could use a little more beauty on the island."

She laughed and stole a look at Alex, but he seemed fascinated by the water.

When the boat docked at the mainland and the familiar worker took her hand and called her Angelina, Alex raised a brow. "Angelina?"

"Like Jolie," she told him as they walked toward the long-term parking garage across the street. "When I came to the island, he checked my ID. I was blonde when it was taken. He told me he liked me as a brunette and that I reminded him of Angelina Jolie. It was silly," she added. *Why do I care if he thinks I'm vain?*

"No, I don't think so," Alex said. "I can see it."

Is he flirting with me?

He didn't offer any other comments; just unlocked the gate and held it open for her. "Why do you keep your cars here instead of just boarding them on the ferry?" she asked.

He shrugged. "We have our reasons." They stopped at the end of a row of aluminum doors, and Alex pulled a remote out of his jeans. She couldn't help but notice the sliver of toned abs that peeked out at her.

The doors complained loudly as they were pulled up. Alex snapped the black cloth off the car to reveal a gorgeous cherry-red vintage Mustang.

"Oh my God. Is this yours?" she asked as he raised the door of the tiny garage.

"That's what the title says."

"It's beautiful," she said. "What is it, a sixty-six? It looks pristine."

"It's not a big deal," Alex said as he opened the door for her. "Just part of who I used to be."

Now that is interesting. The engine roared to life, and they pulled onto the main road. "So what does that mean? Who you used to be?" she asked. Signs for Savannah had already started to appear.

"Nothing," he said. "I just used to live in Atlanta; lived a different lifestyle."

That's all?

He was silent and stared down the road. Maybe she wasn't used to him after all. It had been easy on the ferry with other people around. Now it felt like she needed to engage a brick wall. "I think living in Atlanta would be fun," she said to fill the silence. "It's funny, people think San Francisco's like this big city, but it's actually so small. You know?"

"No, ma'am," he said without a glance in her direction.

"Well, I mean geographically the actual city is small. But it's not just that. All the attorneys and firms know one another. My ex, we broke up a year ago, but I'd still run into him all the time. That's part of why I came here for the summer. I mean, not because of him, I'm totally over that. But just for some change of scenery. You know?"

"No, ma'am," he said again.

She had started to get flustered but couldn't stop talking. "I've been thinking about it since yesterday. I think it would be good to renovate the house on Saint Rose. But you know, maybe keep the land wild."

Alex's eyes widened, but he still didn't look at her. *Finally, a reaction.* "Surprised?" she asked. "What, you didn't think I heard you?"

"No, I know you heard me," Alex said. "I just didn't expect you to listen."

Faith laughed. "Well, after you talked about all those endangered species . . . I'm a Californian, not heartless. There's a difference, contrary to popular belief."

"Will wonders never cease," he said as he transitioned onto a freeway.

"That's the main reason I'm going to Savannah today," she said. "I figured I'd try to look up a couple of contractors while we're in town."

She looked at him expectantly, but he wasn't going to budge. *And I gave him the perfect opening, too.* Surely Alex knew contractors or someone in the industry, and he wasn't even going to offer that up.

Faith glanced at her phone. *Finally, a strong signal.* The reception on the island was hit or miss.

She busied herself with googling contractors in the area. "It says that George Stephanos is the best contractor in town," she said aloud.

Alex let out a little growl.

She looked at him, surprised, and he had a scowl across his face.

"Who says?" he asked.

"Uh, Yelp?" Faith replied. She tried not to laugh. "Why? Do you know him? Do you have another recommendation?"

Alex just shook his head.

"You don't think I should look him up?" she pressed. "It lists his mobile number on his website."

"I think you should do whatever you want. Now, do you mind?" Before she could reply, Alex cranked up the radio to the jazz station. Nat King Cole filled the car.

What is his problem?

She spent the rest of the drive into Savannah checking out contractor bios, websites, and portfolios. *Fine, let Alex act like a child.*

He was a mystery, all right.

6

ALEX

*H*e couldn't believe she even mentioned George, let alone the idea of hiring him.

Alex thought he'd wiped George Stephanos from his memory, but as soon as the name had dripped from Faith's plump lips, it all came back to him. Labor Day weekend six years ago, when he'd brought Rebecca to the island for the first time. When Mama had demanded the whole family go to the beach for the annual barbeque, he hadn't argued. It would be a welcome change from watching Lee moon over Rebecca while she egged him on with her flirtations.

"Alex!" George appeared by their picnic table and clapped him on the back as if they were old friends. "Well, I can see what lured you away from Georgia. You must be the wife?" George looked at Rebecca as if he were about to sit down for a meal.

"Hi!" Rebecca said, twirling a lock of hair around her finger. "It's always great to meet one of Alex's old friends."

"Oh, I don't know about that, ma'am," George said. "We went

to high school together is all. I live in Savannah now, where I operate my contracting business. Just in town for the festivities."

"George Stephanos." Mama was suddenly at the table. Alex stood until she sat. "I haven't seen you since you were eighteen and pumping gas at the island petrol station."

"Mrs. Caldwell, ma'am," George said. *Is he blushing?*

"How's your mother?" Mama asked as she methodically set her plastic flatware.

"She's good, ma'am."

"That's nice. So are you still in the petrol business? Or . . ."

Mama looked up at George innocently, and he turned bright red. "Uh, no. No, ma'am, I own—"

"Oh, well, things change. It was good to see you, dear," Mama said.

Alex suppressed a grin as George stormed away.

"Rebecca, pass me the salt, dear?" Mama asked. When Rebecca handed her the little white tumbler, Alex noticed that she wasn't wearing her wedding ring. That trend had been happening more regularly lately.

It was impossible to keep an eye on his wife the entire day. By midafternoon, she'd disappeared. Not that Alex could ask anyone where his wife was. That wouldn't look too good.

Finally, he found her hidden on the side of the shaved iced stand with George. They giggled like schoolchildren. "Rebecca?" he said, and ignored George entirely. Alex took her by the elbow and led her away.

"What are you doing?" she hissed. "You're embarrassing me!"

"Just be here with me and my family. Okay?"

"Okay, okay! Geez," she said. Rebecca rubbed her arm as if he'd bruised her.

"Y'all enjoy the party now," George called. Alex could still remember that shit-eating grin.

Apparently, George Stephanos didn't have any respect for marital bonds.

Alex gripped the wheel tighter as the memory flooded him. He was ruined when it came to women, that was for sure. Trust just wasn't something he could do anymore. *Not even for a woman as hot as Faith.*

His knuckles had turned white, but he couldn't loosen his grip. Alex hated himself for how he'd let Rebecca ruin him. And Faith probably thought he was an asshole just for the hell of it. But there was no way he'd ever tell her why. If Caleb and his big mouth or Lee and his fawning over Faith spilled the tea, then so be it.

Finally, they reached the heart of the city. Alex maneuvered onto the exit. "It says to turn right at the second light," Faith said.

"To where?" he asked. *I know the goddamned city, Faith.*

"George's office. I texted him, and said I was with you. He'll be in his office till ten."

Alex was surprised he didn't split the steering wheel in two. "Well, then you can tell him I'm dropping you off."

She started to sputter but no words came out. Finally, she managed, "Sorry. It sounded like you knew each other. I thought . . ."

"You thought wrong," he said as he pulled up to George's building. It had been years since he'd driven by, and a lot had changed. The all-glass contemporary building stuck out like a sore thumb amid the otherwise brick buildings on the main drag.

"You mean you're not even going to—"

"Call or text me when you're ready to be picked up," he said. There was absolutely no way he was going to see George. Alex wasn't one to air his dirty laundry, but something about George brought it out in him.

He kept the engine running and stared ahead until Faith got out of the car. In the rearview mirror, he could see that she watched him drive away until he turned a corner.

George would surely spend as much time with Faith as possible. *Probably ask her to dinner, or a show, with promises of showing her around town. Fuck.*

He went to the aircraft supply shop to pick up a few items for the plane. Next, the big supermarket to stock up on the shampoo and soap he liked that couldn't be found on the island. After two hours, there was still no word from Faith. *Screw her, then.*

He'd exhausted his own errands but needed to kill time. Alex drove to the Just Delicious sugar-free bakery and chocolatier on the other side of town. It was Mama's favorite. He still remembered when she'd been diagnosed with type 2 diabetes twenty years ago. She'd been devastated; acted like the world was ending.

But within a week, she'd started to sweeten her tea with stevia leaf and had pinpointed the best sugar-free bakeries and chocolatiers around the country. Still, Just Delicious was her favorite. Alex suspected it was because it was one of the few that didn't deliver.

"Someone's got a sweet tooth," the young clerk said, her hat oversize and comical. He remembered that look, the slow up-and-down assessment that women gave him. It used to give him an ego boost. Now, it did nothing.

"Yeah," he said, adept at avoiding any actual engagement.

Of course, as soon as he was handed the receipt, Faith texted him.

All ready!

Yeah, sure you are. As soon as I'm on the other side of Savannah. He took his time getting there. Faith waited on the ornate white iron bench on the curb, covered by an awning. Thankfully, George was nowhere in sight. *The feeling is obviously mutual.*

Faith hopped into the car, and he knew she expected him to ask about the meeting. He said nothing. "So," she said slowly. "I'm hungry. You? Can we get something to eat?"

You mean George didn't take you wining and dining? He bit his tongue and shrugged.

On autopilot, he drove to Captain Sam's. The casual barbeque joint used to be a favorite of his and Lee's back in the day. It was on the riverfront and known just as much for the views as its burned ends, brisket, and ribs. "This is so cute!" Faith said as they settled at a table on the patio. "I've never actually had real southern food before."

"You can't be serious," he said. Alex pushed the menu aside. He didn't need to look at it.

"I mean, there are so-called southern restaurants in San

Francisco and other places I've traveled, but I know it's not the real deal. It's always fusion or elevated or something. Oh, look, hushpuppies! I've always wanted to try those."

"You've never had hushpuppies." He was flabbergasted.

"Nope. And what the hell. The barbeque sampler platter, too. Might as well go big or go home." She pushed her big round sunglasses onto the top of her head, and he sucked in his breath. Her long, lush lashes and piercing green eyes were almost too much.

Alex went to the counter to order and came back armed with a beer carrier filled with condiments.

"So," she said as she examined the sauce names. "Tell me more about your family. I still don't quite get how everyone at Greystone is related."

"It's not that complicated," he said. "Caleb's my Irish brother, and—"

"Irish brother?"

"You know. When kids are born less than a year apart."

"Oh! I'd never heard that. Maybe it's a southern thing."

"Yeah, you know. Or an Irish thing." She blushed and looked down. For just a second, Alex felt a pang of guilt. *Why am I being so mean to her?* "Anyway, Matt's our cousin, but he's lived with us since we were kids and his parents died."

"I'm sorry," Faith said.

Alex shrugged. "Not my parents. I don't even remember them." It was a dick thing to say, but he couldn't help it.

"And Lee?"

"Lee? He, uh—"

Just then, their number was called at the counter. Alex was happy for the excuse to get up. He couldn't really tell Faith that Lee used to be his best friend until he'd started drooling over Rebecca. "Ain't nothin' fancy," he said as he sat the tray down.

"It looks amazing!" she said.

"Try the hushpuppies first, when they're freshest. That is, as fresh as straight out of the deep fryer as you can get."

She smiled at him, and that guilt kicked at his stomach again. *Why am I always such a jerk to her?*

He took a long pull of his beer as he watched her bite into the fritter. Faith closed her eyes and licked those ripe lips. When she gave a little moan, he couldn't help but smile for a second. "You know, I don't know how everyone around here doesn't weigh a million pounds," she said. "I'd eat here every day if I lived here, calories be damned."

"Yeah, well, you haven't seen the Deep South. I can't speak for everyone else in Savannah, but I run five miles per day minimum. Kind of helps balance things out."

"A runner, huh?" she asked. "I ran one marathon, but that was it. It was my one and done. My runner friends all told me I'd get addicted, but I knew better. I'm more yoga oriented."

He rolled his eyes. "Why doesn't that surprise me?"

"Hey!" she said. "There's nothing wrong with yoga. In fact, it really complements running. There are even yoga classes just for runners. But you know what? I might take up running while I'm down here. It's not very fun in San Francisco. Too busy, crowded, so you're usually just stuck on a treadmill."

"But the hills have to be great for hill work," he said.

"Yeah, I don't even know what that is. But trust me, anyone who lives in the city gets plenty of 'hill work' without having to seek it out." She'd devoured two more hushpuppies and had started to work on the barbeque plate.

"Hey!" he said. "That sauce is really hot. You might want to—"

"I can handle it," she said with a laugh. "You southern boys aren't the only ones who can take the heat."

Alex wasn't going to argue further. He watched her dig into the spice-covered ribs and expected to have to run for a glass of milk. But she was nonchalant. Faith didn't even reach for her sweet tea.

"So, uh, how long do you actually plan to stay down here?"

"Why? You going to miss me?" she asked. Her lips were stained with the barbeque sauce, sticky and sweet.

"No," he said quickly.

She sucked in her lower lip and worried it. Alex dropped his gaze, unable to watch. "I don't really know," she said. "A month, maybe?"

Alex nodded. He wished it was less. Or at least that the piece-of-crap property she'd been left was decent enough for her to stay in. One month was too much of this girl, that was certain. She sparked something in him he'd never even known he had.

By the time they'd finished, she'd matched him cornbread to cornbread, and end to end. After she'd wiped her long fingers on the wet wipes, she groaned and cradled her flat stomach. "I'm never eating again."

"Let's get going," he said. "Or we'll miss the last afternoon ferry."

He couldn't get back to Greystone fast enough, but he knew they'd be stuck in Savannah rush hour traffic. *That's just what I need, to be stuck for hours next to this girl.*

7

FAITH

She didn't know what she was going to do. George had been flirtatious, to say the least. Faith didn't know much about renovations or contract bids, but even she knew the price he quoted was ridiculously low. Of course, she knew it was because George was into her, but who was she to turn down a lust-driven bid? She'd nearly signed the agreement before she walked out the door but told herself not to jump the gun just yet.

"Pleased to make your acquaintance, ma'am," George said as soon as she was ushered into his office. He was the same height as her and a bit stocky. But Faith could tell he had that kind of swagger some women fell for hard. What he lacked in looks, he likely made up for in smoothness.

"Hi," she said quietly as she took in the office. It was different from what she imagined a Savannah business to be. Minimalist design, with the only decorations being shelves of trophies and ribbons from industry-related organizations.

"I see you have a knack for picking out the best," George said.

"Please, have a seat." Faith settled into the stiff, uncomfortable but chic chair. George sat right beside her, foregoing his own cushy leather desk chair on the other side of the stainless steel desk. They were uncomfortably close, but Faith wasn't about to be the one to shift away.

"Thank you for seeing me on such short notice."

"It's my pleasure," George said. "Any friend of Alex's is a friend of mine." She thought she detected a touch of disgust when he said Alex's name.

"Well, we're not exactly friends," Faith said. His knee touched hers. "More like connected through family friends. But he doesn't seem particularly happy that I'm here." *Why am I telling this man all this?*

"Don't you take it personal," George said. He patted her knee, warm palm partially on the bare skin exposed by the high slit of her dress. "Alex has been difficult since the incident."

"Incident?" Faith's ears perked up.

"Oh, well, I really shouldn't say anything," George said. "My apologies, ma'am, I thought you knew. Everybody knows. Anyway, what can I do for you? I must admit, I did a little snooping on you."

"Snooping?"

"What is it they call it? Google stalking? I like to have an idea of who I'm meeting with," he said with a fake laugh.

"Oh. Find anything interesting?" she asked. Faith knew it sounded flirtatious, but it was a calculated risk. Maybe George had stumbled across something interesting.

"Not much," he said. "Saw you're some fancy lawyer in San Francisco."

"Hardly fancy," she said, though she blushed.

"Asked round 'bout you. From friends that came from Saint Rose an' such. Heard you and your daddy used to spend a few summers here, along with some aunt an' cousin from up north."

"Aunt?" she asked. "Cousin? Do you know their names? Are they here now, or . . ."

He raised a brow. "I figured you'd know their names, ma'am."

"I, uh, I didn't really keep in touch with the family on my father's side," she said.

"Well, then, why don't you ask your daddy?"

"He's dead," she said quietly.

"Oh. Oh my. My condolences, ma'am. I didn't know."

He doesn't know that, but he knows some kind of gossip about Alex? Faith didn't want to come off as a gossip herself, especially since George had made time for her. "Thanks," she said curtly. "But in regard to the property, I just inherited it. It's worse for wear, but I'm thinking about having it restored."

"Restored." George repeated the word as if he'd never heard it before. Even though he held her gaze and didn't sneak a look at her chest, it felt like he was skillfully undressing her with his eyes.

"Or something," she said. Her ears burned. "I, uh, sorry. I don't really know anything about that kind of stuff."

"No? Not a professional flipper then," George said with a smile. His teeth were shockingly white and straight compared to the rest of his aesthetic. Obvious veneers, although well done and clearly expensive.

"Hardly," she said. Faith couldn't hold out any longer. She switched the crossing of her legs to direct her body slightly away from him. "I'm actually visiting from San Francisco. I didn't even know Saint Rose existed until I inherited the property. Or, I'd forgotten. Now that I'm here, though, I keep getting, like, flashbacks to the summers here."

"Your Aunt Lydia musta taken a real likin' to you," George said. "Leavin' you her whole island and all."

"Did you know her?"

"Well, not really," George admitted. "But when you grow up on Saint Rose, everyone knows everyone a little bit," he laughed. "She mostly kept to herself, but she was a good, solid woman. I did go to her funeral."

"Oh. I, uh, I wasn't aware of it." Faith felt like she should apologize for missing it.

"Don't you worry. I don't think the dead take attendance," he said, and leaned back into the hard chair.

"So you know the property then?" she asked.

"The big one she kept on the island? I know of it," George said. "Turn of the century, typical Saint Rose plantation home. About four thousand square feet, quite a lot of acreage."

Faith laughed. "Well, you know more than I do," she said.

"I like having leverage," George said. He smiled, but it was loaded with suggestion.

"Do you . . . do you think it's a worthwhile project? To renovate it?"

"That's up for you to say," George said. He leaned forward

again. "What are your plans for it? You Gonna move to the island, use it as a vacation home for yourself, rent it out . . ."

"I'm not really sure," Faith admitted. "Maybe more a vacation home type of thing. But given all the land, I'd like to keep it as natural as possible. Kind of like an unofficial arboretum and wildness conservation, you know?"

"You really are a California girl," George said. "Don't get me wrong, I love me some bleeding-heart liberals. They open their, uh, *wallets* wide up when they come to me." This time, he did let his eyes travel to her thighs, which were buried under the thin material. It was calculated, designed to put her on edge.

"I just thought it might be nice," she said quietly. Faith was used to men flirting with her, but not like this. This felt like a touchless assault.

"I'm sure it'd be real nice, ma'am," George said. He lifted his eyes back to hers. "Just my professional opinion I was sharin', that's all. You know what they say about California girls."

She cocked her head. "We don't mind sand in our stilettos?"

He let out a bark of a laugh. "I was goin' for I wish they all could be California girls, but you right, too."

Faith smiled. Maybe she imagined the whole predatory creeper thing with George. After all, this was the South. There were different rules, and she knew it wasn't nearly as progressive as San Francisco. *You're out of your element, that's all.*

"An' what's Alex think of all this?" George asked. He reached across the table and picked up a small tin of chocolates. He popped one into his mouth, offered the tin to her, but she shook her head.

"Actually, the whole preservation thing was his idea," she said.

"Yeah, I can imagine. He was always an odd one, that," George said. "Never quite fit in here."

"His mom's nice, though," Faith said. "And his brother, Caleb."

"Mama Mae? Caleb? How you know them?" George asked.

"Well, I'm . . . I'm kind of staying at Greystone."

"No shit," George said. "Pardon my language, ma'am. You mean you booked a room there? Or . . ."

"No. I mean, they got looped into the whole inheritance thing somehow. I guess Mae was close with Lydia? Or . . ."

"Yeah, yeah, I got you. That whole island's intertwined in one way or another. Well, Miss Capshaw, let me do something. I'mma write down a figure here. Now, keep in mind it's just a sight unseen bid, but I'm very familiar with those properties. An' you have a think on it."

When he reached for the pad of paper, his leg pressed against hers, but he didn't move it. Faith saw it as a challenge and pushed right back.

*S*he watched Alex cover the Mustang. The entire ride back from lunch had been awkwardly quiet. Whatever his problem was, this whole brooding, angsty teen thing was too much. Why couldn't he lighten up? The few glimpses of being a normal guy she saw at the barbeque joint were rare.

"Coming?" he asked curtly as he made a beeline for the ferry.

Faith sighed and followed. They were fifteen minutes early for the last ferry, and no crew members were on-site. The only other passengers were a group of fat, mean-looking rednecks.

She didn't think much of the motley crew until they reached the boarding area and Alex abruptly stepped in front of her. "Faith?" one of the men said meanly. His knuckles were covered in faded blue tattoos, and his neck was so big it merged his head with his shoulders.

"Yes?" she squeaked. *How does he know my name?*

"Get out of the way, Caldwell," one of the others said. Alex didn't move, but Faith peered around Alex's broad shoulders at the group.

The first man spit a stream of reddish brown chew into the dirt. "Ain't you Gonna give yo' cousin a hug, baby girl?" asked one of them.

"Excuse me?" she said.

The group broke out in cruel laughter. "She ain't even know," said the second man.

"We yo' cousins, Cousin," said the first man.

"I, um, I don't . . ."

"Yeah, you don't know shit is right," said the first man. He eyed her up and down the best he could behind Alex. "Yo' great-*aunt*, Miss Lydia? Crazy ol' bitch done left you the estate when she know good an' well it belong to us."

"You knew Lydia?" Faith asked. She stepped to Alex's side. He grabbed her forearm to keep her from getting any closer to them.

"Know her? Sweetheart, we a hell of a lot better related to her than you ever be."

"Yeah," agreed the man with the menacing tattoos. "And we none too pleased you come up in here like some uppity princess and steal our inheritance."

"Your inheritance? Listen," Faith said as she held up her hands. "I have no idea why she left everything to me. But that's the way it is."

"Oh!" squealed one of the men. "She done gone lawyer on yo' ass."

"You listen here," said the first man. "That property ain't yours. You hear me? And I'll be damned if yo' Gonna take it."

Alex cleared his throat. "Y'all best leave," he said. "I think the sheriff will be plenty interested in the fact that you threatened her. Sheriff's just looking for reasons to lock you up, is what I heard."

"Yeah, Caldwell?" asked one of the men in the back. "You Gonna tell on us? Well, now ain't that a surprise. That Becca fucked you up real good, right? Ain't got nothin' better to do than run round snitchin' on everybody."

Becca?

The men shuffled for a moment but eventually left with scowls plastered across their faces when Alex didn't budge. Most looked over their shoulder at Alex and Faith. "I be watchin' you," the first man called to them from across the street, where they climbed into an old Bronco with a massive lift kit. "*Cousin,*" he added.

It wasn't until the Bronco was out of sight that Faith realized her heart had started to slow. "What the . . . what the hell was that?" she asked Alex. She gazed up at him, but he wouldn't look her in the eye.

"Just a li'l domestic dispute," he said.

Domestic dispute? Are those monsters really her cousins? She wanted to push and ask more but knew it would be impossible with Alex. She held her tongue and told herself she'd ask Mae.

It felt like hours before the ferry came into view. "You enjoy your day in town, ma'am?" the security checker asked.

"Oh, uh, yeah," she said. "It was great." Alex raised a brow at her. *Not gonna blab about the fat cousin brigade?* he seemed to ask.

"Seems y'all my only customers," the clerk said. "So we Gonna get goin' straightaway."

Instead of leaning against the railing like he had in the morning, Alex started to circle the small deck area. Faith heard him swear as he fumbled with a pile of something pushed under a storage seat and wrapped in a gray cloth.

"Hey!" she called to him as he picked up the bundle and tossed it overboard. "What is that? What are you doing?"

"Nothin'," he said. "Just some stupid booby trap."

"Booby trap? But how did you know? Was it for me—"

"I just knew. Okay? Now drop it."

"There's no way in hell I'm going to drop it. What was it? A bomb?" she asked. She looked around the ferry to see if anyone was watching, but the small crew was nowhere to be seen.

"I said drop it," he repeated. Something in his voice made her listen.

A chill crept through her. When they were five minutes from docking on Saint Rose, Alex finally came and stood beside her.

"Cold?" he asked.

She shook her head. "I just can't believe there's been so much friction. I've only been here two days! I didn't even know about those guys." She couldn't bring herself to say cousins. There was no way she was related to those creeps.

"Maybe you should think about whether or not it's worth your while," Alex said, stone-faced. "You're just here for a short while, anyway."

Is it just her, or is he trying to get her to leave?

Faith didn't want to argue with him. What was the point? Getting information out of Alex was a painstaking process.

On the other hand, maybe he was right. She didn't have to be on the island to handle the estate. That's what estate attorneys are for, and there were no rules that she had to keep the property anyway. Surely it could be sold. Not for a huge profit, maybe, but for something. Besides, the real windfall was in the cash inheritance, not the house.

Faith inched away from him as Saint Rose came into view. In some ways the rednecks were right. Who was she to inherit everything? She hadn't even known the woman had existed until the attorney had contacted her.

She sighed. The estate attorney who'd called her about the inheritance only lived a bit away. Maybe it was better to get things handled sooner rather than later.

8

ALEX

*A*lex returned from his morning run late. Instead of the usual single loop, he'd pounded through two. If running couldn't give him peace of mind, the least it could do was wear him out.

As he rounded the last curve of the trail to home, he heard splashing in the pool. It was rare these days for anyone to make use of the Olympic-size pristine water. As children, he, Caleb, and Lee would spend summers racing through the water, but that was long ago.

He saw Faith finish a lap at the deep end. She hoisted herself out of the water with hair that looked even darker and longer than usual. *Jesus Christ, no woman should be shaped like that.* She had legs for miles, taut and toned in the high-cut bikini bottom. *Amazing tits, too,* he thought. The red two-piece showed off every curve, and the halter top emphasized her perfect hourglass shape.

Faith looked in his direction and caught his stare as she wrapped a white towel around her tiny waist. He looked down quickly and walked faster toward the house. *This was way too much of a distraction.*

He'd never realized before just how small the inn could be. His entire life, it had seemed huge. But now? With Faith there, it was like he couldn't avoid bumping into her. All morning and into the afternoon he busied himself with tasks around the house.

"Since when do you cut the firewood?" Caleb called to him. Alex winced. It had taken him ten minutes to get into the meditative, repetitive motion of chopping wood. "Besides, it's summer. How many fires do you think there will be?"

"There're always bonfires," Alex said to himself. After a few minutes, he felt Caleb's presence disappear. Half an hour later, he caught sight of a bright-yellow figure on one of the trails. Matt and Faith walked side by side while his cousin pointed out the wildlife.

But Faith seemed to be looking directly at him. *Is that right?* It was too far away to tell for certain.

By the time Alex had moved on to mowing the manicured front lawn, even at his mama's insistence that the gardeners would be there in two days, all doubts were erased. Faith sat on the front porch sipping sweet tea. The heat of the day had forced her to draw her long dress up over her knees while her feet were perched on the railing. He felt her eyes on him the entire time.

It's not like it's the worst thing for my ego to be looked at by a woman, he told himself. *Especially someone that looks like her.* Alex paused and pulled his shirt over his head. As he wrapped the T-shirt around the handlebars of the old push mower, he was well aware of the show he put on. *Thank God for a diligent workout regimen.*

Alex stole a look at her through his sunglasses. Her own aviators partially hid her gaze, but he could feel her stare like a heat probe.

She could be a model. Or an actress, he thought. *But a lawyer?* In some ways, that made her even hotter. In others, it reminded him that she was a world away from him.

By the time he'd finished with the lawn, Faith had gone back inside, and the sun was starting to set. He was soaked in sweat, but the manual labor of the day gave him a type of energy he hadn't felt in years.

The foyer and sitting rooms were clear, though he heard clangs in the kitchen. Alex took the stairs two at a time and hit the shower. Already, he could feel a minor sunburn had soaked into his shoulders and chest. While he lathered up, he refused to think of Faith. Not now. Even a fantasy could get him into trouble.

Downstairs, he heard laughter and hushed tones. Mama and Faith were huddled in the kitchen at the breakfast table while Gwen and Jessie hunched over the stove. "What are y'all doin'?" he asked.

"Oh, just looking at some old family photos," Mama said.

"What—what family photos?" he asked. He recognized some of the old, thick photo albums Mama had laid out on the table. A couple were historic photos of the inn and Saint Rose from circa 1900. Other albums weren't as familiar.

Faith was totally absorbed in the books and didn't even look up when he walked in. "Who's this?" she asked Mama.

"That's my great-aunt. She swore the secret to a long life was two gin and tonics plus half a pack of cigarettes every day. Of course, she died at sixty-three."

Alex rolled his eyes and peeked over Gwen's shoulder. "Collard greens?" he asked.

"Yeah, wit' pork, baby," she said. "Now, you know how I feel about having noncooks in my kitchen. Get. Y'all Gonna eat real soon."

"Yes, ma'am," he said. There was nowhere to go but the table.

Mama had pulled out yet another album, and this one was newer. Alex still didn't recognize it, but Mama was always archiving family photos. She refused to switch to digital, though he and Caleb had been trying for years. "And what am I supposed to do when the computer crashes again?" she'd asked.

"Mama, if that happens, the pictures will be safe in the cloud."

"In the what now?"

He shook his head at the thought. Some things never changed.

"Now see, here's the whole family 'bout seven years ago," Mama said. She pointed to a posed shot of the extended family from Alex and Rebecca's rehearsal dinner. "Flew in from all over the world! Alex 'n Caleb's aunts and cousins from Luxembourg, right here. And this—"

Alex's heart quickened. He knew what Faith's next question was going to be. He remembered the shot well, with him and Rebecca right in the center. It couldn't be another page or two before it became obvious that it was his wedding album.

"Hey, Mama, think dinner's ready yet?" he interrupted. It was a stupid question, but it was the first thing he could think of.

"Hey? Hay is for horses," Mama scolded him. "And didn't I

just hear you bothering Gwen about it anyway? Why are you asking me?"

"I just thought—"

"Dinner's ready," Gwen said as she turned off the gas.

Mama sighed. "Saved by the bell, you are," she told Alex. She snapped the album shut. "Go get your brothers. I'll help Gwen serve."

"I'll set the table," Faith said and jumped up.

"Well, bless your heart, that's real sweet of you," Mama said. "You could learn a thing or two from her," Mama said to Alex. "Real helpful. What you been doing all day, anyway?"

Alex opened his mouth to tick off the list of nonstop chores but then snapped it back shut. What was the point?

He ran back upstairs and called out to Caleb, Matt, and Lee. It didn't take much to get them to rush downstairs for Gwen's collard greens. She wouldn't even give the recipe up to Mama. It was the one dish she cooked completely by herself.

As they settled down in the formal dining room, Mama and Gwen glided into the room with arms full of steaming home cooking. Dishes of blackened catfish with Cajun spices, jalapeño-infused cornbread, slices of tomatoes from the garden with salt and pepper, and pimiento cheese were spread out across the table.

"This looks amazing," Faith said. All four men remained standing until both Mama and Faith sat.

"Gwen's amazing," Mama said. "I swear, she and I are nearly the same age, but I learned more about cooking from her than I ever did my own mama."

75

"Thank you much, ma'am," Gwen said as she delivered the last dish to the table, baked mac 'n' cheese with bread crumb topping.

"I heard Alex took you for some barbeque in Savannah," Caleb said to Faith.

"Yes! My first time. It was fantastic. I'd never had hushpuppies before. Or, you know, *real* southern food."

"You never had hushpuppies?" Lee asked. "What they servin' out in California?"

"Oh, you know," Faith said as she speared the greens. "Kale was huge for a while, kale everything. But that's not really trending anymore. I still love a good quinoa bowl for lunch. Local sashimi is great. And I guess avocado toast is having a moment, but I just can't bring myself to order that at brunch when I could make it for two dollars at home."

"All right. I understood about half of that," Lee said with a laugh.

Faith followed suit. "I guess it does sound pretty pretentious," she said. She closed her eyes and let the flavors of Gwen's greens take over. "But trust me, even the best sushi in California can't compete with this."

"Next time you go to the mainland, I'll take you," Matt said. "I know this great little New Orleans Creole-style restaurant. It's got just the right amount of French influence."

Alex rolled his eyes. *Of course Matt would try to impress her at one of the most expensive restaurants in town.*

"That sounds great," Faith said with a smile.

Alex surveyed the table. He could tell all three of them were into her. The flirtations were passed around like hors d'oeuvres.

"Mama?" he asked suddenly. Alex didn't care if he interrupted the game between Faith and the rest of them. "I was thinking, I'm going to move back into the cabin."

"What on earth for?" she asked.

He shrugged. "I just need a little more space. Plus, I can get up for my morning runs and make breakfast in the morning without worrying about waking anyone."

"Alex, I just don't see the point," Mama said as she cut off a piece of catfish. "The room upstairs is perfectly fine."

"So is the cabin," he pointed out. "Besides, it's not being used, and Jessie cleans it every weekend for no reason. It's just on the other side of the property."

Mama sighed. "Fine. Get as far away from the family as you can. But if we get any booking requests for it, you best bet you'll be outta there quicker than a fox out a henhouse."

"Yes, ma'am," he said. No guests had requested the cabin in three summers. Most came to Saint Rose looking for the full plantation experience. A log cabin that looked like it belonged more in North Carolina than a Georgia island wasn't exactly what anyone had in mind.

"Where's the cabin?" Faith asked. She looked around the table, but it seemed like her eyes lingered on his.

"Oh, just at the end of the trail that heads toward Alex's plane. Remember how it forked, and one trail was bark chips while the other was pavement? You just follow the bark chips," Mama said.

"And it's usually just empty?"

"Well, didn't used to be," Mama said. "Their daddy built it as a caretaker home when we thought we'd be retiring elsewhere. But here we are," she said with a smile.

Alex finished up the last of his greens. While he sopped up the juices with the last of his cornbread, he watched Faith toss her head back and laugh at something Caleb said.

"May I be excused?" he asked the table but stood up before anyone could argue.

"Think you done made up your mind 'bout that, already," Mama said pointedly as she sipped her tea.

Alex shoved the contents of his dresser into a tote bag and jogged to the cabin. *I just can't be in that house with her anymore.* Something about Faith just got to him. There was no way he could sleep two doors down from her. He'd be up all night.

In the cabin, the lights bathed the rooms in warmth. Jessie had kept the cabin flawless for years, dutifully cleaning, dusting, and changing the bedding every weekend without fail.

He fell into the cushy bedding and waited for sleep that never came. Instead, images of Faith in that red bikini flooded his mind. The way she'd looked at him as she emerged from the water, her nipples stiff from the morning breeze below the wet material. Before she'd wrapped that towel around herself, he'd seen how her round ass had swallowed half the bottoms. From the looks of it, the suit clung to her with just a few bows and knots. All it would take was a few pulls in the right places.

Alex groaned and rolled onto his side, but it didn't get rid of the image. Instead, he just started to replay the image of Faith getting out of the pool. How the water had dripped down her curves, and how her hips had flared out just right.

Alex felt himself get hard, but he refused to touch himself. If he gave in, there was no telling what he might do the next time he saw her. All day long, it had seemed like she'd watched him like she couldn't get enough. Then at dinner, she'd been open to flirtations from Caleb, Matt, Lee, all of them.

He grabbed the phone and texted Erica on a whim. *Busy this weekend?* he asked.

Immediately, he saw the ellipses start. *Sorry, babe. Last-minute trip to Seattle for work, I'll be here all summer.*

He growled and tossed down the phone.

Shit. His only outlet was gone. *What's wrong with me? Why does one woman affect me so much?*

9

FAITH

Faith signed up for yet another Georgia community forum. She copied and pasted her plea for the sixth time that morning.

My name is Faith Capshaw, 26F. I was born in Eureka, California. But my father was born on Saint Rose and had a sister named Lydia Capshaw. I've heard I had a paternal aunt and female cousin, around my age, who were on Saint Rose in the summers about 20 years ago. I'm looking for anyone who might be related . . .

So far, she had no bites. Nobody seemed to know her aunt Lydia except those terrifying redneck "cousins" of hers. And George, though he said he knew of her, not that he knew her. Still, he'd gone to her funeral and made it sound like there was a decent turnout.

Faith didn't know what she expected to figure out even if she did find someone who knew Lydia. What would she ask? *Why did she leave everything to me?* Who could answer that? *Where's my other aunt? My cousin? Why didn't we keep in touch?*

She watched the forums fill up with comments that had nothing to do with her. It seemed like all over Georgia and the South, people were reconnecting.

Faith tried searching for Capshaws in Georgia on Facebook, but it was such a common surname there was no way she could wade through them all. *Besides, what would I even message to them—do you think we might be related?*

She closed her eyes and tried to picture Lydia's face or the face of her other aunt but came up blank. She remembered an outfit or a pair of shoes. But it seemed like her memories were from so long ago, she'd been so small that she only knew people by their smell and clothes. "It's pointless," she said to herself.

She waited until the firm opened back in California to call and check in.

"Faith!" the receptionist squealed. "Mr. Parsons is out for a breakfast meeting with a client this morning, and Hank won't be in until ten o'clock. But I'll be sure and tell them you called."

"Thanks," Faith said. She could hear the familiar sounds in the background. The unique ring of the phones and the typical morning chatter. She didn't feel any twinge of longing at all. Instead, she was flooded with relief not to be there. *Man, I really have lost my taste for corporate law.*

Not that she felt at home here. It was clear that Alex didn't want her around. *I mean, my God, he moved into a cabin to get away from me!* Mae was sweet, of course, but Faith didn't know how much of that was from ingrained southern hospitality. After all, she'd said, "Bless your heart" to her the other night. It hadn't seemed to be used as a negative, but Faith had seen enough movies to know that was often the southern version of an "eff you."

As for Caleb, Matt, and Lee, they followed her around like puppies. Sure, they were innocent and nice enough, but she felt a bit bad about the whole situation. *Did they think she was leading them on?* She had no idea how a polite southern woman was supposed to handle such attention.

She'd told Mae last night that she planned to work through breakfast, but that was a lie. What she really needed was a break from it all. From the smiling, from dodging flirtations, and from Alex's scowl across the breakfast table.

When she heard the last of the morning clatter come to an end, she sneaked downstairs and selected a peach from the big wooden bowl on the kitchen island. Curled into the chaise in the front room, Faith gazed outside at the regal oaks and cloudless sky. *It really is paradise here.* But like all paradises, something lurked below the surface.

Alex appeared in the distance, shirtless but with white running shorts. Faith hid behind a piece of gauzy curtain and watched him approach the house. *Damn. He's perfectly shaped. Not an ounce of fat on him. Too bad he's so antisocial.*

She watched him until he reached the largest magnolia tree near the house. Alex hosed himself off, his muscles strong and defined. His hair was getting a bit shaggy, and it suited him. Faith chewed at a nail and felt that tug of warmth between her thighs.

Her phone buzzed with an email. *Yes, reception.* She had two bars, just enough to text Natalie. *Contrary to popular belief, there's actually quite a bit of beefcake here on the island,* she wrote to Natalie.

What they lack in education they make up for in muscles, huh? Natalie replied.

Surprisingly, the boys aren't all dumb, either, she replied.

Alex had just finished up with the hose, and Faith snapped a photo of him on the sly. On the little table beside the chaise was a group photo of the boys from what looked to be about a year ago. Faith took a photo of it, too. She sent them to Natalie and leaned back on the velvet cushion.

Natalie's reply was simply an eggplant, kissy face, and heart eye emoji. Faith laughed just as Alex walked through the front door.

"Alex!" she called. "I need to go to the house to meet George about the reno project. Mae said you could take me?" She was emboldened by her texts with Natalie. Mae had said no such thing, but she knew the woman would back her up if it came to it.

He glared at her as he pulled his shirt back on.

"So? What do you say?" she prompted. "He and his crew are going to be out there all morning taking measurements."

"Fine," he said. "I'll be ready in fifteen."

As he jogged off to the cabin, she started to wonder why Alex's attitude always got worse at the mention of George. *Had something happened between them?* She knew small towns could be gossip mills, and it was probably even worse on an island.

Ultimately, when she'd told George she'd take him up on his bid, he was all business on the phone. Maybe she'd imagined the extreme flirtations at his office. Or maybe when you took everything except verbal cues off the table, things just got a little more efficient.

While she waited for Alex, she went back upstairs and changed. She remembered how overgrown the property was —and how dangerous the house seemed. Faith pulled off her romper and stepped into her worn jeans. Wearing a light-weight tank top and Converse sneakers, she felt like this was as business casual as she could get on a decrepit plantation site.

Back on the chaise, Alex saw her as he was halfway up the steps to retrieve her. "C'mon," he called to her through the window. "We haven't got all day."

As she expected by now, he was silent on the way to the plane. "Thanks for taking me to see George," she said as they climbed into the small aircraft.

"Don't have much choice, do I?"

She sighed. "Why are you so unfriendly every time George is brought up?"

He looked at her in surprise as the plane ascended. "Me? It isn't any of my business who you hire."

"Shouldn't you, uh, keep your eyes on the road. Or sky, or whatever?"

"This isn't like driving a car," he said.

"Look, if there's something up with him, I'd appreciate it if you'd let me know. I mean, I'm trusting the guy to renovate a freaking plantation."

He sighed. "In terms of his business, from what I hear he's solid," he said.

This time, when she saw the tiny island with her home—her home!—come into view, she saw it in a new light. It really was beautiful. Just as when she was a child, it looked like a magical jewel in the water. Like that island in *The Beach* or *Blue Lagoon*. Faith laughed to herself. *Not like those movies are particularly happy.*

She remembered a landing with her father and her cousin. "Paradise," her cousin had said.

Her dad had laughed, and she remembered thinking how rare that was. "How do you know such a big word?" he had asked.

Her cousin just smiled and repeated it. "Paradise."

"Absolutely gorgeous," she said aloud as he landed. She felt his eyes on her and looked at him. Simultaneously, they blushed and looked away. *Did he really just blush?* she wondered.

This time, Alex didn't have such a fast clip as they deplaned, though she still trailed behind him through the forest to the house. "You know, I used to play in these woods a lot as a child," he said over his shoulder. "They still look the same as when the Native Americans lived here."

"Is that a piece of *information* about the mysterious Mr. Alex Caldwell?" she asked with a laugh.

"Just telling you," he said, though she thought she heard a smile in his voice.

"Do you . . . do you ever remember seeing a couple of little girls here?" she asked.

"You mean you an' your cousin?"

Does everyone know except me? "Well, yeah," she said.

He shook his head. "Not that I remember. I don't recall Lydia being overprotective of her land, but Mama woulda whooped me good if she knew I was on other people's property. Mostly sneaked around here durin' the off season."

They saw the crew's rigs and materials before the house came into view. "Wow," Faith said. "Looks like the entire company is out here." Workers covered the property with men walking on the roof, measuring the porch, and surveying the land.

"Miss Capshaw, ma'am!" George called from the porch, his arms outstretched. He looked out of place in the stiff jeans and awkward button-up shirt that a middle-aged dad might wear. *He looked more himself in that suit in his office*, Faith thought.

"Hi, George," she said as she extended her hand and bounded up the steps to greet him.

He ignored the hand and pulled her in for a two-cheek kiss. "Don't you look stunning," he said. He held her out at arm's length to study the length of her body.

"Um, Alex brought me," she said. But when she turned around, Alex had busied himself inspecting something on the patio landing.

"Man, you really do look a vision. Don't you think, Alex?" George said. Alex glanced at him and shrugged. "Not much for lavishing a woman with the compliments she deserves," George said to her with a knowing grin.

Faith was uncomfortable. She'd never experienced the kind of flirtations George showered her with. And she didn't know how to best respond to keep him at bay. "I think he has other things on his mind," she said to George kindly.

"I don't know how," George said. He blatantly stared at her chest. "I don't mean to be too forward, ma'am, but if I was sharing a house with you? You'd be the only thing on my mind."

"Well, actually," Faith started. "Alex is living out in the cabin now."

George let out a laugh. "I can see that," he said. "And honestly, can't blame him. Who wants to be almost thirty years old and livin' with their mama?"

Her instinct was to smile to soften the situation, but she wasn't about to go along with making fun of Alex just to stroke George's ego. "I don't know," she said. "I know a lot of people in their twenties and thirties living with their parents —or vice versa—in San Francisco."

"That's different," George said. "I read about them housing prices out there." He let out a whistle. "Now that's where I should be doin' what I do. Can you imagine the profits? That who you live with, ma'am? Your parents?"

She blushed and looked down. "No. I—"

"I see. Got a boyfriend. Yeah, that whole livin' in sin thing's got trendy here now, too. Not that I'm one to judge," George said.

"No, no boyfriend. I, um, I live alone."

"Alone? A pretty thing like you? Now that can't be safe. I guess maybe that's why you're lookin' at this here property then. It's a real good family home. Now you just need the family," he said with a wink. "Who knows? Maybe I can help you out with that, too. Every woman needs a good man at home."

"Excuse me?"

He laughed again. "I'm just playin' with you. Don't get too serious."

"I really don't think—"

George ignored what she'd started to say completely. "I've got some good news and some bad news, as per usual on these renos. Which would you like first, ma'am?"

"Um, I guess let's start with—"

"I'm goin' on a walk," Alex said. He interrupted both of them and although his voice was calm, the anger was palpable. He looked only at Faith and blocked George out entirely. "Be back in thirty."

"Okay?" Faith's voice was tiny.

"That boy," George said and shook his head. "Always runnin' round them woods since we was kids. Dunno what he sees in it."

"Yeah," Faith said quietly. They both watched Alex disappear into the woods. "George? I know this is none of my business, but why does Alex hate you so much?"

George's smile dimmed.

"I'm sorry. God, that was rude. It's so none of my business. It's just, whenever I mention you, he gets so upset."

"Well, ma'am, I don't like to air dirty laundry. 'Specially other people's. But . . . I guess I could say, Alex's first wife wasn't particularly faithful."

"His *wife*?"

"Oh, shoot, you didn't know that, either? Well, yes, he was

married. Some girl named Rebecca, if I remember right. And, I 'spose I did flirt with her a bit. Just to get Alex's goat, you know. High school rivalry silliness."

Faith narrowed her eyes. This was getting a lot messier than she'd expected. She didn't know what she'd thought George would say, but it seemed like there were secrets on this island that went deeper than she'd imagined. "Sorry to pry," she said. "Anyway, what were you saying about the good and bad news? I guess I'll take the bad first. It can only get better from there." She forced a smile onto her face.

"Well, it turns out the requirements for flood plains have changed since the home was built. So you have two options . . ."

George talked, but Faith's mind reeled. *If George is willing to admit to flirting, there's probably a lot more to the story. No wonder Alex hates him!* It also made a lot of other things make sense.

And what happened to his wife? Why hasn't anyone mention that? Divorce was pretty normal, unfortunately. Maybe that's why Alex seemed so upset about being on the property. And maybe it wasn't about her at all.

"Ready for the good news?" George asked as he interrupted her thoughts.

"Sure," she said.

He began to rattle something off about the insulation but not much registered. Given the situation between Alex and George, it was clear that George wasn't the contractor for her. But she'd still pay for today's survey and let him give his spiel.

Faith looked toward the woods where Alex had disappeared.

She frowned. *Am I the one who can finally get him to loosen up a little?*

10

ALEX

"Where y'all goin'?" Mama asked.

Alex looked at Caleb, who just shrugged. "Boat work," Caleb said.

"And you?" Mama looked hard at Alex, who slumped his shoulders. He thought attending breakfast would have been enough to keep her off his back.

"Onto the mainland for the day, ma'am," he said somberly.

"The mainland?" Faith perked up. She sat beside his mama at the breakfast table, nursing her second cup of coffee. "Can I come?"

"I don't know—"

"Alex," Mama said sharply. "Of course, he'd love to take you," she told Faith.

"Since when do you go to the mainland?" Caleb asked.

"Since now," Alex said.

"Where you goin'?" Matt called from the sitting room.

Jesus Christ, doesn't anyone have anything better to do? Alex thought.

"Mainland!" Caleb hollered back. "You wanna go?"

"*M*iss Jolie, ma'am," the ferry worker said with a wide smile as he took their tickets. "Y'all goin' to raise some hell?"

"How'd you know?" Caleb replied.

"It's Friday. Why else go inland?"

"So what's the plan?" Faith asked. She tied a loose braid into her waist-length hair to keep it at bay in the breeze.

"*My* plan was to go into town and have a couple of low-key drinks. Alone," Alex said.

"Don't be such a party pooper," she told him.

"He was goin' to Redskin," Caleb said and nudged Alex in the ribs.

"Redskin? Isn't that racist?" Faith asked in a whisper.

Caleb burst out laughing. "Maybe so. But the bar was named after the peach. So I guess if whoever named the peach was racist . . . round and round it goes."

"It's Georgia. Of course they are racist," Matt said with a sniff.

"So what kind of bar is this?" Faith asked.

"You'll see," Caleb promised.

Alex didn't like sharing his bar with anyone. When he, Caleb, and Lee turned twenty-one, they'd favored the slick lounges in the city, while Alex always found himself pulled in by the neon glow of the roadside Redskin.

"Wow," Faith said as they walked in through the saloon doors. "This is just like the bar in *True Blood*."

He looked at her with her wide eyes as she took it all in. Alex could see it coloring her perspective. The place was a bit of a dive. A touch dangerous. "You know, they say every time someone tells you a 'walked into the bar' joke, you always picture the same one. Whatever that might be."

"Really?" Faith asked. "I never thought about it. I guess I do. Mine's like the one in *Desperado*."

"Sorry to hear that," Matt said with a grimace as he surveyed the crowd. It was largely mixed. Rednecks, city college kids who thought they could slum it, retirees, and underage travelers.

"Hey, darts!" Faith said. "Y'all game?"

"Y'all?" Caleb asked. "Didn't take Georgia long to rub off on you."

"I'll get the first round," Alex said. "Y'all get set up. What'll it be?"

"Beer—"

"Whiskey," Faith interrupted Caleb. "On the rocks."

"Yes, ma'am," Alex said. The guys looked at him strangely—he never drank whiskey. "Lady's choice," he said with a shrug.

By the second round, it was clear that Faith was in her element. "You're a shark!" Caleb said, tipsy before he took the last pull of the amber liquid.

Faith laughed and covered that beautiful mouth with her hand. "Hardly," she said. "I can just hold my liquor better than you guys."

"Speak for yourself," Matt said. He still worked at the first round and made a face with every sip.

"Sorry, they don't serve appletinis here for you," Alex said. "I asked."

Faith grinned at him.

The combination of the whiskey that warmed him from the inside and her smile that lit up the room was undeniable. He stood up from the barstool to take his turn at darts and felt the room start to shift. It had been a long time since he'd let himself get buzzed like this.

"Okay, final round!" Caleb said. "Winner takes all. Or chooses the next game. You know, same thing. Alex, make this round so Faith doesn't make us play truth or dare or some girly shit."

"Hey!" Faith said.

He took the dart, but it was as if his arms were simultaneously too heavy and hollow as a bird's. He barely made it onto the dartboard at all.

"We win!" Faith said and gave Matt a side hug.

"Yay," Matt said, underwhelmed.

"All right, all right," Caleb said. "What's it gonna be, Faith? Makeover madness in the bathroom?"

"You wish," she said. "No, the billiards table just opened up. Let's do classic pool, stripes versus solids."

"Works for me," Alex said. Finally, a game he actually liked. As he started to walk toward the cue sticks, Faith put her hand on his arm and stopped him.

"*And* truth or dare," she said.

Caleb groaned. "I knew it."

"You're the one who gave me the idea!"

"Fine," Caleb said. "How is this going to work?"

"Alex and I are stripes, you two are solids," she said. "Whoever misses, scratches, whatever has to take a truth or dare from someone on the opposite team."

"This is stupid," Alex said under his breath.

"*You're* stupid," Faith shot back. But with that smile, he couldn't be mad at her.

Matt was the first to scratch, to no one's surprise. "Yes!" Faith said. "Okay, Matt, truth or dare?"

"Truth, I guess." He gripped the cue stick like it would save his life.

"Hmm, let's see," she said. "How old were you when you had your first real kiss?"

Matt turned bright red. "I don't remember," he mumbled.

"Bullshit!" Caleb said. "Everyone remembers."

"I don't—"

"C'mon!" Caleb said.

"Fine! Nineteen. Okay?"

Caleb burst out laughing. "Shit, man, what were you doing hanging all over . . . what was her name? Vicky? That whole time in high school for?"

"Vicky was just a friend!"

"Well, obviously," Caleb said with an eye roll.

Faith banked three solids before she missed the fourth by a hair. "Yes!" Caleb said. "Truth or dare?"

"Truth," she said. Faith picked up her third whiskey, which had started to sweat.

"Oh, come on!" Caleb said.

"Lady's choice," she said with a smile.

"Okay, fine. Have you ever had a one-night stand?"

"Sure," Faith said as she put the glass down.

"Really?" Caleb asked. Clearly, he'd expected a different answer. "How'd it happen? What did—"

"That's two questions," she said. "I don't have to answer the second."

"Cheater!" Caleb said as he shook his head.

"First rule of truth or dare. Always ask an open-ended question," she said.

"Women and their manipulations," Caleb said under his breath.

Pool was usually Alex's game, but the pressure of the children's game over it put him on edge. He didn't just miss the first stripe he tried to bank—he put a solid away for the other team. "Damn, Alex, out of practice much?" Caleb asked.

"Out of practice when drinking three glasses of whiskey? Yeah. I'd say so," he said.

"What's it Gonna be?" Caleb asked. "Truth or dare?"

"Shouldn't Matt ask me?"

Before Matt could respond, Caleb cut him off. "Nah, you know it'd be lame. C'mon."

"Fine," Alex said. He looked hard into Caleb's eyes that were so much like his own. Caleb knew him better than anyone, and they were on dangerous ground. He didn't like the direction the questions were going. "Dare."

"Oh! We got a live one!" Caleb said. "Hold on a minute. I need to confer with my partner." He pulled Matt aside and put their backs to Alex and Faith.

"What do you think they're going to do?" she asked him.

"I have no idea. It's like they're at their first slumber party and on a sugar high. Maybe make me take my bra off so they can freeze it. Or a pillow fight."

She slapped him lightly. "You have no idea what girls really do at sleepovers, do you?"

"Okay! We got it," Caleb said. "I dare you . . . to kiss . . . Faith." There was a devilish look in his eye that Alex hadn't seen in a long time.

"What? Hell, no. Are you crazy?" Alex asked.

"Hey!" Faith said. "Rude."

"Not about . . . not about *you*," he said.

"Oh, come on! You know the rules," Caleb said.

"This is childish."

"Come on!"

"It's stupid!"

"Oh my God, just come here," Faith said.

Alex wasn't sure if she kissed him or if he kissed her. All he knew was that suddenly his lips were on hers, and they were softer and sweeter than he could have ever dreamed. Somewhere far in the distance there were whoops, hollers, and an old jukebox hummed. He felt her hands on his chest, and somehow his arms were around her waist. They fit perfectly in that deep curve right above her hips. He wasn't sure, but he thought he felt the tip of her tongue against his. Alex let out a noise in the back of his throat.

Faith pulled back, unable to look at him. Alex could feel his face as it burned.

"That was something," Caleb said. All the play had drained out of him. Matt stared at a television in the far corner.

Faith picked up her drink and downed it, while Alex and Caleb followed suit. "Should we keep playing?" Faith asked. *They have to know this is a terrible idea*, Alex thought, but everyone picked up their cue sticks.

The next couple of truth or dares were much milder. It made Alex think maybe whatever strangeness had happened was over. Still, the next time it was his turn to choose, he picked truth.

"Truth, huh?" Matt asked. He scratched his chin. "Okay. Do you feel like you're over Rebecca?"

"Matt," Caleb hissed.

"What? I'm curious."

Alex looked at Faith. *How much does she know?* He didn't have a clue what Mama or the guys had told her.

She looked back at him. A soft expression spread across her face. "I know about Rebecca," she said.

He was taken aback but also flooded with relief. "Yes," he told Matt, though he still looked at Faith. "I'm over her."

In one pull, Alex finished the nearly full drink they'd poured two questions ago. "I'll be at the boat when y'all are done drinking."

"Ferry's gone, man," Caleb said.

"*Our* boat, idiot," Alex said.

He didn't make it far toward the Saint Rose community dock before he heard steps behind him. "Hey!" Faith called. "Wait up."

Alex glanced behind him but picked up his pace.

"Alex! I'm sorry," she said as she caught up to him. "I didn't mean to make things awkward."

"It's fine," Alex said. "Really. You're not the one who made it awkward anyway."

"Will you stop?" she asked out of breath. "Just for a second."

Alex halted sharply and looked down at her. "What?" he finally barked.

"Are we . . . are we good?" Faith asked. "Because I thought, back there at the bar when you kissed me—"

"*I* kissed you?" he asked.

"Or when I kissed you! Whatever! I just . . . you didn't feel anything? Because I—"

"You're drunk. Go back to the bar."

"I'm drunk? Not any more than you! And you and I both know we're nowhere near buzzed enough to—"

"Faith! Please," he said.

"You don't get to do that!" she said. "You don't get to pretend you didn't feel anything. Or blame it on the drinks or the game or whatever."

"It was a stupid game," he said.

"Yeah! It was. Okay? I was just playing around. I didn't think Caleb and Matt would, you know. But how can you deny what was there when—"

"Faith, seriously. Go back to the bar."

She looked at him with big eyes, lips partially parted. Most of him wanted nothing more than to lean down and kiss her again, but he stopped himself. She was clearly frustrated, but she'd just have to stay like that.

"I can't believe you," she said. She licked her lips, and that just made him want her more.

Alex didn't say anything. He knew if he started to walk away, she might follow. This was a showdown, and one he'd have to wait out.

Faith stared down at the grass. The pink neon from the bar lit up her skin and made her glow like something magical. "Fine," she said finally, and turned on her heel. He watched her leave and listened to her Converse sneakers in the gravel.

Alex didn't turn toward the boat until she was out of sight. *I can't think about how it felt to kiss her,* he told himself. *Don't be an asshole. Or how it felt when she said Rebecca's name.*

No. It was all too much, and it was better not to think about right now.

11

FAITH

She groaned and pulled the pillow over her head. The hangover pounded into her brain, and the sunlight that streamed through the window dug into her eyelids. *How much did I drink last night?*

As Faith rolled over, flashes of last night appeared. She remembered the darts and how she'd gone drink for drink with all the guys—except Matt, of course. Then the billiards. *No, it wasn't just pool. Truth or dare.* And the kiss. *Oh God, the kiss.*

The more she thought about last night, the more details emerged. How it had gone from a stupid dare to something more. She was sure of it. Alex had to have felt it, too. Right?

Even if he did, I didn't have to go running after him! Did I think throwing myself at him would do something? But she couldn't help it. Faith pushed the heels of her hands into her closed eyes and let out a moan. *Maybe it isn't as bad as I think.*

She reached toward her phone on the bedside table. After she'd stumbled home drunk with Caleb and Matt, she couldn't remember the details. Mascara had rubbed off onto her hands, and her phone was nearly dead. Clearly, she hadn't had enough sense to wash her face or plug in the iPhone.

It was early in the morning in California, but Natalie would answer. She called Natalie on FaceTime and checked her smeared makeup on the screen. She looked nearly as bad as she felt.

"Why are you calling so early?" Natalie asked groggily. Faith could make out the familiar floral duvet cover and baby-blue pillowcases. "Jesus, what happened to you?"

"A lot of whiskey happened to me," Faith said. She rolled onto her back and held the phone above her head. "Whiskey and a lot of stupidity."

"Oh yeah?" Natalie asked with a yawn. "The two tend to go together. What'd you do?"

"Why do you think I'm the one who did anything?"

"Because you always instigate," Natalie said with an eye roll.

"Okay, fine. I went drinking with all the guys here I told you about. Well, almost all of them. We went to some dive place on the mainland."

"You? You went to a dive bar?" Natalie asked. "Why do you always tell me no when I ask you to go—"

"Listen!" Faith said. "Anyway, we'd had a couple of drinks already, then I said we should play pool."

"Okay . . ."

"And truth or dare."

"Oh God, Faith," Natalie said. "All right. Who'd you kiss? It was the hot one, right? The brooding one you told me about?"

"Shh!" Faith hissed into the phone. She glanced around the room. "Yes, okay? God, how did you know?"

"How did I know? You always go for the mysterious ones, Faith! You act like I don't know you at all."

"Yeah, well, that wasn't the worse of it."

"No?"

"After, you know. He booked it out of there, and I followed him."

"You followed him."

"Okay, I, like, ran after him."

"Oh my God." Natalie rubbed her eyes. "What happened? Was he drunk, too? Maybe he doesn't remember."

"I mean, we all drank the same amount. He pretty much blew me off and left. I don't—I haven't seen him since then."

"Well, don't worry about it," Natalie yawned. "I'm sure it's no big deal."

"Maybe," Faith said. "Ugh, my phone is about to die. I need to let you go, go find the charger."

"Okay," Natalie said. "But seriously? Don't worry about it. Even if he remembers, you can write it off as being drunk."

"You think?"

"You *were* drunk, weren't you?" Natalie asked. "It'll be fine."

Faith blew Natalie a kiss and scrambled out of bed to look for the charger. As soon as it was plugged in, she started to search for other contractors in the area. Downstairs, she heard the occasional door close and pot bang, but all was quiet. Mae must have figured out they were all hungover and wouldn't bother with a grand breakfast.

She pulled a granola bar out of her bag and tore through the sweetness as she perused contractors. Most were available on Saturdays and answered her calls. The first couple had accents so thick she could barely make out what they said. The next handful provided ballpark bids so astronomically high she almost choked. *George really is giving me a deal*, she thought. It was tough to give up such an attractive bid, but she knew she had to. If he'd screwed over Alex like that, there was no way she'd hire him.

Finally, she called Just Peachy Contractors and an upbeat man with a voice that reminded her of her dad's answered. "This is Craig."

As soon as she introduced herself and gave him the address, he interrupted.

"You mean Lydia's old place, ma'am?" he asked.

"You know it?" By now, she wasn't surprised.

"I know all the properties on Saint Rose."

His bid wasn't nearly as good as George's, but it was doable. *Remember the inheritance*, Faith told herself. She hadn't touched the cash Lydia had left her, so it still didn't seem real. Still, even if she used that cash for the renovations, she'd have plenty left over.

She hung up with Craig feeling lighter and with a verbal agreement to meet at the site to finalize the bid and planning.

Now for the tough part. George. Faith sighed and kicked her

long legs out from under the covers. She felt a little bad about George having already done some of the groundwork but knew she shouldn't. After all, she'd still pay him for the survey work and what he'd done so far. She couldn't be the only client who'd pulled out early in the process.

Faith scrolled through her recent contacts until she found a 912 area code from the day she'd talked with George. "Faith!" his voice crowed when he answered. "To what do I owe the pleasure?" He lingered over the word "pleasure" in a way that made her feel dirty. *I'm doing the right thing.*

"Hi, George," she said and adopted the professional voice she used when speaking with troublesome clients. "I just wanted to give you a call and tell you that I've decided to go a different direction. With Lydia's property. So, I, uh, I'm sorry, but I can't hire you."

"*You* can't hire me," George repeated. His voice had changed, gone nasty. "Don't you mean Alex won't let you hire me?"

"Alex?"

George gave a mean laugh. "C'mon, Faith. How stupid do you think I am?"

"I don't think—"

"Alex put you up to this and don't try to say otherwise." She heard him spit a stream of chew. "Little fuckin' cunt."

"What?"

"Alex," he said slowly, but not until after a long pause.

"Look, George," she said. "I can assure you that I made up my own mind about this. And after talking to you now, I know I made the right decision."

"Y'all are goddamned morons if you think any contractor in the state is going to offer the kind of bid I did. That was a fuckin' friends 'n' family discount. Hear me? I was doin' y'all a goddamned favor—"

Faith hung up before she could hear any more. She longed for the days of landlines, when she could have slammed the phone down, especially as she noticed her shaking hands. *Where did that come from?*

She set the phone screen-side down on the table and swung her legs off the bed. *Coffee.* That was what she needed. Something to help clear her head.

Faith made her way downstairs in a pair of little pink pajama shorts and the matching lace-trimmed cami. A silk robe wrapped around her felt cool and comforting against her skin.

"She lives," Mae said as Faith entered the kitchen.

Faith offered up a little smile.

"Coffee?"

"You read my mind," Faith said.

"Hardly. You're just not the first guest I've had who overimbibed the night before." Mae set down a steaming mug of coffee in front of Faith. "No cream, no sugars?" Mae asked.

"You remembered," Faith said.

"Hard to forget something like that," Mae said with a raised brow. "Never been able to drink my coffee black, as many times as I've tried over the years." She poured a spoonful of heavy cream into her own mug along with a lump of white sugar.

"Mae, can I ask you something?"

"You just call me Mama, sugar," she said.

"Oh, um, okay," Faith said with a blush. "Do you know George Stephanos?"

"Unfortunately," Mama said. She didn't stop stirring.

"Oh. Well, I had been talking to him about renovating the property."

"I know," Mama said.

"Well, I called him this morning. Just now. And told him I've decided to go in another direction."

"Oh? You find someone better suited?"

"I guess you could say that." Faith took a big swallow of the hot rich coffee. *How much does she know? Did Alex talk to her about this stuff?* "But when I called George to tell him? He got really nasty with me. And I don't know why. I'm paying him for the work he's done so far."

Mama tsked and put down her mug. "Doesn't surprise me."

Before Faith could ask her why, Lee and Caleb came into the kitchen. "'Bout time," Mama said to them. Lee looked at her with surprise. "Oh not you," she said.

"Morning, Mama," Caleb said. His voice was scratchy from the hangover.

"Y'all know what George Stephanos did to Faith?" Mama asked.

Faith looked at her with big eyes. *So this is how gossip spreads so fast in the South.*

"What's that?" Lee asked. He sat down beside Mama and leaned in for the gossip.

"Went off on her somethin' ugly. All on account of her choosing another contractor." Mama took another sip of her coffee.

"Figured," Caleb said. "'Cause of Alex?" he asked as he brewed his own mug of coffee.

Faith pinched her brows together. "I just don't want to work with anyone who has no integrity," she said, eager to get off the subject of Alex.

"Integrity's important," Lee agreed.

"You bet it is," Mama said. "Why else do you think I took you in when you were just a kid? I mean, besides you and Alex always bein' two peas in a pod. Back then at least. But it was 'cause you had real integrity, even after what happened to your poor parents."

Lee opened his mouth to say something but snapped it shut as Alex walked into the kitchen. Lee looked at Alex but didn't say a word.

Faith was reminded of that first day she'd arrived at Greystone, back when she'd thought Lee was just a hired hand. Caleb and Alex had really been going at one another that day, and Alex had been flippant toward Lee. *There is a lot more going on under the surface than I know.*

She'd pieced together how Lee factored into the equation, but not why he and Alex had killed their friendship. Why Mama had kept Lee on though, she could see. Lee couldn't have broken any real trusts, or Mama would have kicked him out. *So what is it?*

There were tensions between all the men, and she couldn't even begin to unravel them. Clearly, there were still a lot of disagreements happening behind the scenes. She felt Mama's hands on hers. Across the table, the older woman's warm blue eyes were filled with concern. "Poor thing," Mama said. "That's a nasty hangover, isn't it?"

Faith just nodded, embarrassed now that Alex was in the room.

"One of y'all should take her to explore the ocean today," Mama said. Faith's stomach lurched at the thought of trying to handle sea legs. "Don't you worry," Mama said. "The salt-water is known for its healing powers."

"Lee and I are busy today," Caleb said. He finished his mug of coffee and rinsed it in the farmhouse sink. "Boat work on the fishing rig. But maybe Alex is free." It was more of a statement than a question, and Caleb didn't even bother checking Alex's expression.

Faith looked up and saw Alex's glare toward Caleb's back. She blushed and looked away. *What is Caleb trying to pull? Just the other day, he would have jumped at a chance to flirt with me on a boat for an afternoon.*

"What's going on?" Mama asked. "Y'all better speak up real soon."

Faith racked her brain for an excuse, but fortunately Alex spoke up—somewhat. "I'll take her," he mumbled, barely audible.

"Now that's more like it," Mama said. "I swear, sometimes it's like you boys were raised with no manners at all. And what do y'all s'pose that says about me?"

Faith smiled. "I'll go get my suit on, then," she said.

"Make sure you wear a shirt," Alex called after her. "And shorts, too. And covered shoes!" She ignored him as she raced up the stairs. *I swear, sometimes it's like dealing with a stepfather!*

In the bedroom, she pulled out the collection of swimwear she'd eagerly packed back in San Francisco. At the time, she'd envisioned a lazy, leisurely summer of sunbathing and had gone overboard with the bikinis and monokinis. Natalie had gone shopping with her, encouraging her to get both a yellow string bikini and a tropical-print mesh monokini. "You can never have too many sexy swimsuits!" Natalie had said. Faith opted for a skimpy white bikini.

In the mirror, Faith noticed that she'd somehow already turned a golden bronze from the Georgia sun. It was just the right amount of glow to warrant the bright-white bikini that barely covered her. She wiggled into the stonewashed short shorts with pockets that peeked out and kissed her thighs.

At the bottom of the duffel bag, she found the white crop top with the peach graphic across the chest she'd purchased before her trip. It hung off one shoulder, and she could easily make out the bikini underneath. "You *have* to get this!" Natalie had crowed. "It's so Georgia!"

Alex had told her to wear shorts and a shirt. He hadn't specified how modest they had to be. As she pulled on the beat-up black Converse that she'd had since law school, her heart began to race. One more look in the mirror, and Faith had to admit she was a vision. A sliver of taut golden stomach could be seen between the shorts and crop top. She pulled her long hair into a messy topknot and slid the vintage Ray-Bans on.

She couldn't tell she was hungover at all. *If this doesn't pique Alex's interest, nothing will.*

12

FAITH

Faith sauntered onto the front porch, where Alex waited. He'd changed, too, into knee-length board shorts and a tight white T-shirt. She took in his muscled chest and broad shoulders before she glanced away.

"Come here," he said. "I want to show you something."

She followed him wordlessly, aware of the warm summer breeze that whipped around her thighs and stomach. Alex walked ahead of her but not at that lightning-fast clip he normally took. Still, Faith hung back and admired the span of his back. He'd hoisted a small red backpack over his shoulders. She couldn't quite put her finger on it, but there was something about him that was addictively intriguing.

"So," she said as she approached his side. "What was it like growing up here? I can't even imagine."

"Oh?" he asked, though he didn't look at her. "I thought all these memories were comin' back to you. But sounds like it wasn't exciting enough for you to remember much."

She faltered. "That's not what I meant when I said that," she said. "About forgetting about summers on Saint Rose. I mean, I was just a kid. I don't really remember kindergarten, either. Honestly? I'm kind of jealous, if you want to know the truth."

"Jealous?"

She shrugged. "I grew up in Southern California. We had beaches, obviously, but not like this. They were super crowded, unless you wanted to get up at five in the morning. And even then, there were countless surfers who had the same idea."

"You surf?" he asked, surprised.

"No," she blushed. "My cousins who I grew up with did. Still do, actually."

"Oh. Well, a childhood on Saint Rose is great for learning about nature. But it was hard being so far away from everyone else."

"I guess the grass is always greener," she said. What she really wanted to ask was who "everyone else" was.

"What about you?" he asked.

She nearly tripped in surprise. *Is he really asking about me for a change?* "Not much to tell," she said carefully. "It's a pretty cliché California story. When I was really young, we lived in Los Angeles. My mom was an actress—"

"Have I seen her in anything?" he asked.

"Probably not. She died when I was a baby. I don't even remember her, and the movies she was in were mostly really small parts or made for television type of things."

113

"I'm sorry," he said.

"It's okay, it was a long time ago," she said. "She gave up acting when she got pregnant with me—well, gave up acting *and* drinking, or so I was told."

"Did she . . ."

"She was an alcoholic," Faith said simply. "That's not exactly the word my dad used, but it was obvious. Any money she made with her acting, it went to lavish parties and expensive liquor."

"And what about your dad?" Alex asked. They'd reached a small cliff where the tall grass tickled their bare legs and the view of the water was magical.

"He worked a lot," she said. "Attorney. I guess that's why I went into law, too. He was pretty distant, like a lot of men from his generation were. And I don't know. It's hard to say how much of it was because of my mom. A lot of people tell me I look just like her."

"Well. At least you had a father," he said.

It stung when he said that, like it all circled back to Alex no matter what. "I guess that's true," she admitted. "Though, him dying when I was a teenager wasn't exactly easy. Sometimes . . . God, this sounds bad, but sometimes I kind of wish I'd never known him, either. So you know some of my darkest secrets. Tell me one of yours."

"Like what?" he asked. She couldn't read his eyes through the sunglasses perched on his aquiline nose.

"Like what's the deal with you and Lee?"

Alex was quiet so long she thought he planned to ignore her

entirely. "Lee and I were best friends. For a long time, all through childhood."

"Yeah, I gathered that. And then?" she asked as she navigated around an abandoned sandcastle.

"And then I found out he was in love with my wife."

"I'm sorry." Now it was her turn to apologize, though it sounded fake. The shock reached all the way to her marrow.

Alex sighed. "I didn't know until after Rebecca died," he said. "And it's not like Lee ever *said* it to me. They didn't have an affair or anything. But I could tell, you know? That he was into her. And then, afterward, it just became obvious. And I started thinking about all these little times when I saw Lee sit up straighter when she walked in. I think she was oblivious. But Lee . . . he still blames me for it."

Faith's breath caught in her throat. *Blames him? What happened?* But she didn't want to push.

"I mean, hell, I can't blame Lee for that. For him thinking it's my fault, at least." Alex walked on in silence for a few more feet. "I blame myself, too. That night. Christ, I should have stopped her. I knew she'd been drinking."

She wanted to thank him for trusting her with this, but the shock at the revelation stole her words. Divorce, sure, she'd assumed that. She'd never thought his wife had died.

Faith searched for something to say, the right thing to say. "Get undressed," Alex said suddenly. He shrugged the backpack off and pulled off his shirt.

She was shocked at the forwardness, but she felt a jolt of excitement shoot through her. As if she couldn't resist his commands, she hooked her thumbs into her shorts and bikini bottoms—then realized Alex just meant for them to strip to their swimsuits.

Embarrassed, she pulled off just the shorts and shirt. "Here," he said to her, and held out his hand for her shorts and shirt that were wadded up in her fist.

She suddenly felt too naked, too exposed, in the tiny white bikini. Alex stuffed their clothes into the backpack.

"Come on," he said, and headed toward the water. She tried not to stare too obviously at his body as he scrambled down the steep sandbank. Faith realized he was wearing rubber-bottomed water shoes, perfect for climbing and handling the beachy terrain. Her own feet felt heavy and waterlogged.

He was already waist-deep in the jewel-colored water by the time she made it to the frothy shore. She bent over and pulled off her shoes. The warm water tickled her feet while the sand pulled at her toes. She was surprised by the warmth of the water, nearly bath temperature though it was before noon.

Alex turned and looked at her. She couldn't read his expression behind his aviators. "Hurry up!" he said.

With every step, the water licked higher up her legs and reached toward her thighs. When she was an arm's length from Alex, he held out his hand.

"Come on," he said. "We can wade all the way there."

"Wade?" she asked in disbelief.

"It'll be fine, I promise."

"Where?" She grabbed his hand and he pulled her to his side. "Where are we going? I thought there was a boat—"

"You'll have to wait and see," he said with a grin. Alex pulled the backpack as high onto his shoulders as he could with one hand, but didn't let go of his grip on her.

Faith was stunned by him. He was almost playful. It was a side she hadn't seen before.

As they splashed onward, she was surprised that the depths of the water seemed to have stabilized. They were no longer going deeper into the water but seemed to be on a level surface that led them into the unknown. "Ready?" Alex asked.

She didn't know how to answer and couldn't have responded if she'd wanted to. Suddenly, the sand took a dip and the water was at her chest. She gasped and he let out a laugh. Faith looked up at him and the blazing white smile that spread across his face. He was gleeful, in his element, and the beauty of it stole her voice.

As quickly as the sand had deepened, it began to rise. The land started to slope upward again, and the water was back at her hips. She was aware of the wet swimsuit fabric that clung to her chest, and how her nipples had hardened in response to the wetness followed by the breeze. Faith glanced down to see just how transparent the suit had become. *That was one thing I didn't check on in the Neiman Marcus dressing room!* But she couldn't tell.

Alex led her onto dry ground. "A sandbar!" she exclaimed. It was a big one, too, nearly a tiny island. Faith laughed. She hadn't known what to expect, but certainly not this. "How do you know about this?" she asked.

He smiled at her. "I know all the island's secrets," he said. "Actually, this has been my spot since I was a kid. I've never seen anyone else here."

She marveled at the secret spot. It looked completely untouched by humans. At the water's edge, perfect sand dollars and gorgeous shells peppered the white sand.

Alex let the backpack slip off and pulled out bottled water and sunblock. "Here," he said as he tossed the sunblock toward her. "I didn't want to have you do this until we were out of the water."

She stole glances at him while she rubbed the lotion up her calves and along the span of her hips. Faith covered her belly, chest, and arms in the thick SPF and handed it back to Alex.

"Hey," he said as he finished coating himself in the lotion. "Get my back?"

She bit her lip as she began to work his back. He was warm, wet, and the feel of his muscles beneath her hands was almost too much to bear. Faith finished in a hurry so she wouldn't be tempted to drool too much.

"Thank you, ma'am," he said. "Want me to do you?"

A flurry of flirtatious comebacks came to her, but she simply turned her back instead and tucked stray strands of hair into the knot.

She closed her eyes as he began to work the lotion into her back. Alex started at her shoulders and slid a finger underneath the strip of her halter top. He worked his way down, across her shoulder blades. She let out a moan as he hit a tense muscle in her lower back.

Alex paused, and a flicker of embarrassment washed over her. She expected him to stop, but instead he did it again, deeper. She moaned again, and the rest of her body started to respond.

His touch didn't just release that tight muscle in her back. It started a fire throughout her entire body. *Damn,* she thought. She could drift away, let this man touch her all over like he was touching her right now.

His thumbs expertly glided across her lower back as he worked out the kinks. Faith's breasts tightened, and she felt her nipples pebble. She sucked in her breath, head bowed, and could see her nipples as they responded to him.

A warm wetness began to spread between her legs. Normally she'd get flustered. She shouldn't be getting turned on right now, but how Alex touched her . . . it had been so long.

She arched her back and pushed back against him. Faith could hear his breath right behind her. His shadow fell over her.

He stopped rubbing her back so suddenly that she nearly fell backward. Alex stood up and waded into the water alone. He tried to play it cool, like it was natural, but the awkwardness was obvious.

Faith watched him, aware that the tiny window of time to let seduction take over was rapidly closing. *If only I were bold enough,* she thought. She had been before, with other men. But that was different. It was clear they'd wanted her, and she'd been equipped with liquid courage. Seduction was easy in the dim lights of a big-city bar. But here? On this secret sandbar with a man she sometimes felt hated her? The risk of getting embarrassed or worse, turned down, was too much.

What is wrong with me? she asked herself as she watched him dip below the water. When he came back up, the seawater glistened on his back. *Getting all turned on when he was just putting sunblock on me? Rubbing my back because it was tight?*

Alex didn't look at her and certainly didn't ask her to join him. *I'm reading way too much into this. The guy seriously just told me about his best friend being in love with his dead wife!*

She leaned back on her elbows and let the sun soak into her skin. *Alex didn't even want to take me out here. His mom made him.*

Faith looked toward the horizon and tried to enjoy the natural beauty. Here she was, squarely in paradise, and all she could think about was how horny she was. And Natalie was probably right, anyway. She did always go after the men who made her wonder if they even liked her. The moody, brooding type, and Alex certainly fit that description.

He swam lazily in the water and didn't look at her once. Although Faith willed the swell between her thighs to go away, it was a slow process. Her nipples were still hard, too, though she could blame that on the breeze.

Alex must have thought she was totally crazy. Either that, or a complete nymphomaniac. She could blame the other night on the whiskey. But today? That was all on her.

As she watched him dive into the water again, she tried to think about anything except how he looked without a shirt. How the water trickled off his perfectly sculpted muscles. How he seemed to know exactly how to touch her and could turn her on without even coming close to where she wanted him to touch her.

13

ALEX

*A*lex stood beneath the rainfall showerhead in the cabin and hoped the soothing spray would wash away the shame of the day.

It didn't work. He mentally kicked himself repeatedly. Why he thought it would be a good idea to take Faith out into the middle of nowhere—his middle of nowhere—and rub lotion on her, he had no clue.

He tried to tell himself it had been an honest mistake. That the lotion thing had just been a fluke, and he'd honestly been trying to avoid burns. But even he knew that was mostly bullshit, no matter how he twisted it in his mind.

But now? He couldn't stop thinking about how her skin had felt on his. Or how she'd groaned and pushed into his hand. He'd seen her nipples harden at his touch and couldn't stop himself from responding in turn. Alex had stiffened instantly the moment he'd touched her but had kept a large enough distance between them that she hadn't noticed.

I gotta stop. But it was like he'd opened a floodgate and there was no turning back.

He'd been in this shower with its lukewarm water for ten minutes already. Alex turned the tap all the way to cold and flinched as the cool spray caressed his skin. But it did nothing to lessen his hardness. It ached painfully, but there was no way he would let himself get any kind of release. He was afraid he'd come with images of Faith in that nothing of a see-through bikini in his mind.

After another ten minutes, he gave up. He shivered as he turned off the tap and grabbed a towel. As he stomped around the cabin to dry off, he tried to think of anything but Faith.

Alex pulled jeans and a T-shirt out of the dresser and gave his hair a final rub with the towel. There was no way to deny his attraction for her. *Don't forget that she's not sticking around*, he told himself. *Yeah. Who needs that kind of trouble, anyway?*

And that's exactly what she was. Trouble. For the past week he'd avoided the house as much as possible. At first, it had been easy. In fact, it was kind of nice to take a break from Caleb's jokes at dinner and Lee's perpetual "woe is me" expressions. But days of making bonfires on the beach and living off his meager catches was starting to get old. He hated to admit it, but he craved company. Specifically, *her* company.

Alex sighed as he combed his damp hair. Mama wasn't going to put up with "another damn day" of him avoiding dinner. That was how she'd put it when he walked Faith back to the inn that afternoon.

"You avoiding us?" Mama had asked.

"No, ma'am," he said sullenly. He felt like a teenager getting reprimanded in front of Faith.

"Good. Then I expect to see all y'all for supper tonight," she'd said.

Everyone else was already in the formal dining room when he made his way to Greystone. Matt bombarded Faith with questions about firms in San Francisco, while Caleb snatched chips and pimiento dip from the table. Gwen swatted his hand.

As soon as Mama strode into the dining room and set down the mashed sweet potatoes, Alex went to his chair and waited for her to sit. He groaned inwardly when he saw Faith approach him.

"Can I sit here?" she asked, that sweet smile on her face.

"Do what you want," he said. "But it's quiet time."

She made a face and sat down anyway. The dinner felt forced, though Mama commanded it like a queen. She only asked Faith once how the afternoon had been before she directed the conversation toward Caleb and Lee.

Gwen served the still-warm peach pie à la mode, and the table was pleasantly quiet save for the occasional scrape of the last plump peach slice from a plate. Caleb leaned back with a hand on his stomach. "I'm stuffed," he said. "May I be excused, ma'am?" he asked Mama. She shooed him away.

"Alex," Mama said. "Why don't you take Faith on a walk? It's good for digestion."

"I'd love that!" Faith said. He thought he saw his mama give a conspiratorial smile but couldn't be sure. And Alex was too full to argue anyway.

The sun had just started to descend as they walked toward the trail that led to the water's edge. The rays got caught in her locks and gave the loose waves an almost amber look. She was every bit as beautiful as that sunset, if he were honest.

"So," he stammered, "when, uh, when are you going to meet with George again?" He hated the way that man's name sounded on his tongue.

"Ugh," she said. "I'm not. Another contractor is coming tomorrow to take a look at the property, though. And give a concrete bid."

They'd reached the water. The still surface reflected the pastel rainbows of the setting sun. "Really?" he asked. He wanted to push more, ask what had happened to George, but he was conflicted.

Obviously, Faith had fired George because of him. But what was he supposed to say? To feel? Did she expect him to be grateful? *I should be grateful, asshole.* "Thanks." It sounded awkward, but she smiled up at him.

"It's no big deal," she said. "I didn't exactly want to feel indebted to him anyway. Besides, he kind of gives me the creeps."

She could make it sound like she did it for herself all she wanted, but he knew the truth. The silence began to stretch into uncomfortable territory. He racked his brain for something to say, but it was blank.

"It's beautiful here," she said. "But, I don't know. It doesn't seem to suit you."

"Thanks," he said sarcastically.

"That's not what I meant," she said and elbowed him in the ribs. They stopped simultaneously to take in the sunset. "I mean, where did you think you'd end up? When you were a kid?"

"I don't know," he said with a frown. "Not here, that's for sure."

"Yeah, well. I thought I'd get the hell out of California the first chance I got," she said. Faith popped a mint between her plump lips. "And look at me. San Francisco's as far as I got."

"I don't know how it happens," he said. "I made mistakes, plenty of them, in my early twenties. Mistakes that didn't look like mistakes at the time, but they derailed me. Not that you'd know what that's like," he added pointedly. The satisfaction from that little dig settled nicely into his stomach.

"What, like I never made a mistake?" Faith asked. There wasn't any accusation in her tone, just curiosity. For a split second, Alex felt badly for the assumption.

"Well, it certainly seems like you have it all together," he said. He stared out at the water, unable to meet her eyes.

She laughed that tinkling giggle that made him weak. "Me? The only reason I majored in prelaw, then went to law school, is because my dad once said when he was pissed off at me that I'd never get in. I wanted to prove him wrong."

"But you did, obviously," Alex said.

"Yeah," Faith agreed quietly. "That's a lot of time, work, and money just to prove your daddy wrong." She squinted into the lazy sun. "I had this dream, you know?"

"Like Martin Luther King?"

"No!" she said with a laugh. "I mean, I imagined my dad in

the audience at law school graduation, and he'd be so proud. Like, he'd realize how wrong he was about me."

"And?" Alex asked.

"How does that saying go?" Faith crunched down on the mint, and Alex could smell the rush of peppermint. "If you want to make God laugh, make plans? My dad died during my first year of law school. And we were as far apart as ever."

"Yeah, I . . . I didn't know that. When you first arrived. And when you told me the other day, I didn't respond right," Alex said. Suddenly, he didn't know what to do with his hands. "I'm sorry."

She shrugged. "Don't be. The past is the past. I just, you know, kind of have a chip on my shoulder about being told I can't do something. Obviously. It makes me want to do it more."

"But you still finished law school. Not just that, you're an attorney. Surely you're not still proving your dad wrong," he said.

"I don't know." She gazed into the distance. "Maybe I am."

"You sound like me, though," Alex said. "The whole proving people wrong thing. At least, until a couple of years ago."

Faith was quiet for a beat. "It must have been hard," she said slowly. "Losing someone like that."

He thought he'd feel that familiar pang in his chest, the one that came every time Rebecca's death was mentioned. But it didn't come. "It was," he said. "And it wasn't. And hell, the more I think about it, I don't even know why I still carry a grudge against Lee. He never acted on how he felt about

Rebecca, or nothin'. Matter of fact, probably did better than most, harboring that crush for so long. "

"I know exactly what you mean. About how we 'should feel' when we lose someone. I felt that way when my dad passed away."

Alex looked at her and saw her face full of sincerity. *She's nothing if not truthful.* Maybe she really did know how it felt. How it felt like you were just blundering along when people heaped how sorry they were onto you. Of course he wished Rebecca hadn't died. Their relationship hadn't always been so shitty—had it? There had to have been good times. He wished he could remember those.

But he also wished Lee hadn't been in love with her, whether he could help it or not. *Who the hell knows? Maybe it was just a little crush, not love at all. But he'd lugged that grudge against Lee around so long, it was a part of him now.* He wished George and Rebecca hadn't had that *thing* on the long weekend. But it was like as soon as someone died, they could do no wrong. Everything was forgiven, and the living were left to bear their crosses.

Alex's gaze dipped down to Faith's lips, glazed with a gloss and smelling of Christmas. He wished he'd had the time, the mind-set, to enjoy those lips the first time he'd tasted them. His eyes continued downward to her breasts. From this angle, he could see straight down the button-up gingham shirt to the pink lace bra below. Her cleavage was deep and deliciously tempting, though he was disappointed he couldn't make out her nipples. When they'd hardened in that little swimsuit, he was so turned on he could almost taste them between his lips.

The urge to kiss her was almost unbearable. To nibble on

those lips and run a thumb across her breasts. *Hell, I even know what she tastes like.* But this time it would be different. It wouldn't be under the guise of a game or with Caleb and Matt cheering him on.

Alex leaned down and she tilted her head up. He watched her close her eyes, those thick lashes fluttered shut. But at the last second, when those lips he craved more than anything were only an inch away, he straightened up. "It's gettin' dark," he said. "We better head back."

He turned and stalked toward the inn before she could say anything or he could see the disappointment on her face. *What's the matter with me? She's already nearly begged me once!*

"Hey!" she called as she caught up to him. "What's the matter? You—"

"I gotta get up early tomorrow," he said.

"But—"

"C'mon, I'll walk you back," he said.

They didn't say another word all the way back to the inn. He thought he saw someone, probably Mama, through the window, but he couldn't be certain. The crickets had started to chirp, which helped ease the awkward silence.

"Well," Faith said as they made their way onto the porch. "Thanks for . . ."

She couldn't finish. Thanks for what? "Get some rest," he said. For a moment, he felt like a teenager again. All left feet and in the spotlight below a girl's front porch light. As much as he'd hated those years, it had been a long time since he'd felt that kind of flutter in his chest. And Faith looked so goddamned beautiful with the sun-kissed freckles across her nose.

"Rest," she repeated, as if she really had to mull it over.

"Night," he said and took off toward the cabin.

"Good night," she called back. He heard the front door swing open and Mama's voice asked how the sunset walk had been. Faith's voice gushed, but by now he was too far away to make out the words.

Too far away, and the stiffness that ached in his jeans was so overwhelming it was all he could think about.

14

FAITH

*T*he sunset cast a pink glow across the dusty abandoned plantation home. Faith made her way through the rooms and scrawled down notes. Since she didn't know much about construction or architecture, she thought her notes would be few. But it didn't take long until she started to notice the magnitude of problems.

Mold, maybe even black mold, had settled into bathroom corners. The exposed wiring for the chandelier and sconce lighting looked dangerous even to her untrained eye. She sighed and perched on the windowsill. It was wooden and ornate, but she felt it give slightly. *What kind of mess am I signing up for?*

For the past few days, she'd trotted around the property with Craig and Alex. Craig was solicitous and likable. Even Alex had grunted his approval. However, not even the best contractor in the world was going to be able to turn this neglected home around for anything less than a small fortune.

Outside, she watched Craig and Alex finish up another round of the property. It wasn't just the house that needed salvation. It operated off an old well system, and the pipes seemed to be pierced by tree roots. Craig had promised to bring out a "water guy," who he promised was honest, but honesty wasn't going to pay that bill.

Faith dusted off the back of her denim shorts and went outside. "Okay guys, what new problems do you have for me?"

Craig smiled up at her. He was middle-aged and had started to go silver, but he still had a boyish smile that always lightened up bad news. "Not so bad today, ma'am" he said. "Although I'd recommend getting an arborist out here to look at some of the trees close to the back porch. One of 'em looks diseased if not dead, and you don't want it fallin' on the new roof."

"And how much is that going to cost?"

"Hard to say, ma'am," Craig said. "Fallin' trees aren't my business. Couple thousand, maybe? With stump removal?"

She cringed. The figures just kept climbing higher.

"All right, ma'am, that's all we got for today," Craig said. He tipped the baseball cap emblazoned with his company logo. "Y'all have a good night."

Faith bounded up the front steps to look for Alex. She thought she heard something in the abandoned laundry room. She turned into the small room off the mud room and was smacked with a flashback.

There was no Alex, and suddenly the room sparkled bright and white. She could smell bleach in the air, and the addictive scent of fresh cotton. But everything seemed taller, bigger. The ancient washer rumbled, and at her feet was a basket of clothespins.

"Daddy?" her own child voice was instantly recognizable. Still, she couldn't make out her father's face.

She saw his hands pull up the jeans that were at his knees, his rough fingers as they struggled with the belt. "Faith! Get on outta here," he said.

"Fate! Fate!" her cousin's voice, with that tiny lisp, bellowed from just a few feet behind her.

She still didn't look up. But she saw Lydia's short, clean nails pull down her housedress and smooth the skirt. One sensible heel had fallen off, and the other clung to her nyloned toe. "Little ladies should knock before they come into a closed room." Aunt Lydia's voice was also, in an instant, recognizable.

Faith's breath stuck in her throat. Her father and her aunt? His sister? A sickening hook sunk into her stomach.

That's why I didn't remember. That's why we never came back. Why the family cut us off.

"Ready?" Alex asked her. She jumped at his voice. "You okay? Look like you seen a ghost."

"Uh, yeah," she said. Her voice wobbled. "Fine. Just, um, remembered something."

"Anything important?" he asked. The concern consumed his face.

Can I trust him? "I don't . . . I don't know," she said. "I, Jesus, this sounds messed up. I think I walked in here when I was a kid. And, uh, caught my dad. With Lydia."

"Your *Aunt* Lydia?" he asked.

"Yes," she said quietly.

He let out a breath and put an arm around her as he guided her out of the house. It was firm and solid, strong enough to steady her.

Thank God he is here. She'd figured that by now he wouldn't stick around for these walk-throughs and consultations. It had been a few days since their near kiss, and the tension between them was intense. But day after day he kept hanging around while she took care of items related to the property. Craig had even mistaken him for her boyfriend.

On the walk back to the plane, she tried to push the memory out of her head and focus on the house. *What is the point in dwelling on it?* She didn't question its validity. She knew what she'd seen and was confident in her assumptions of why they'd never returned—and why she'd never had contact with her dad's family.

Instead, she tried to focus on the project at hand, secure with Alex's arm around her shoulder. The reality of the renovation work began to really sink in. Craig told her it would take at least eight weeks to complete, and that was assuming no bumps. "But there're always bumps," he'd cautioned with a laugh.

"I can't believe I've been here two weeks already," she told Alex. The change of topic was awkward, but he went along with it.

"Time flies," he said.

"I told Mae—er, Mama—that it would just be a couple of weeks. But with what Craig said about the project, I don't know. I think I'll need to talk to her about staying a month."

"A month?" he asked. He stopped so fast she nearly ran into him.

"At least," she said. "I don't know. With how things are sounding, it might be a whole summer here."

Alex didn't reply but did continue to walk. She couldn't tell if he was upset about it, happy, or something else. But he certainly didn't return his arm to her shoulder.

"So yeah. I'm hoping to go into town tomorrow and start looking at flooring. Maybe check out the door and window shop Craig was talking about."

Alex didn't say anything, and she gave up. There was only so long she could force a one-sided conversation. They climbed into the plane and spent the short flight back in silence. By now, Faith could recognize a lot of the landmarks with new adult eyes.

Faith stole glances at him out of the corner of her eye. Even with his quietness today, it seemed like he'd warmed up to her in the past couple of days. Or maybe she'd imagined it all. *Or maybe he just felt sorry for me when I realized my dad was screwing his sister.*

Faith focused on the confidence he showcased while he expertly maneuvered the plane. She'd toyed with the idea of getting a pilot's license but hadn't gone beyond an orientation course. It had been on a whim, an effort to get rid of a lingering fear of flying.

Her heart no longer banged away in her chest when he landed the plane. *When did I get used to this? Taking little planes to tiny islands off other islands?* It had only been a few days, but she'd surprised herself by how easily she'd settled in. Natalie couldn't understand how Faith wasn't bored out of her mind, and she couldn't explain it, either. Every time she got an email from the firm, she dreaded it. How easily she could just leave her life in California behind amazed her.

"What's for dinner tonight?" Alex asked her as she helped him pull the canvas cover over the plane.

"Gwen didn't say this morning," Faith said. "And I'm not sure if I'll even make it down. I'm exhausted."

"Renovating a plantation is tough work," Alex said. He tightened up the cables.

"I bet. And I'm not even the one actually doing it."

"What kind of flooring you got in mind?" he asked as they began the walk to the inn. *Is he actually taking an interest in the project? Or just trying to keep my mind off what I'd remembered?*

"I don't know. Wood, definitely, but I'm torn between a nice, rich dark or a lighter, walnut-colored one. Wide planks, either way. What do you think?"

He shrugged. "Wood's wood, if you're just talking about the stain. But given the temperature and humidity here, I'd go with an oak."

"Oak?" she asked.

"Or something else native. Something that's meant to be here. And doesn't have to adjust. Of course, any good contractor would let the planks sit a few days anyway."

She nodded as if she'd thought of all that herself. "And as for the doors and windows, I don't know. Obviously it would be best to go with the most energy efficient possible in the long run, but that'll really add up. And this whole project is already costing way more than I expected."

"Houses always do," he said. She tripped over a root that shot up out of the sandy trail, and he caught her arm.

"Careful," he said. She blushed and let go of his hand.

"Maybe I should start watching some of those HGTV shows," she said.

"What now?"

"You know. The home and garden channel."

"That magazine has a whole channel now?"

She rolled her eyes. "Yeah. One of my roommates back in law school was totally addicted to it. I didn't get it at the time, but I do now. I just wish all of that secondhand television forced onto me had actually sunk in."

He shook his head. "You start watching all that, and you'll be more confused than you are now. If I were you, I'd trust Craig to make most of the selections. He knows what does well here, what looks good, and what's high quality."

"You don't think it would be fun?" she asked as she looked up at him. "Picking everything out, making all the choices—"

"Nah," he said. "It's like planning a wedding. It might sound fun at first, but as soon as you get into it . . ."

He trailed off, and she didn't want to push. Every time he mentioned Rebecca, she felt like she saw the pain fresh all over again. "Maybe you're right," she said. "Besides, I didn't come all the way here to spend my time streaming television."

"Streaming?"

She shook her head. "Never mind."

Alex took off his baseball cap and ran his fingers through his thick hair. Faith could watch his hands all day. They were perfect, though she'd never fancied herself a "hand girl" before. But Alex's were big with thick fingers that looked just as adept at manual labor as a roll in the sheets. She blushed at the thought but couldn't help herself. She imagined, if she could ever explore them, that they would have just a few calluses. Enough for a touch of roughness without it being too much.

"Yeah?" Alex asked. She realized he'd caught her staring at him.

"Nothing," she said and looked away. "It's just you keep your nails really clean. For, you know, a guy who works on planes."

He gave a short laugh. It was so rare that it sounded delightfully foreign. "You're judging my fingernails?"

"Don't worry. You passed," she teased. "Women look at these things, you know."

"Good to know."

Mama was sitting with Lee on the front porch as they approached, a pitcher of sweet tea between them. "Y'all have a productive day?" Mama asked.

"As productive as it can be when you're basically building a home from scratch," Alex said. She shot him a thankful look, being glad that she wouldn't have to make house-related pleasantries with Mama.

"That place has good bones," Lee said. He wiped the back of his hand across his mouth. A hand that was nothing like Alex's.

"And how would you know?" Alex asked. Lee just shrugged.

"Boys," Mama said. "I swear, they can be like a couple o' cats in a duffel bag."

Faith smiled at Mama, impeccably dressed as always. She wore cream linen wide-legged trousers, a perfectly pressed turquoise silk blouse, and matching jeweled sandals. "Got any more sweet tea?" Faith asked. It was strange how she'd come to crave it every evening. But something about that sugar rush was irresistible.

"I'll go grab you a glass," Mama said and started to get up.

"No!" Faith said with a laugh. "I'll get it, I know where they are."

She listened to the three of them talk as she pulled one of Mama's tea glasses with the lemons etched into it out of the cupboard. Gwen was nowhere in sight, but she could smell her signature pork and beans as they simmered on the stove-top. *This is how life could be. It's how it is for some people*, she thought.

On the porch, she downed a glass of the sweet tea and felt a new wave of exhaustion wash over her. "You tired, baby?" Mama asked.

"Yes, ma'am," she said. "I don't know. The worrying about finishing the house, being out there in the heat all day. It feels like I ran a marathon."

"Well, I wouldn't know how that feels," Mama said. "A lady shouldn't *run*, let alone run twenty-something miles. But I know how tiring it can be to manage a house being reno-vated. Why don't you go on and take a rest? Gwen can bring you up something."

"Actually, I think I might just make something light and hit the hay early tonight." *Hit the hay? When did I start talking like that?*

"You sure, baby?" Mama asked. "Gwen picked up some great pork cuts this afternoon. There's some extra in the fridge if you want."

"Thanks," Faith said with a tired smile. "Well, good night, y'all."

"Night," Lee said softly over his shoulder. He still looked at her from time to time as though he had a schoolboy crush on her, but it was lessening. And now that she knew about what had happened with Alex, Lee, and Rebecca, when Lee looked at her like that it made her nervous. Mama offered up her signature megawatt smile. But Alex barely glanced at her. He gave a slight nod in her direction but continued to stare into the horizon.

Faith slathered some mustard onto the home-baked bread Gwen and Mama prepared nearly every morning. It was crusty yet soft on the inside—the kind of bread she paid six dollars a loaf for at the upscale market on the way home from the firm.

She shook her head and laughed at the insanity of it. Who paid six dollars for bread? And it had nothing on what she'd become accustomed to on Saint Rose. Mama hadn't been wrong about the pork. It was thick, juicy, and smelled heavenly. Faith layered it with the local cheese Mama picked up regularly from the dairy farm in Savannah and stuffed lettuce leaves from Greystone's little vegetable garden into it. Now *this* was living.

Upstairs, Faith slipped into her satin pajama shorts and tank top before she washed her face. She looked dog-tired in the mirror and barely had enough energy to plait her hair. After she spread moisturizer on her face, she perched on the edge of her bed and tore into the sandwich while her laptop booted up.

There was an email from the firm, but she could tell by the subject line it was just a checking-in email. *Thank God*, she thought as she archived it. A bunch of spam, a cursory summer letter from her aunt, probably with updates on all her cousins' accomplishments, and an automated message from the dating site Natalie had made her sign up for six months ago.

"We miss you!" the subject line read. She groaned and almost deleted it. At the last minute, she clicked it open, scrolled down and unsubscribed. *The last thing I need is a reminder of just how single I am.*

Although she didn't have any emails from any genealogy forums, she logged into the forums just in case. Nobody had responded directly to her. *Of course.*

She'd polished off the sandwich in record time. Faith closed the laptop and returned to the bathroom. *Flossing can wait till tomorrow*, she thought as she performed a cursory tooth brushing. As she watched herself in the mirror, she scrunched up her nose and turned from side to side. *What is it with Alex?* she wondered. She was cute, right? Why was he so freaking standoffish?

"Stop thinking about him, Faith," she told herself as she climbed into bed. She didn't even have the energy to set an alarm before sleep claimed her.

15

FAITH

She'd been dreaming of the sandbar, of Alex's bare and muscled back, when the crash came. The sound of glass as it shattered all around her made Faith jump. She was confused, and the big bedroom seemed wildly foreign. *Where am I?*

The wispy curtains flailed on the other side of the night-stand. She peered over the bed and saw a dangerous jigsaw of broken glass on the dark wooden floors. It wasn't the safety glass she was used to, the kind she'd hoped to shop for soon. The pieces were big, and the edges dangerously sharp. *What the hell?*

Faith eased her legs over the edge of the bed so she could toe her flip-flops closer. The rubber soles crunched across the glass as she looked out the window to see a fist-size stone headed straight toward her. *Shit.* She ducked just in time. The stone flew silently into her bedroom to hit the dresser at the far end of the wall with a thump.

She crouched as low as she could and made her way to the

hall. As she scurried downstairs, she saw a light on in the kitchen and the sound of a shotgun being cocked. It sounded just like it did in the movies.

"Faith!" Mama hissed under her breath. The older woman was hidden behind the table in the formal dining room, shotgun at the ready.

"What's going on?" Faith asked in a whisper, but Mama just held one finger to her lips.

Mama took Faith's wrist and pulled her down beside her. "Don't worry," she said. "These hooligans are about to be scared off real good."

"But who are they?" Faith asked. Mama just shook her head and listened.

Faith's heart thumped like crazy, loud enough that the blood that rushed through her head was deafening. Soon enough, male voices could be heard on the patio. Their boots were heavy on the planks. There was no reason for them to be quiet.

Mama rose to her knees and angled the shotgun through the narrow window opening that led directly to the patio. Faith couldn't make out what the men murmured, but one of them let out a low chuckle. Mama fired a shot that rang in Faith's ears. By the time her hearing returned to somewhat normal, she could still hear the men swearing.

"Jesus fucking Christ!" one yelled. His voice seemed much farther away.

"Did you . . . did you hit him?" Faith asked. Her own voice sounded funny. It trembled in a way she'd never heard before.

"Of course not!" Mama said. "Just scared 'em off."

"Oh thank God," Faith said, though she didn't know why. *Wouldn't it be better if they had been shot?*

"Honey," Mama said as she lowered the gun to her lap, "if I wanted to hit 'em, I would've."

In the distance, they heard an engine roar to life. Headlights flooded the living room. Faith saw that Mama still wore her nightly white face cream and a carefully buttoned-up pajama gown. Pink spongy curlers were in her hair. Even through the craziness of the night, Faith had to stifle a laugh. There was something too contradictory about seemingly sweet Mama cradling a smoking shotgun across her legs.

"Mama?" Caleb's voice hollered through the house. "Mama? Faith?"

"In here, honey," Mama said. She stood up as the tires outside squealed away. It took Faith a minute to realize Mama held out her hand to help her up. She felt like an outsider, a big-city outsider, to accept the hand, but it was her only choice. Her legs felt like Jell-O, and she immediately looked outside. "They're gone, baby," Mama said with oceans of comfort in her voice.

"Long gone," Caleb agreed. "Thanks to Mama's eagle-eyed shot."

"It was nothing," Mama said. She engaged the safety and put the gun on the dining table.

"What the hell is that?" Lee asked as he came into the room. He stared out the window into the front yard.

"What in the Lord . . ."

Mama squinted and pulled the window up. "Oh my . . ."

Faith, Mama, Caleb, Lee, and Matt rushed outside to the fire. "What the fuck?" Matt said under his breath.

"Language," Mama said automatically, but nobody listened. Perched on the front lawn was a burning cross at least seven feet tall. It was nothing like the modest nod to the Christian upbringing Mama had originally installed on the property, right alongside the American flag. This one was big and mean—and burning bright with gasoline. Throughout the yard and into the flower garden, little sparks of flames popped up everywhere.

A flash of yellow appeared in the distance. Faith made out Alex's shape jogging toward them. "Hey!" he yelled. "What's going on?"

"I have no idea," Mama said quietly. However, it only took her a moment to take charge. "Caleb, Lee, y'all get to puttin' this out. Grab the hose. Matt, take a look around, but be careful, baby. Make sure there's nothing round here that can catch fire. Put out what little flames you can with them blankets in the bed of Lee's truck."

"Yes, ma'am," he said, and started to circle the cross.

"What's going on?" Alex asked again as he reached them.

"Some no-good intruders, that's what," Mama said. "And burning up my rose garden like this! What nerve."

"Mama?" Matt asked as he approached them.

"What? You find something, baby?"

"Well, maybe not what you were looking for," Matt said. "But, uh, you need to take a look at this."

"What . . . what is this?" Mama asked. They walked carefully around the little clumps of flames in the grass and the rich garden soil.

"You gotta see it from here," Matt said. He took Mama's elbow and directed her away from the house.

Faith and Alex followed in silence. She didn't realize how heavy her breath was until Alex put a hand on her lower back to calm her.

"What in the ..."

Mama was speechless. They all were. Facing the house, thirty feet away from the porch, the flames crudely spelled out a warning. LAST CHANCE BITCH was emblazoned in the yard.

Faith's hand shot to her mouth in shock. Last chance? And the cross? She wasn't sure how, but she knew those big burning crosses were a KKK symbol. Or was it just an homage to Mama's little cross they'd burned earlier? "This makes no sense," she said.

"Honey, there's nothin' these lunatics do gonna make any sense," Mama said. She sighed. "And they had to go and ruin a full season's worth of planting."

"But, I mean, clearly this is for me," Faith said. "And the whole KKK thing, the race thing, I don't get it."

"How so?" Mama asked.

"I'm French and Irish!" she said.

Alex's hand moved from the small of her back to her waist. She felt him resist, uncertain, but she threw herself against him. Tears threatened to spill down her cheeks, but somehow she kept them in check. "This is crazy," she said into his chest.

145

His hand gently rubbed her waist, and in that moment she felt safe even as the flames burned all around them.

Mama sighed. "Alex, you take Faith inside, all right? Y'all have some tea, I'll have the rest of the boys handle this."

Faith and Alex were silent as they ascended the porch steps. The fire lit up the house and made their shadows dance.

"Are you all right?" Alex asked when they reached the kitchen. He put on the kettle and pulled the tea bags out of the cupboard.

"I guess so," Faith said. "God, I'm so sorry."

"Sorry? For what?"

"Well, really I should say sorry to Mama. For everything! These burning crosses, her ruined yard, and—oh God, I forgot."

"What?" he asked as he sat down beside her. Their knees touched.

"Those guys, they threw stones through my bedroom window. Shattered the glass, and I don't know what other damage."

"It's fine, Faith," he said. Alex reached across the table and took her hands. "It's just a window. I'll take care of it. You said there's glass broken?"

She nodded. "I don't know how bad it is," she whispered.

"For tonight, you'll stay in one of the guest rooms. That glass is old, I don't want you cutting yourself."

She bit her lip. "I should go home," she said. "I'm just making a mess and trouble. For all of you," she added. Faith looked up at him and couldn't help but notice how boyishly handsome he was even with mussed up hair and tired eyes.

"Don't be ridiculous," he said. The kettle started to whistle, and he stood up. "None of this is your fault."

"Clearly it is! You think any of this would be happening if it weren't for me?"

He shrugged with his back to her. "I have no idea. But I do know this island—and the people on it—better than you. There's a lot of history here that you know nothing about. Hell, that I don't know much about."

"But the whole KKK thing . . . that just makes no sense," she said.

"Who knows," he said as he sat down a mug of steaming hot tea before her. "Maybe they're confused, maybe there's more to it than we think, I have no idea. But what I do know is that you shouldn't go running back to California just because a few rednecks get fire happy."

She sighed. "Maybe you're right," she said. "I don't know. But I feel terrible, dragging your whole family into this."

"You didn't do anything," he said. Alex sat down beside her and blew on his own tea.

"Do you . . . do you think it's those same guys? From the ferry?" she asked. Faith couldn't bring herself to say "cousins."

"Maybe, I don't know," Alex said. "I didn't get a look at them. But judging from the size of your so-called cousins, I'd think they'd be pretty easy to identify."

"I didn't get a good look at them," she said sadly. "I just—I woke up because of the window breaking, and when I tried to look outside, all I saw was another stone coming my way. Maybe Mama saw more than I did."

He shook his head. "I doubt it. Mama's blind as a bat without her contacts."

"But she was shooting a gun!" Faith said, flabbergasted.

"Yeah, might not want to mention that to her," Alex said. "She swears she doesn't need good vision to shoot. Instinct, she calls it. But my bet is she couldn't tell you if those guys weighed one hundred or one thousand pounds."

"Great," Faith said with a moan. "Do you . . . do you think they'll be back?"

"Hard to tell. Anyone with a lick of sense would steer clear of Mama and her shotgun."

Faith smiled. "She's a tough woman," she said. "You know, they make it sound like you need to be hard to live in the city. San Francisco, New York, whatever. But I've never seen grit like what your mama has."

Alex smiled. "That's a country woman for you. But with Mama, I think it's more than that. She basically had to raise a whole brood of boys on her own. That'll thicken anyone's skin real quick."

Faith laughed. She cupped her hands around the hot mug and let the warmth soak into her. Suddenly, she realized she no longer shook with terror. The flames were still getting doused outside, but at the breakfast nook with Alex, the horror of the evening felt a world away. "This isn't what I expected," she said.

"What's that?"

"This. Everything. Life on the island, your mama. You." She blushed at how it sounded, but didn't want to take it back. It was all true. *People really can surprise you.*

"Think we got it all," Lee said as he stomped into the kitchen like an overzealous puppy.

"Any other messages?" Faith asked as she finished her tea.

"Not that I could tell," Lee said. "They sure were generous with the starter fluid, though."

"—thing tomorrow. You tell that nursery manager I don't care if they're not in season. I want my garden . . ."

Mama shot directions at Caleb in the mudroom as they kicked off their boots. Faith smiled slightly. Everything was already en route to normal again. Mama worried about her flower garden, and Faith could just picture Lee as he took mental notes of tomorrow's tasks.

"I smell like I work at a gas station," Matt complained as he came in behind Caleb and went directly to the sink to scrub his hands.

"A little manual labor'd do you good," Caleb said.

"Manual labor and pumping gas aren't exactly comparable," Matt said.

Alex rolled his eyes at Faith, and she giggled.

"What's so funny?" Matt asked as he dug through the cupboard for soap that wouldn't dry his hands to hell, according to him.

"Nothing," Faith said with a smile. "Can I do anything to help?" She tried to stifle a yawn.

"Y'all go on back to bed," Mama said as she appeared in the kitchen. "That's enough excitement for one day."

"Yes, ma'am," Matt said, and bolted out of the room.

"Well, that's one way to start a Friday," Caleb said.

16

ALEX

*H*e was exhausted, but Alex dragged himself into the cabin shower as the sun started to rise. He reeked of smoke and was covered in debris from the aftermath of the fire. Still, through the exhaustion, he had to admit it felt good that Faith had turned to him. In the midst of everything, he was the only one she'd turned to for comfort.

Alex had almost forgotten what it was like to be someone's protector. *It's addictive, that's for sure*, he thought as he stepped under the piping hot water. *And Faith's body. She was so soft in my arms.*

After he'd put her to bed, he'd joined Caleb, Matt, and Lee to clean up the yard as best they could. The entire night, from holding Faith to the adrenaline rush of the attack, had him bursting with energy.

As he rubbed a bar of soap across his torso, he toyed with the idea of getting himself off after the shower. It had been a while. Actually, he couldn't remember the last time. He'd spent so many days resisting the urge to feel anything because of how Faith got to him that now he was a bundled up mess.

He sighed and turned off the shower. Alex dried himself off and tousled his hair. The bathroom was thick with steam, and the summer heat had already crept throughout the cabin. It was equipped with ceiling fans but no air conditioning. "To give it that touch of southern authenticity," the builder had said.

Alex let out a huff when he remembered his clothes were still in the bedroom. *I really am out of it today*, he thought. Though when he tossed the towel onto the bar, he brushed his hand across his rock-hard cock. Even that small of a touch made him ache with want—and an image of Faith in those barely there shorts she always wore flashed through his mind.

He was blinded by the steam when he exited the bathroom but knew his way around the cabin without seeing it. Alex reached forward to where he knew the back of the sofa would be and ran smack into Faith.

"I'm sor—" she started but stopped. They were just inches apart, and her eyes went directly to his groin. He knew he should be embarrassed, cover himself or do something, but he was frozen. Her eyes on his cock somehow made him even harder.

She parted her lips and started to take quick breaths. When he glanced down, he saw that his tip was already slick with precum.

"Alex," she started, but he couldn't hold himself back anymore. It took less than a second to close the distance between them. His lips were on hers, exploring. Faith parted her lips farther to welcome his tongue against hers. *God, she tastes sweet.*

With one hand, he cupped her chin upward to him. The other pulled her close against him. His hardness slipped with ease between the heat of her soft thighs. *Those little shorts really are good for something besides a tease.*

Alex needed more, wanted more, and by the way Faith responded, he knew she did, too. He started to walk her backward, through the open bedroom door. When the back of her knees hit the bed frame, she sat down, those readied lips inches from his cock.

Before she could react, he lifted her shirt over her head. Below, she wore nothing. Pink nipples were already hard, and his length slickened more, desperate for her.

But he wasn't about to give in yet. Instead, he twisted the thin cotton shirt around her wrists like makeshift handcuffs. Slowly, he lowered her bound hands and gently pushed her onto her back. Faith lifted her head to watch while he lowered his lips to the full breasts he'd fantasized about for so long.

As Alex began to nibble on one nipple, he pinched and squeezed the other. Faith let out faint gasps and wriggled against her T-shirt, which held her captive. His cock pressed against one of her thighs, covering her skin in his wetness.

When she began to whisper, "Please," and whipped her head from side to side, he moved down her stomach with soft kisses. He only needed one hand to unbutton those denim shorts and pull them off her legs. Beneath, a thin lace thong barely contained her wetness. She'd soaked nearly entirely through the light-pink material.

Alex kissed her through the material and tasted her sweetness. She let out a loud groan, spread her legs wide, and pressed herself to his mouth. He smiled up at her, though her eyes were screwed shut. *When was the last time someone wanted you like this?*

He kissed her again, deeper, through the material. Her clit was swollen and plump. With his every touch, she responded. With one hand securely holding the T-shirt around her wrists, his other hand ripped down the thong in one fluid motion. Alex traced his tongue up the inside of her thighs and across the crest of her mound. Faith panted his name when he came close to her glistening clit, but he teased her mercilessly. Instead of the kisses and licks she craved, he blew across her clit and made her open her legs wider.

She was so ready; her juices had already started to drip from her opening. He tested her with a finger, which she pushed against greedily. As his finger entered her, slowly, he tasted her clit and felt her muscles tighten around his knuckles. He pulled his finger out, though she did her best to press against his hand and keep him inside.

His index finger was covered in her viscous juices. He held his hand up to her and pressed his thumb and forefinger together so she could see just how wet she was. Faith leaned up to suck his hand, but he pulled away and traced her areola with her sweetness. "More," she murmured.

"More what?" he asked. Alex tightened his grip on the T-shirt as she started to struggle again. At the same time, he teased her opening with two fingers and kissed her clit.

"Give me more," she said.

He slid two fingers into her. Faith cried out as he began to work her clit, licking and sucking. When she began to fuck his hand, he let her and matched her rhythm with his mouth. When he could tell she was close, he made her slow down. Alex raised his head, switched his mouth for his thumb, and took her in.

With her head tossed back, eyes shut, and mouth open, she was an absolute vision. "Are you going to come for me?" he asked as he started to fuck her faster with his hand.

"Yes," she said. Faith opened her eyes and looked at him. He released her wrists just enough so she could prop herself onto her elbows and watch. "I'm close," she said.

"I want you to come in my mouth," he commanded. "I want to taste you."

"I can't—"

"Come in my mouth, Faith," he repeated. Alex's tongue returned to her clit. He explored every crevice of her. When he could tell she was close to coming, he slowed down. Alex removed his finger from her even as she cried out in frustration—only to begin to moan when his tongue dove into her center.

"Please," she said when he trailed his tongue from her opening to her readied clit.

"Come for me, Faith," he whispered. Alex released her hands.

Immediately, she wove her fingers into his hair and pulled his lips against her center. He gripped her hips on either side of his face and met her furious pace. She fucked his face, his mouth, like it was all she'd ever wanted and every time she cried out his name it made him want her more. "I'm coming," she said. "Oh, fuck, right now."

He'd readied himself for the flood of her sweetness, but what she gave him he'd never have expected. Along with the gush of her coming, the juices that poured onto his tongue, he felt the stream of her squirting across his face. It drizzled along his throat and to his chest.

She was wetter than anyone he'd seen before. Carefully, he licked up every last drop of her. The trails of her come and squirting coated her legs. When he kissed her clit one last time, she shivered.

As he raised his head, he saw that she was flushed. Faith clutched the balled-up T-shirt to her face. "I'm sorry," she said. "It doesn't usually happen, and I thought—"

"Sorry?" he asked. "For what? That was the hottest fucking thing I've ever seen."

"Really?" she asked. Faith chewed at her lower lip and gave him a half smile. Alex got up from his knees and she looked down. "You're still hard," she said, almost surprised.

"Yeah, well, I kind of blame you," he said with a laugh.

"You were hard when you came out of the bathroom," she said. Faith sat up.

"Because I was thinking about you."

"Really?" she asked. Faith looked up at him through those thick lashes.

"You're all I've been thinking of since you got here."

"You're just saying that," she said with a glint in her eye. She brought a hand to his length, but he caught her wrist. "Please?" she asked.

He smiled at her. "Good manners are hard to find," he said. "Please, what?"

"Please let me have your cock," she said. She reached for him with her other hand, but he caught it, too.

"I don't know," he said. "What do you want to do with it?"

"You'll see," she purred. "Please." Faith leaned forward and took his tip between her lips. Alex couldn't resist anymore. He dropped her wrists and combed her hair back with his fingers so he could watch. Those lips he'd dreamed of for the past two weeks were finally on him and felt better than he'd hoped.

Faith licked the full length of his shaft and sucked gently on his tip. With her hand at his base, she took him slowly all the way to the back of her throat. "Jesus," Alex said, but he resisted the urge to hold her head.

She made satisfied little sounds in the back of her throat as she licked and sucked. "You're going to make me come," he said, his fingers twisted in her long hair.

Faith released him. "Come in me," she said as she stroked him with a hand slick with saliva.

"What?"

"Come in me," she repeated. "Please, Alex, I need you to fuck me." She pushed herself back along the bed and opened her legs to him. One of her hands pulled at a nipple while the other circled her clit.

"Say it again," he demanded as he crawled toward her.

"Please fuck me," she whispered into his ear.

He slid into her with ease and called out in surprise at how good she felt. Tight, wet, and warm.

Faith dug her nails into his lower back to keep him deep inside her. "Slow," she said. "I want to feel you."

He started to fuck her, slow and controlled, while he kissed and sucked her neck.

"Stay," she said suddenly as she pulled him as tight as she could against her. "Fuck, I'm coming again."

He felt the waves of her orgasm squeeze against him. It was so intense she brought him along with her.

"Faith," he said. "Jesus, you're going to make me come right now."

"Come in me," she panted through her waves of pleasure. "Please, I need it."

He released himself into her with a cry, and Faith yelled his name as another wave of orgasm hit her. Alex wasn't sure if it was just their combined orgasms or if she'd squirted again, but he felt nothing but the heat of their juices.

"Oh my God," she repeated over and over.

He felt the aftershock of orgasms roll through her, and each one squeezed out more of his come.

Alex propped himself up on his forearms and looked down at her. *God, she is beautiful. More so now than ever before.* "I didn't even get to fuck you properly," he said with a smile.

She laughed. "There's plenty of time," she said. "It's just, you know, been a while for me."

"Yeah, I probably have you beat," he said. Alex rolled to her side and lifted his arm for her to spoon into his chest.

Faith nuzzled against him and traced the outline of his

muscles with a finger. "You have no idea how much I wanted this," she said.

"Oh, I think I can guess," he said. "The feeling was mutual."

"The least I can do is clean you up," she said as she got onto all fours.

"What do you have in mind?"

"Just a little of this," she said, and started to work her way downward. He was sensitive but still half-hard. Faith lapped up their mixed juices. By the time she'd worked her way to the tip, he was nearly fully hard again. "Round two?" she asked sweetly.

He groaned. There was no way he'd ever get enough of her. "Come here," he said and pulled her against him.

17

FAITH

Faith woke up groggy and alone. She ran her hand along Alex's side of the bed, but it was cold. She furrowed her brow and searched for a clock. After the night —and, more importantly, the early morning—her internal clock was a mess.

She squinted her eyes at the little old-fashioned alarm clock that rested on Alex's side of the bed. *Seven in the morning? Where is he?*

Faith groaned and buried her face in the pillow. *Is he regretting everything? Stop overreacting. Maybe he just went for a run.*

She found some instant coffee in the kitchen and boiled water. Outside, the morning chores were being handled by Mama's team. Faith pulled on her shorts and blushed slightly at her balled-up ripped thong that had been tossed beside them. Her shirt was a mess, wrinkled and stretched from being used as handcuffs.

In Alex's dresser, she found one of his old college T-shirts and pulled it on. By the time she'd downed the coffee, he still hadn't returned, and it was no longer officially dawn. She'd have to sneak back into the inn soon if she were to avoid questions.

As she rounded the curved trail toward the house, there was no sign of Mama or any of the guys. Jessie swept the front porch, which meant all the exterior doors were probably unlocked. The remains of the cross were still evident in the front lawn. It pulled at Faith's stomach as she jogged behind the trimmed hedges toward the back door.

Fortunately, Mama's home still had most of its original design. That meant the back door was reserved for servants and deliveries, with almost a completely separate compartment. However, there was a hidden back staircase she could take up to the second floor. It would just require some wiggling through a never-used children's nursery storage door to get to her bedroom.

Miraculously, she didn't run into anyone en route to her bedroom. Matt's bedroom door was closed, and she could hear the faucet running in the bathroom Caleb and Lee shared.

Faith sighed in relief when she finally made it to her room. She leaned against the closed door and was greeted with a neatly swept-up floor. *The glass. Shit.* Who had cleaned it up? Mama? Jessie? And at what time? Did they realize she never went back to bed?

Of course, Alex had told her that she'd have to stay in a spare guest room anyway. *Is that what they think?* It would be strange for Mama not to at least check in with her and make sure she was comfortable in a new bedroom. *How much do they know?* For all Faith knew, the whole house had seen her run off to Alex's cabin before dawn.

What's the point in stressing about it? she asked herself as she stripped off Alex's too-big shirt. Faith gasped as she caught sight of herself in the vanity mirror. Her chest and neck were covered in hickeys and bite marks. She examined her throat and pressed her fingers into the blue and black marks. *Jesus, were we that rough?*

Faith brushed out her tangled hair and turned on the shower of the en suite. Whoever had cleaned up, they'd gone all-out. The new bedding smelled of fresh cotton, and there were new towels in the bathroom.

As she stood under the water, she ran her fingers through her folds and winced. She was still incredibly sore. *But then again, it had been a while*, she reminded herself.

Her hair was still damp and hung in long ropes when she finally made it downstairs. She'd carefully arranged it around her neck, which was also partially covered with the collar of a button-up blouse. Mama sat at the breakfast table with a mug of coffee. "Sleep okay, sugar?" Mama asked. Faith scanned her face for a tell but found nothing.

"Pretty good," she said. "Mama, I've been meaning to ask you. With all the renovations at the property and everything? It's going to take a lot longer to get started than I thought. So I was wondering—"

"You wanna stay a spell longer?" Mama asked.

"I mean, if it's not too much trouble."

"No trouble at all! Don't be silly."

Alex walked into the kitchen and nodded to Faith. "Morning, Mama," he said.

"Morning, baby. Y'all headed out to Faith's property today?"

"Don't know," Alex said. "You'll have to ask her."

"Excuse me?" Mama said at his tone.

"You'll have to ask her. Ma'am," he corrected himself.

"No, not today," Faith said quietly.

Alex's gazed lingered on her a moment, just enough to make her self-conscious of their shared night. But eventually, he took his coffee to go. *How can he just act like nothing happened?* Faith fumed inside but had to hold it together in front of Mama.

"That boy," Mama said with a sigh. "Well. You know how he can be."

Yeah, I'm starting to see, Faith thought. *But why am I so mad anyway? It's not like we promised each other anything.* Still, he could have at least given her a sign of how things were between them. Or he could have at least not sneaked out at the crack of dawn!

"Well, that's just fine," Mama said. "If y'all aren't doin' any reno work today, how about we spend some time together? I can show you round the island. Tell you a little more 'bout its history. Say, an hour?

"That sounds great," Faith said with a smile.

*a*s soon as she heard Mama's bedroom door close upstairs, Faith rushed outside to the cabin. "Hey," she said as she walked in unannounced. Alex looked at her in surprise. He stood in the kitchen, shirtless, prepping his usual high-protein afternoon snack.

"Hey, yourself."

"What was that all about?" she asked.

"What?"

"What? You acting all normal in there? Like . . . like nothing happened? How can you—"

"Whoa, whoa," he said as he held his hands up. "I, Faith, I'm sorry. Leaving this morning, that was a dick move on my part."

"Yeah, well," she said with a huff. Faith slouched onto one of the barstools at the island and grabbed a strawberry from the cutting board.

"But, shit, this is hard," he said as he put down the knife.

"What?" She had a sinking feeling in her gut.

"What we did last night? It wasn't right."

"Wasn't right?"

"It shouldn't have happened," he said, though he couldn't look her in the eye.

"You're telling me this *now*? I'm about to go on a historical drive with your mother! What am I supposed to do?"

"You go," he said simply. Alex rested his hands on the island and looked up at her.

"Well, of course I'm going! But tell me why. What happened? What could have possibly changed in the past twelve hours?"

He sighed. "It's, damn, it's clichéd. I want to say it's not you, it's me, but—"

"Damn right, it's you," Faith said. He winced, and she knew it was a low blow. *But it hurts me, too.*

"I'm sorry," he said simply. "It won't happen again."

"Yeah," she said as she stood up. "You're telling me."

"Don't be upset," he said to her back.

Faith turned slowly. "Upset? I'm not upset," she said. "In fact, I'd rather know now, rather than later."

"I like you," he said. "I do. But it's just not that easy with me."

"And whose fault is that?" she asked before she turned and walked out.

She met Mama on the porch right before noon, still angry about her talk with Alex but determined not to let it show. Mama directed her to another garage on the other side of the property and revealed a little green Alfa Romeo. "I didn't know you had this!" Faith squealed when Mama pulled it out of the garage.

"Don't drive it much anymore," Mama said. "But when I do? Girl, you better watch out. Hop in."

As they left the property, Mama took a different road than any of the guys ever did. "Pirates used to own this land, near 'bout," Mama said. "Ran the whole coast of Georgia. Sneaking in liquor and all sorts of goods to the mainland via this very island. And all the nearby ones. Including yours," she said with a smile.

Mama with her hair wrapped in a silk handkerchief and the white-framed sunglasses looked just like a movie star. Faith kept ahold of her own long plait and hoped the baseball cap she'd pulled on would be enough to keep the tangles at bay. The little convertible handled the curves of the road surprisingly well.

"So are there still any pirates out and about?" Faith asked. She let her hand glide in the wind.

"Oh, shush," Mama said. "Don't be silly."

"I'm just saying," Faith said with a laugh. "I mean, I wonder if the islands *could* be used for smuggling, though. It seems like the perfect setup. I'd never even heard of them before I got that letter from Lydia's estate attorney."

"I don't know nothin' 'bout that, dear," Mama said. "Anything's possible, I s'pose. Lots of young girls and boys are trafficked through here."

"What?" Faith asked. Mama had said it so nonchalantly, like she was talking about dairy farming.

"Oh, you know. Run up through a bunch of farms where they're used as slaves. Or sex slaves. Human trafficking's big business, you know!" she said. "Always has been. Just doesn't get the media attention as much as some other things, but it hasn't gone anywhere."

"Huh," Faith said. She felt like she shouldn't show how shocked she was. *Sex slaves? Human trafficking? On Saint Rose?* "How, um. How big are the islands? Population-wise?"

"Oh, I have no idea, sugar," Mama said. "That's something for the goggle."

"The what?"

"The goggle or whatever it is. What y'all kids use to look things up on the World Wide Web."

"Oh, Google."

"That's what I said."

Faith made a mental note to look into it. Surely if it were

common knowledge, and even Mama threw it around like it was cocktail conversation, there would be plenty of articles available.

"I'm surprised you slept so well," Mama said. Faith braced herself for the change of topic.

"Yes, ma'am," she said. "I guess with the scare and excitement last night, I just—"

"That bed in the cabin's not too comfortable," Mama interjected.

"Excuse me?"

"Oh, please," Mama said with a laugh. "I might be in my golden years, but I'm not stupid. I see how Alex looks at you when he thinks no one's lookin'. And how you look at him."

Faith blushed. *I guess I wasn't that discreet after all.* "How much . . . how much do you know?" she asked.

"Oh, I reckon plenty," Mama said. "That's what happens when you get to be my age. You notice a lot more. Thanks to experience. And, well, not havin' much else to do."

"I'm . . . I'm sorry," Faith said, though she wasn't sure why. "I didn't . . . I didn't expect to come here, and—"

"Sugar, you got nothin' to be sorry for," Mama said. "I'll admit I'm a bit biased, but I made some good-lookin' boys, both of 'em. But I know Alex got that dark mystery 'bout him that drives young girls crazy."

"Yeah, well. I think that might have come back around to bite me," Faith said. Mama had turned the car onto a narrow road that hugged the water. "It's clear he doesn't want anything serious. Not that I necessarily do, either. But . . ."

"I think you're wrong," Mama said.

"What?"

"I said I think you're wrong. Look at you," she said, and glanced over at Faith. Even with the glasses, Faith discerned the worry on her face. "Gettin' all upset over how some silly boy acts. I can say that, 'cause he's mine," she said. "But you . . . you gotta look deeper than the surface with Alex."

"How so?" Faith asked. She was eager for some kind of secret, the key to Alex's lock. She partially hated herself for letting him get to her like that, but she couldn't help it. She couldn't stop thinking about him. Maybe Mama had that key. "I mean, I know about his wife. About Rebecca. You can't get over something like that so easily. It makes sense that he's still steaming over it—"

"Oh, it's been plenty of time," Mama said as she downshifted for a hill. "That *girl*, that wife of his? Never liked her. Nobody did. I'm not even sure Alex did, but she was his first. Puppy love an' all that. And she was a big-city girl, so for him that meant exotic and wild and different."

Faith bit her tongue when she thought about telling Mama she was a big-city girl, too.

"But she wasn't like you," Mama said. "Don't think us island folk assume everyone from the city is the same. You might come from San Francisco, Miss Capshaw, but you don't have that big-city mind-set."

"I was born on the beach," Faith said quietly.

"What's that now?"

She cleared her throat. "I was born in a little beach town an hour from Los Angeles," she said. "My mom was an actress but gave it all up. I don't . . . I don't remember much of the early years. But I grew up in another beach town not far away. I think I made it into the city maybe once a year."

"The beach is in your blood," Mama said with a nod.

Is it? Is that why it feels so much like home here?

"But believe me, Faith, when I tell you. Alex's wife? That girl had a strange hold on him. An unhealthy one. The way she'd flirt with—well, never mind 'bout that. But it's over now. I know that. Seems all it took was another pretty woman to have remedied any lingering spell she had on him."

Mama didn't take her eyes off the road when she said it, and Faith was grateful. Her entire face flushed pink.

"Just," Mama started slowly. She reached over and took Faith's hand. "Don't hurt my boy, all right?"

Hurt him? Alex? Faith nearly laughed at the thought. It would be about as easy to hurt him as it would a porcupine.

"'Cause if you do, I'm afraid I'll have to come after you," Mama said. Her smile told Faith it was all in fun. "And remember, now. I do know where you live. Just one island over. Lydia mighta kept to herself, but that's not your style, that I can see."

"Oh now I don't *live* there, Mama," Faith said with a laugh. "That would be a death wish at this point. But did you know much? About Lydia, I mean?" She couldn't bring herself to say "aunt" anymore, it shot a chill up her spine.

"Nah, not much," Mama said, though she paused too long. "And maybe you don't live there yet," Mama said. "But you wouldn't be puttin' so much work, time, and love into that land if you weren't thinking on it. I've heard how you talk about that place. It's a home of yours. Well, here we are," Mama said.

Faith looked up and saw they'd come full circle. Greystone Inn loomed like a majestic castle at the end of the long drive. She glanced at her watch and saw they'd whittled away nearly two hours on the road, though it felt like just a few minutes.

Mama pulled up to the front of the inn via the circular drive and left the engine running while Faith stepped out. "Why don't you let me help you put it in the garage?" Faith asked as she leaned over the little green car.

"Nonsense, I've been taking care of this baby on my own for decades," Mama said. "Now, shoo, you go on in and get some of Gwen's sweet tea for yourself."

"Thanks, Mama," Faith said.

"And, Faith? Remember what I said. You be good to my boy now." Mama smiled as she drove to the garage.

Yeah. You might want to tell him the same thing about me.

18

ALEX

*H*e'd breathed a sigh of relief when he heard Faith would be gone for the afternoon. She'd be with Mama, which did give him pause, but then again Mama was full of traditional southern manners. He doubted Mama'd give in to gossip even if Faith pushed. *Besides, it wasn't like Mama knew him anymore anyway.*

Alex had thought that a move to the cabin would be far enough to avoid Faith. He'd been wrong. Ever since that time between night and morning when she'd shown up unexpectedly, it was like he couldn't avoid her.

She was there making coffee in the morning, even when he thought he'd planned it well enough that she'd still be asleep. Every dinner was awkward as hell. He thought she'd be staring at him, but when he'd focus his eyes on her, she would be caught up in a conversation with Mama or Caleb.

Faith drove him crazy. Plain and simple.

It had been a week since their *incident*, and he'd thought that giving in once would satisfy his craving for her. But it just made him want her more. Every time he saw her, whether it was a glimpse of her legs as she went up the stairs or the way she pushed her hair out of her face in the morning light, he was reminded of that time together.

In a second, he could go from putting honey in his tea to remembering how she sucked her lip as he tasted her. Those long fingers that helped Gwen prepare lunch he imagined once again on his cock.

The past week had been even worse. Her face always held a perfectly blank expression. It made him mad, nearly enraged him. *I might not know her perfectly, but I know her well enough to realize she always has an expression.* Puzzled, engaged, laughing, about to explain or debate—she always did *something* with her face. Until now.

"Y'all all right?" Mama had asked the two of them when she found them in silence one morning. Alex stood watch over the Keurig while Faith scraped at her toast.

"Yes, ma'am," Alex had said automatically.

"Just fine, Mama," Faith had said.

He didn't look at her face, but he could hear the warmth in it. *Why doesn't she talk to me like that anymore?*

Alex pulled on some clean clothes for another dinner at the inn where Faith would pretend he didn't exist. "Shit," he said. There was a tear in his shirt and a button was missing. *How the hell did that happen?* There was no way Mama would let "such riffraff" at her formal dining table.

By the time he'd changed and raced across the lawn to the inn, everybody was seated and waiting for him. Gwen arched one of those perfectly shaped brows at him while she put down the last pot but didn't say anything.

"Thought you'd plumb forgot," Mama said. She whipped the cloth napkin open and settled it on her lap—a cue for everyone else to follow suit.

The only seat was between Faith and Mama. "Sorry, ma'am," he mumbled to her. Faith didn't even look up. She busied herself with complimenting Gwen and Mama on the spread.

"Care to lead us in grace?" Mama asked Alex pointedly.

He sucked in his breath through his teeth and took Mama's hand. Faith didn't readily offer hers up, so he grabbed it harshly and held it on his thigh. Even as he went through the familiar prayer, eyes closed, he was well aware of the heat of her body against his. *Her hand is just so soft.* He was tempted to squeeze it, do something to let her know he was onto her, but by the time the amens rang through the dining room, he'd lost his nerve.

"That was lovely, thank you," Mama said. He knew it had been rushed, but he'd take any compliment Mama would dole out at this point.

"Grits at dinner, my favorite," Caleb said.

Gwen circled behind him and swatted his hand as he reached too far for the dish. "Manners," she said. "Y'all act like you's raised by wolves and not your fine mama."

"Thank you, Gwen," Mama said.

"So you were saying?" Faith asked Caleb. "Earlier, about the scuba? I've always wanted to try that."

"I'm surprised you haven't, coming from Southern California and all," Caleb said. Finally, Matt passed him the grits topped with golden cheese, and he piled his plate high.

"My cousins were really into it for a little bit, but at the time I was studying for the LSAT all the time." Faith sunk her fork into the pork shoulder, which fell off the bone like butter. "Amazing, Gwen. Mama," she said.

"Well, if you're interested, I can get you started," Caleb said. He dug into the grits with gusto. "I'm technically able to certify new divers, but it's been a while."

"Oh, I don't know . . ."

"Nonsense, baby. Caleb's a good teacher. Great diver. He'd be happy to take you out."

Was it just Alex's imagination, or did Mama have a certain tone with the "take you out?" *Is she trying to push Faith and Caleb together?* Mad as hell, he tucked into his own plate full of just pork and the steamed broccoli Gwen made on the side just for him. Everyone else happily ladled the buttered, creamy blend of vegetables onto their plates.

"It does sound fun," Faith said with a smile. "But I don't know. I have a lot of work to do on the property still. I swear, it's like Craig thinks I'm part of his crew now. Well," she paused. "Part of his crew that doesn't even know how to hold a hammer right."

"Well, the offer's open," Caleb said. "Anytime. If you think the island's pretty as is, you won't believe what's underneath the water."

Alex stole a look at her from the corner of his eye. *Really, maybe Faith was the same as always. Polite and cordial, even when his brothers flirted with her. Maybe she wasn't so mad after all.*

Like most dinners at Mama's table, there were long stretches of silence. "Sure sign of a good supper," Mama and Gwen always said. They were right. Even through his discomfort and worry about Faith, Alex couldn't help but lose himself in the rich flavors of Gwen's pork.

When their plates had been thoroughly cleaned, Gwen came in with her staple cinnamon peach pie. "I couldn't," Faith said as she cradled her flat belly.

"You can and you will," Gwen admonished. "After all, you helped make it."

"You did, Faith?" Mama asked. "Well, now we've all got to try a piece."

Gwen knew not to push Alex for a slice of carbs and sugar. He was the only one who ever got away with turning down dessert. But when Gwen sidled by this time, he touched her arm lightly. "Just a little piece," he said.

Gwen didn't change her expression or even meet his gaze. But she did cut the smallest of pieces and slide it onto a dessert plate for him.

Alex didn't know if it was because it'd been so long since he'd had dessert, or if the pie really was that good, but every bite tasted like heaven. Every mouthful had a piece of Faith in it.

"Let me help you wash up," Faith said when they finished. Surprisingly, Mama didn't argue. The two women picked up the dishes and went into the kitchen. Lee and Matt followed with their own plates smeared with sweet peach curd.

"Guess we should help," Caleb said uncertainly. Alex shrugged. The two of them picked up the remaining unused flatware and the vessels scraped clean of the comfort food.

In the kitchen, Alex watched how Faith interacted with Mama—with all of them, actually. She was a natural fit, like she'd always been there.

"A shark?" she asked Caleb. "Don't tell me anymore! If you thought that would entice me to go scuba diving with you, you're dead wrong."

"It was a little shark!" he said. "I swear, ma'am. If you went with me, you'd be totally safe."

"A shark is still a shark, doesn't matter the size!"

"What is that? Some kind of Dr. Seuss logic?" Lee asked.

Faith let out a laugh. Alex smiled with his back to the rest of them. He didn't realize how much he'd missed that laugh until that moment.

"Caleb," Mama said. "You best be telling Faith the good things about scuba if you want her to go."

"All right, all right," he said. "Let's see. There are fish, colors like you've never seen before. Bright neon, and big, too."

"I like fish," Faith conceded. "But I don't know if I like them enough to risk my life. I mean, there are aquariums."

"You don't get it," Caleb said with a shake of his head. "It's different. Down there. And the white sand on the beach? It's like another world down there."

"How so?" Faith asked as she helped Mama load the dishwasher.

"Quiet," Caleb said. Something in his voice made everyone slow down and listen. "It's just quiet, you know? Like you've never experienced before. But then it's not. The sound of the ocean, your own breath, it's like another world."

"It sounds like magic," Faith said.

"It kinda is, ma'am," Caleb said. "It's an escape, I guess? Like this secret place where it's just you and all these bright creatures."

"I can see why you go," Faith said quietly.

Alex kind of could, too.

After they'd done all they could, and Gwen shooed them out of the kitchen, he saw Faith pick up her steaming cup of nightly tea and head to the porch. He hung around the inn for a bit, uncertain if he was up to walking past her in silence toward his cabin.

Usually, Mama would join Faith for their evening tea on the porch. But this time, she made a show of being tired. "I think I'm just Gonna head to bed. Y'all all right?" she asked the boys. "You need anything?"

"Nah, Mama," Caleb said. "You go on. You work too hard."

"Really?" Mama said. "Glad to know somebody finally noticed."

Caleb rolled his eyes at Alex. "Think I'll hit the shower before bed," he said. "Don't know if I'll be up for it with that five in the morning wake-up call."

"Five?" Matt asked.

"Fishin'," Caleb said and pretended to cast and reel in a line. "Me and Lee both."

"Ah," Matt said. He'd already curled up into his favorite leather chair in the sitting room with a thick book.

Soon enough, Alex was left alone on the first floor with just the occasional flick of the page from Matt in the corner.

"Headin' out," he told Matt. He saw Matt's hand raise in farewell.

As soon as he stepped onto the porch, he saw Faith with bare feet perched on the rail. She slouched back into the swing and swayed herself slowly. Faith looked at him with big open eyes but didn't say a thing. Instead, she took a long sip of her tea.

"Hey," he said. His voice sounded strange. *Hey? That's what I have to say to her.*

"Hey," she repeated.

"You know," he began. Alex searched for words as he approached her. He thought if he stood over her, he'd have some leverage, but he might as well have been his knees. "About the other day . . . women, they don't understand what they want." Instantly, he knew the words came out wrong, but he couldn't suck them back in.

"No," she said and put down the mug. "You don't get to turn this around on me."

"I'm not—"

"I'm not interested in continuing this conversation," she said. Faith removed her feet from the rail. "I'll be real with you. I think you're hot. Okay? I mean, I'm not going to deny that," she said with a laugh.

Alex felt red creep up his neck. *She thinks I'm hot?*

"But I'm not here to get a shit show of emotions dumped on me. Especially when they have nothing to do with *me*."

Alex clamped his mouth shut. She was right, of course, but how could he admit that to her? "I don't know what—"

"Yeah, you don't know," she said. "That's the problem. But I'll tell you one thing, I'm not the one who has problems understanding what I want."

"I never asked for any of this." That wasn't what he'd wanted to come out, had expected to come out, but there it was.

Faith looked down at her lap and nodded. Her expression was set in stone. "I'm not even going to validate that with a response," she said. "But all of this? Your attitude and everything? That's you. Projecting onto me. And I'm not going to allow it."

He was stunned into silence. Faith stood up and walked right past him into the house. The scent of her perfume lingered around him long after the door clicked shut.

A woman had never spoken to him like that before. He'd grown used to Rebecca's manipulative crying fits and yelling, but not this.

Is Faith right? Is he really dragging all of his crap with Rebecca around with him now?

19

FAITH

aith couldn't get last night's conversation on the porch out of her head. *If you could even call it a conversation*, she thought. She shook her head and dug into a sugary bowl of cereal. She knew she'd get a look from Mama for foregoing breakfast made from scratch in favor of Cap'n Crunch. *But sometimes a girl needs her comfort food*, she thought, even as the rough cereal scratched the roof of her mouth.

"I see you got started early," Mama said as she breezed into the kitchen. One brow was raised in question at the bowl.

"Sorry, Mama," Faith said. "I just had a craving."

"I remember those," Mama said with a sigh. "Brace yourself. They just get worse after a certain age." Mama put on a fresh kettle and wrapped her morning robe tighter around her. "What are y'all's plans for the day?"

"Oh, um, Alex and I are going into Savannah to meet up with Craig in his office." Faith hated how Alex's name felt in her mouth. But she was staying in his mama's house, so she at least had to put on a front of nonchalance.

"Uh huh," Mama said. "Think y'all will have time to go to that bakery I like? I'm running low."

"Of course, Mama," Faith said with a smile. A box or two of chocolates might do her some good, too.

As Mama went off in search of Jessie, Faith lifted the sugary bowl of milk to her lips and drank with abandon. *Screw manners*, she thought.

"Thirsty?" Alex's voice broke through the drone of the kettle hard at work.

Faith set the bowl down with a thud and wiped her lips with the back of her hand. "Parched," she replied without a look in his direction.

Alex got two of his little, hard, low-carb slices of "bread" out of the cupboard and popped them in the toaster. As if on cue, Caleb came into the kitchen armed with plenty of crap to talk about Alex's diet. "Mmm, whip me up some o' them cardboard toast coasters," Caleb said.

"Yeah, you could use some," Alex said and pretended to inspect Caleb's biceps.

Caleb laughed. "Don't need no fake toast crap when you actually put in a full day's worth of manual labor. Check these babies out," he said. Although he presented his flexed biceps to Alex, Faith saw him as he stole a glance in her direction.

"I'll pass," Alex said. "By the way," he called to Faith, "Caleb and Matt are coming with us to Savannah."

"Oh!" Faith said. "Great, great." It drove her mad that he acted like nothing had changed. Like they hadn't had the best mind-blowing sex of her life just a few days ago. *Is he just playing it cool in front of his family?* Even if he didn't feel anything for her beyond lust, how could he act like everything was the same as it was when she had arrived?

Or maybe he just doesn't care, she told herself. That was one possibility she didn't want to linger on for long.

"We got some business ourselves out that way," Caleb told her. He sat down at the table with the leftover grits from last night, cold.

"Ew," Faith said as she wrinkled her nose. "You eat them cold?"

"It's like pizza," he said. "I like all toppings, hot, cold, whatever. It's all good."

"Right," Faith said. "I think I'll stick with pizza."

"I'll come get y'all in about thirty," Alex said. He grabbed his toast to go, wrapped it in tinfoil, and headed back to the cabin.

"Things movin' forward with the property then?" Caleb asked. He ate like a little boy, full of gusto and without a care for how it came off.

Faith smiled at him. "I guess," she said. "I don't have any context, so I can't say if it's on schedule or not."

"Ah, it'll be fine," he said.

Matt walked into the kitchen in a light-gray suit perfectly pressed. "Wow, fancy," she said. For the first time, Faith really looked at him. Matt was handsome in his own way. Even dressed as a typical attorney, which she'd been surrounded by for so many years, there was something about him that was different. A softness, maybe a sort of southern charm, that wasn't in California lawyers.

Matt shrugged. "Sometimes I can clean up okay."

"I didn't mean that," Faith said softly. In the few weeks since she'd been here, she'd figured out Matt liked to cover his insecurities with sarcasm.

"Thanks," Matt said. He picked through the bowl of fruit on the table for the ripest apple to slice into his oats.

"You're not dressing up?" Faith asked Caleb.

"Me? Hell no," he said. "Matt's got the brains and the corporate looks. All I got to bring is the brawn."

"Nice," Matt said. He rolled his eyes as he sat down with them.

"Guess Gwen an' Mama's skipping the grand breakfast spread today," Caleb said with disappointment.

"I think it's because of me," Faith said. "I told her this morning Alex and I were headed out. Maybe she knew y'all were joining us."

"I like that southern accent on you, ma'am," Caleb said with a wink.

Faith blushed. She didn't mean to pick up their slang and accents, but she heard it as it slipped in occasionally.

"Y'all still eating?" Alex called from the front porch. "Hurry up! We don't got all day."

Caleb let out a huff and raised his eyes at Faith. "The timekeeper's upset," he said.

*T*hey arrived at the dock just as the ferry was about to set off. "Close call, y'all," the ticket taker said.

The breeze was warm and the water just as gorgeous as always. Today, it was exceptionally crowded for the small ferry. "Market weekend," Caleb told her. "Whole island heads to the mainland to stock up for the rest of summer. And to sell their goods," he added.

Faith looked around. There did seem to be an inordinate number of bins and boxes on board.

For the entire ride, Alex stayed a few steps away from them. Faith watched him gaze into the distance and commanded herself to forget him.

If he is going to act like a brat, why should I get dragged down with him?

"So what kind of business are you guys going to Savannah for?" Faith asked. She pushed her sunglasses up her nose.

Caleb glanced at Matt. "Oh, just, you know. Property stuff ourselves."

Matt cleared his throat. "Mama prefers us to handle estate planning and management at this point," he said. "She oversees the paperwork from the inn."

"Estate planning?" Faith was worried. *Is Mama ill?*

"It's nothing," Matt assured her. "Just precautionary, is all. When you have the kind of assets Mama does, you can't be too careful. Plus, with the tourism industry exploding nearby, the value of her property is always changing."

"Exploding?" Faith said with a laugh. "It's rare if we cross another car on the roads on Saint Rose!"

"Yeah, well, you can't imagine what it was like even five years ago," Matt said. He shook his head sadly. "There was a time you knew the name o' every person you passed. Every car. Heck, even every horse. But now?" He chewed his lip. "It's just like anywhere else."

"Did you, I mean did either of you ever meet Lydia?" she asked. Behind their sunglasses, Faith couldn't read their expressions.

"I think I met her once," Caleb said. "Yeah, 'bout ten years ago? Lee and I used to manage a produce stand at a market on the island that's defunct now. I think she bought some strawberries from us."

"You think?" Faith asked. This wasn't exactly the kind of insight she was looking for.

"Maybe it was blueberries?" Caleb asked.

"Right," she said.

"I never met her," Matt said.

"Big surprise," Caleb said. "You've always had your nose buried in a book too deep to notice anyone else."

Once they'd docked on the mainland, Faith was disappointed in herself when she realized she scanned the parking lot for the rednecks' truck. Her heart rate slowed slightly when it was nowhere to be found. *I'm not going to let those jerks get into my head.*

"All right," Caleb said as he slapped Alex on the back. "We're Gonna take the Chevy. I'm guessin' you'll be in the Mustang."

"You guessed right," Alex said.

"Chevy?" Faith asked. "How many cars do you guys have here?"

"Enough," Alex said, and Caleb let out a laugh.

The Chevy's garage was right next to the Mustang's. Faith watched as Caleb and Matt uncovered a pristine 1950s truck with glistening chrome trim. "Wow," she said. "That's beautiful."

"Sounds beautiful, too," Caleb said with a wink.

She tried to help Alex uncover the Mustang, but he whipped the cloth off so quickly it nearly seared her hands. "Hey!" she said.

"Sorry," he muttered.

She thought he might have said more, but the roar of the Chevy drowned out everything else. He did look over and inspect her hands, briefly, before they set off. The touch of his skin on hers made it nearly sizzle.

In the Mustang, she waited to see if he'd reach for the convertible switch, but his hand remained firmly on the stick shift. Faith recognized some of the landmarks as they headed into the city. When they passed the exit for the barbeque joint, her stomach rumbled. *The last time in Savannah seemed like ages ago. And we are farther apart now than ever. What had happened?*

"Home Depot first?" Alex asked.

"Sure!" she said. Faith tried to sound upbeat, but it came off as fake even to her.

Alex parked far from any other cars in the expansive parking lot. He commandeered one of the bright-orange shopping carts and started to methodically go through the aisles. Faith tried to tick off the shopping list items she had, but it seemed like he had his own agenda.

"Doorbells!" she said as he barreled down the aisle. "Craig told me to pick one out. I guess Lydia never got around to putting one in. What do you think about—"

"Can't you shop for this useless stuff another time?" Alex asked curtly. "We have some real high-need items to take care of."

Faith had an oil-rubbed bronze doorbell in one hand and a brushed nickel in the other. It took all her willpower not to throw one directly at his head. "What's your problem?" she asked coolly.

"My problem?" Alex glanced around the aisle, but they were miraculously alone on a Saturday morning.

"Yes. Your problem. Are you still upset about the other day?"

"The other day?"

"Oh my God. Are you just going to repeat everything I say? *Yes*, the other day. Look, you told me it was a mistake, and I heard you. Loud and clear."

"Oh."

Is he blushing? What the hell?

"You want me to be honest?" he asked. Suddenly any trace of embarrassment was gone.

"Yeah," Faith said. "That would be nice for a change."

"Yeah. I'm still kind of weirded out by the other day. And, Jesus, the other *night* just keeps replaying in my head. I know it was a mistake. You know it. But that doesn't exactly make it easy to be around you."

Faith was so taken aback she nearly stumbled. "Well. Thank you for being honest. And I'm sorry you feel like that."

"Faith," he said in dismay. He let go of the shopping cart and stepped toward her, but she matched his stride and kept her distance. "It's not like that. Shit, I don't know how to say this."

"Don't worry about it," she said. She put back the nickel doorbell and tossed the bronze one into the cart.

"I am worried about it," he said. "I know how it must seem—"

"Oh, do you?" she asked. "Good, then I won't have to explain it."

"Faith—I can't. I can't even *look* at you without thinking about how you looked that night—"

"I'm not interested in talking about this anymore," she said. She brushed her hair from behind her ears to hide her crimson face. "I'm going to go look at floor tile. If you want to help, go pick up the bathroom piping Craig asked about."

Faith stalked off into the depths of Home Depot without a clue of where she was going. She didn't hear Alex follow her. After a few minutes, she glanced behind her, but he was nowhere to be found.

"Morning, ma'am." A young, handsome salesclerk in an orange apron appeared in front of her. "Can I help you with somethin'?"

"Uh, yeah, thank you," she said, and plastered on her brightest smile. "Floor tile?"

The man whistled. "Floor tile. That's a big project. You doin' it yourself?" he asked as he led her to the other side of the store.

She laughed. "I wish," she said. "I have a contractor."

"Your husband's no good with his hands?" the clerk asked. "Or boyfriend?"

She blushed. It had been a long time since someone so overtly flirted with her. It was nice. Refreshing. "No husband," she said. "Or boyfriend."

"Well, ain't that a shame," he said, but his smile suggested otherwise.

Faith let the clerk flirt with her as he explained the difference in the tile. Still, she kept an eye out for Alex and kept checking her phone. *Where the hell is he?*

"There you are," Alex said from behind her. He was armed with loads of plastic piping.

"Well, hey there," the clerk said. He looked confused.

"I told you I'd be in tile," she hissed.

"This what you wanted?" Alex asked as he raised the pipes up.

"I don't know," she said and stormed off again. This time, she left two men in her wake.

She might be a lot of things, but she was nobody's mistake.

ALEX

$\mathcal{H}$e couldn't wait to get out of that Home Depot. Alex didn't know if Faith was oblivious to how the salesclerk ogled her, or if she relished it because he couldn't do or say anything about it.

She'd dragged him around that store for another hour. Alex had worked doggedly to get through Craig's list, but Faith tended to linger. "You want this or this?" he'd ask her, as he held up two different lighting options.

Her answers were either immediately, "This one," or "You choose." Alex couldn't accuse her of ignoring him since she answered all his questions. Yet her tone was frosty.

There were only a few items on the list that demanded much debate on her end. *Thank God,* Alex thought. It was like Craig knew better than to send a California girl into a home improvement shop with much wiggle room for choices.

Alex watched her as she started to head into the appliance section. *Oh God.*

"You know, you'll get a better deal on appliances at Best Buy."

"Oh," she said but continued to check features and prices.

"Generally lower prices and free financing for something like eighteen months," he said.

"I don't need financing," she replied.

That's right. She's rich as hell now. Alex didn't know exactly how much the inheritance was, but it was basically an entire island. A tiny island and a rundown plantation, but still.

"Seriously, if I were you I'd wait till the Labor Day sales," he said.

"That might be a good idea," she agreed and angled the cart out of appliances.

Alex was in charge of what Faith called the building stuff. It included the literal nuts and bolts, wires, pipes, and materials that Faith didn't care much about selecting.

"I think that's it," Alex said as he dumped the last of the shopping list into the cart.

"I'm not sure if I should look at paint here ."

"Craig said the local shop by his office was better."

Faith sighed. "Fine," she said.

By the time he'd loaded up the trunk, Caleb had blown up his phone with texts. *Lunch?* Caleb had asked at noon. *LUNCH?* repeated in three strings of texts by one.

Never take a woman to Home Depot, Alex texted back. He glanced at Faith in the passenger seat. *Ate yet?*

No. CBP. Our ETA is fifteen min.

"Hungry?" Alex asked as he slid into the front seat.

"I could eat," Faith said. She rested her chin on her hand and stared into the distance.

Alex couldn't get to the Crystal Beer Parlor fast enough. He wove through the streets of Savannah well above the limit, but Faith acted like she either didn't notice or didn't care.

"'Bout time," Matt said as they sat down. He and Caleb had already finished one IPA each.

"This place is cute," Faith said. She pulled her sunglasses on top of her head and smiled at Caleb and Matt.

Where had that cheeriness been earlier? Alex wondered. He made a huff and pretended to look at the menu, though he always ordered the same thing.

"Not as cute as the company," Caleb said with a wink. "And I don't mean you," he said to Alex.

"Stop!" Faith said with a giggle. She slapped Caleb's arm lightly. "Hey, look, they have fried green tomatoes for starters. Like the movie."

"Yeah," Matt said. "Or, you know, like the southern dish that everyone's eaten for ages."

"I already ordered some plates to share. The tomatoes, fried okra, and the onion rings."

"Well, that sounds healthy," Faith said with a laugh.

"Muscles and curves require a healthy appetite," Caleb said. He winked at Faith. "Figured you'd know that, ma'am."

"Yeah, well, I've figured a few things out," she said. Faith bit her lip and looked unabashedly at Caleb's biceps that burst out of his shirt.

Alex steamed behind the menu. *Since when had Faith shifted all her attention to Caleb? Hell, he is an outrageous flirt even without her encouragement!*

"What do you recommend?" Faith asked the table.

"Au poivre burger," Caleb and Matt said in unison.

"Where's that?" Faith asked as she scanned the menu.

"Got cracked pepper, peppercorn brandy, grilled onions," Caleb said. "Trust me, try it."

"Oh, what the hell," Faith said. "And a beer, too."

Alex went to the bar for a round, happy for any excuse to get away from Faith and Caleb. He took a shot of whiskey at the bar, even though the waitress cocked her eyebrow. "You have no idea what I'm dealing with," he told her.

That made her smile. "I got you, baby," she said and covertly poured the whiskey into a soda glass topped with Coke.

Back at the table, the group grabbed the beers from Alex and ignored him once again. Matt was buried in his phone, while Caleb and Faith had eyes only for each other.

"I think you'll really like it," Caleb told Faith as Alex settled back in.

"I'm nervous!" Faith said. "You shouldn't have told me about the whole shark thing."

"Don't worry, I'll keep you safe," Caleb said.

Alex half listened to their plans for diving while he let the whiskey and beer do their job on his empty stomach. *I did tell her we were a mistake. Or that she was a mistake?* Hell, he couldn't remember exactly. Either way, it sure didn't sound good, and it certainly hadn't come out right.

"Stop it!" Faith said as Caleb pinched her thigh and imitated a shark. She giggled and put her hand on his forearm.

"Hey, now, I'm just giving you a preview," Caleb said. "I'm sorry, ma'am, but you're Gonna have to do as I say on that boat if you wanna stay safe."

"Okay, okay," Faith said. "I'll be good."

"Not all the time, now," Caleb said.

"But tell me how you got started," Faith said. She took a pull of the beer. "Diving, I mean."

"Oh, me and Alex were always in the water as kids," Caleb said. "Swimming, snorkeling, everything. Dang near drowned each other all them summers. Remember that, Alex?"

Alex grunted in agreement.

"But I dunno, I got the diving bug when I was 'bout sixteen I guess. Mama was happy to send me to the mainland for a month of scuba lessons for the summer. One less boy to deal with, she'd say. And that was that."

"It just took a month?" Faith asked. "That's not too bad."

"Lots o' people get certified on vacations," Caleb said with a shrug. "But there are all kinds of levels."

"And what level would you say you're at?" Faith asked.

"The level where I oughta know better than to take a beautiful distraction out on the water," Caleb said.

"A distraction!" Faith said. "That's hardly complimentary."

"I s'pose that depends on who you ask."

"Matt, do you hear this?" Faith asked.

"Huh?" Matt said as he tore his eyes away from the screen.

"What's so interesting in that phone, anyway?" she asked.

"I'm surprised you're not on yours. Isn't your firm bombarding you with emails?"

Faith sighed. "I think they've given up on me for the summer. I'm pretty much a glorified virtual administrative assistant at this point. As long as I log the documents daily, they're happy."

"That doesn't worry you?" Matt asked. "What about job security?"

"I don't know," Faith said. "I was stoked when I first landed that job. But now? Maybe . . . maybe law isn't for me after all."

"Awful young to decide that," Matt said.

"Better now than later, right?" she asked.

"I suppose."

"You can always come work for me," Caleb said. "I could always use a hot assistant."

"There's no way I'd be your assistant!" Faith said. "We'd never get any work done."

"You don't think? How come? What you imagine we'd be doin' instead?"

"Oh, I don't know . . ."

"C'mon, you can't leave a guy hangin' like that." Caleb nudged. "Gimme some ideas."

"Some ideas for what we'd do instead of work?"

"Sure."

"Probably fight off sharks and start drinking way too early."

"There's no such thing as drinkin' too early. Especially since, well, you know what they say."

"No, what?"

"The more you drink, the better I look," Caleb said with a wink. "And the whole lowered inhibitions thing don't hurt, either."

"Right, like you really need help looking better," Faith said.

"Why, is that a compliment, Miss Capshaw?"

"You take it however you like."

Alex couldn't take much more of this. Matt might be totally oblivious, but it felt like he was the fifth wheel on a date that was headed straight for a hookup.

I can't be mad at her. Or Caleb, he reminded himself. *Caleb's clueless, and I might as well have told Faith that I regretted having anything to do with her.*

"That's so bad!" Faith's giggle burst through his thoughts. He didn't even want to know what was so bad that Caleb had said or done.

Shit. But just because he'd backpedaled, that didn't mean he wanted to sit around and watch her flirt with his brother. The two of them were putting on a show that was too embarrassing to bear.

"Excuse me," she said. "Ladies' room before the food arrives." Alex had to lean back to let her out, and as she passed him her ass was right in his face. The same sweet ass he'd kissed and nibbled on just a few days ago. Those shorts were so tiny, he thought he could still see a hickey between her thighs.

"Damn," Caleb said as Faith made her way to the far end of the restaurant.

Alex realized they both ogled her ass as she swished away.

"They don't make 'em like that round here," Caleb told Alex.

"Maybe you don't look hard enough," Alex said.

"You're one to talk," Caleb retorted. "You just literally had the finest thing I've ever seen in your lap and didn't do a damn thing about it."

"Maybe I don't feel like going to battle with my brother for a piece of ass," Alex said. He regretted the words as soon as they left his mouth, but it was too late now.

Caleb didn't seem bothered by it. His face lit up as the waiter arrived with their order. "Excuse me, y'all," Alex said as he got up. Caleb and Matt didn't even seem to notice.

He headed straight toward the restrooms. Faith waited in line for the women's restroom. *Jesus, she is hot.* "I need to talk to you," he said. The older woman behind Faith gave him a hard look.

"Right now?" she asked.

"Yes, right now." He took her elbow and led her out the back kitchen door.

"Hey, y'all aren't s'posed to use that!" the woman hollered as the door slammed shut.

"What the hell are you doing?" Faith demanded. *Finally, some kind of emotion.*

"What am I doing? What do you think *you're* doing?"

"Uh, trying to pee," she said. "If, you know, I hadn't been interrupted."

"You know what I mean," Alex said. He wanted to tell her to stop toying with Caleb, but the words wouldn't come together in his mouth.

"What, do you want to tell me again how hooking up with me was a mistake? I got the message, Alex," she said. "You weren't exactly subtle about it."

"Look, I get that you can flirt with whoever you want, okay? But my brother is off limits."

Faith laughed and rubbed her hands along her bare thighs. "Then you tell him to stop flirting with *me*. Okay? I'm not going to be rude to him just because you don't know how to act after a one-night stand. At least he's nice to me."

That stung, but Alex knew she had a point. *But one-night stand? Is that what she thought it was?* "That's how he is with everyone," Alex said. His effort to brush it off landed flat.

"Oh, is it now? You're telling me that he's just being friendly? How much do you want to bet that I can get him to kiss me?"

Alex went tense, and Faith noticed.

A smile crept across her face. She crossed her arms over her chest.

Even with the rage that bubbled inside him, he couldn't help but notice how it pushed up her ample cleavage.

"Huh?" she asked. "You like games, don't you? That's how this whole thing got started."

"You wouldn't," Alex said.

Faith looked at him closely. Whatever considerations and calculations she made, he couldn't gauge. "No," she said finally. "I wouldn't. But not because he's your brother. It's because I slept with you, and I'm not ready to move on just like that. Not all women are your late wife, you know."

Alex looked at her. At her lips. *Maybe she is right.*

Faith took two steps toward him and closed the distance. Her arms still crossed, she raised up on her toes and kissed him just beside his mouth. With an unreadable expression, she turned and walked back inside.

Alex looked after her, flabbergasted. *I bit off more than I can chew this time,* he told himself. *Did it the first time I had a dirty thought about that woman.*

21

FAITH

She hadn't had a tension headache like this since law school. Faith rubbed her temples and squeezed her eyes shut. Even the short break from the screen felt like a luxury.

For the past four hours, she'd hunkered over her laptop in the bedroom. The numbers for the property project had all started to run together. Armed with that lump sum from Lydia, she was tempted to just approve figures and projects left and right. However, her father's conservative voice rang in her head. *The more you save, the more you'll have.* "Yeah, yeah, Dad," she said aloud with a sigh. She did her best not to tarnish what little memories she had of him with what she'd remembered in Lydia's laundry room.

It still shocked her to see all those zeroes when she logged into the account Lydia's estate agent had set up for her. Faith had thought when she'd signed on with the firm that she'd be rolling in dough. But her salary was nothing compared to this.

"I highly suggest you invest," the estate agent had told her over the phone. When he'd first told her the figure, she'd stopped breathing. "It's not my place to say, and it's not my specialty, but with this amount of money, it should really be working for you."

"Working for me?" she'd squeaked.

"Well, yes. Assuming you don't have the lifestyle of a champion boxer, I imagine you'd never have to work again."

"But I want to work," she'd said.

"Suit yourself."

Yeah, I was crazy, she thought as she refreshed the latest spreadsheet. This one was even more of a mess than the last. Maybe she did want to work, but the more she stayed on Saint Rose, the more she realized she didn't want to work as a corporate attorney in the Bay area.

She hovered the cursor over the Facebook tab but resisted. It wouldn't take much to get sucked into hours of scrolling through a newsfeed, and then nothing would be accomplished. Instead, she opened up a new tab and googled "human trafficking Saint Rose Georgia."

"Oh my God," she whispered. There were pages of results, though most of the hits were in forums and reeked of urban legends. However, when she started to filter results, there were a few news hits.

"Fifteen-Year-Old Freed from Massive Florida Child Trafficking Ring"

"Florida-Georgia Line a Hot Spot for Sex Trafficking"

"Four Arrested in Georgia Sex Trafficking Ring"

Faith clicked on one of the local news stories based out of Baxley. *Why don't I remember seeing any of this on the news?* The article detailed how human trafficking filtered up from Florida to Georgia. "Reminiscent of slave trade," the reporter claimed. From the looks of it, this had been going on for decades.

The Georgia farms were particularly popular as "holding cells," said the report. "The relative isolation, large parcels of lands, and 'look the other way' attitude of Georgians make former plantations and farms ideal for human, child, and sex trafficking," claimed the reporter. As evidence, a small ring had been busted three years ago. It involved two men and one woman as the smugglers, along with three girls who were barely legal.

One of the victims claimed that she was lured to Florida from her Boise, Idaho, hometown with the promise of success in a legitimate adult-film industry," the article said. "She answered an ad in the Boise Craigslist Gigs section titled *Sexy Girls Wanted*. The victim says that within one week of responding to the ad, the poster booked a first-class ticket for her to Miami."

"Jesus," Faith said.

The other girls in the ring, who were seventeen and sixteen at the time of their arrival in Miami, told similar stories. "I thought I'd just be doing, you know, regular porn," one of the unnamed victims said. "I was okay with that. I'd watched a lot of it, and it seemed all right. But as soon as we got to the house in Miami, it was nothing like what the manager said."

For three years, the girls had been used as sex slaves in what authorities had thought was an abandoned farmhouse in rural Georgia. They were never paid, and the conditions were deplorable, according to the sheriff who responded to the eventual call for help.

"They fed us just enough to stay attractive, that's what they said," reported one of the victims. "But no money, no clothes, no essentials."

"Did the customers, as you call them, did they use protection?" asked the reporter.

"Sometimes," said one of the victims. "They had to pay a lot more for bareback. I don't know how much, we were never told the amount. But I think it was a lot more because only about half paid it."

The victims were described as malnourished, and two of them hadn't bathed in a week. The third girl was found recently showered with "an excessive amount of makeup" but drugged nearly to the point of being comatose. "Rape test kits revealed that she had recently been assaulted by at least three men within the past twenty-four hours," reported one medical staff member. "She can't recall and has difficulty telling time and dates at the moment due to the Rohypnol in her system. However, semen from three men were found, and DNA from two others were discovered underneath her fingernails."

Faith's stomach lurched. There were thumbnails of the girls as they were taken out of the house—a house that looked very much like the one Faith had inherited. However, this one was on the mainland. She couldn't bring herself to enlarge the photos, even though it was obvious their faces were blurred. The mug shots of the ringleaders were bigger. *They look like they could easily be related to the rednecks from the ferry*, Faith thought with a shudder.

She was pulled out of her research by the ding of a new

email. *You've received a response from your I Dream of Genealogy forum query.*

Faith's heart started to pound. After she'd seen the reality of what was happening all over Georgia, her hunt for family suddenly seemed exceptionally minor.

Hi, Faith. My name's Hannah, and I think we might have a connection? I think, actually this is crazy, but we might be cousins. I'm a realtor, so I'll be in your area today and tomorrow. Do you want to meet up?

Faith chewed at her lip and checked Hannah's member profile. She seemed legitimate, though she hadn't included a photo. *But that's normal these days,* Faith thought. However, the account had been created two years ago, and there was a string of posts Hannah had commented on. Faith clicked on a few, and they seemed innocent enough. Hannah hadn't included a surname, so there was no way to dig deeper.

What are you getting all paranoid for? Faith sighed. That's what digging into the underbelly of the news could do to you.

Thanks for the reply, Hannah, Faith wrote. *I'd love to meet up. How about dinner at Pirate Cove tonight? It should be convenient for both of us, and it's open late. My number is below. Let's figure out the details.*

She bristled at the name of the restaurant, but it was the only one that would be open late and was easily accessible. Five minutes later, Hannah replied with a text to confirm the time.

Faith stood up from the vanity table and stretched. It was nearly noon, and she hadn't even showered yet. Still, she needed to make sure she could even get a ride to the restaurant.

All was quiet downstairs. Mama was likely puttering around in her garden, and today was Jessie's day off. Faith started to search for Caleb, worried that he might be out and about in his boat. Without changing out of her satin pajama shorts and matching camisole, Faith grabbed her denim jacket from the mudroom and slipped on her flip-flops.

As soon as she walked outside, she saw Caleb and Alex chopping driftwood. She stopped abruptly and stepped behind a pillar.

They were shirtless and sweaty and she felt an instant heat flush between her thighs. They were competitive, too. Who knew how long they'd been out there, but the pile of chopped wood was impressively high.

Faith peered around the pillar and drank in the sight of them. *Irish twins is right*, she thought. At just one year apart, they might as well have been fraternal twins. Both were gorgeous with bulging muscles covered in a sheen of sweat.

She couldn't help but be drawn especially to Alex, though. That wouldn't normally be the case. *After all, I've already had him*, she thought. Faith didn't normally sleep around or have one-night stands, but she knew she loved the thrill of the chase.

Maybe this chase isn't over yet.

"Faith?" Caleb's voice cut through her admiring of Alex.

"Oh. Hi!" she said, embarrassed. She pretended to dig through the pockets of the jacket for something. "I was just coming out to look for you."

"Seems you were lookin' for a while, ma'am," Caleb said with a smile.

She was thankful that he was too far away to see how deeply she blushed. Alex didn't even stop with his chore. But did it seem like he started to chop harder, faster, after he realized she was there?

"You wish," she said with a smile.

Caleb flexed his arm. "Can't say I blame you, ma'am," he said.

Finally, Alex stopped and turned toward her. She expected to see him looking exasperated or angry that she'd interrupted them. Instead . . . did he actually look sheepish? That would be a welcome change.

"So." Faith started as she walked toward them. "Any chance you could take me to the ferry tonight?"

"What for?" Caleb asked. He slammed the ax into a stump and pulled a red handkerchief out of his back pocket to wipe the sweat off his face.

"I need to go to Pirate Cove tonight," she said.

"Why's that? Got a hot date?" Caleb teased. Out of the corner of her eye, she saw Alex stiffen.

"If you call a hot date Hannah, and she might be a cousin."

"Hannah sounds like a sexy name," Caleb said. "The cousin part, not so much. I'm not that southern."

"God, do you ever stop?" she asked with an eye roll.

"Only if you know the safe word. But, nah, for real I can take you, though. But I don't want you takin' the ferry alone. You'd be comin' back alone when it's dark and might miss that last ferry. I'll take you on the boat."

"Great," Faith said. "Thank you. And, obviously, I'm happy to buy you dinner for the trouble."

"Dinner sounds mighty nice. Been a while since I was at Pirate Cove," Caleb said with a nod. "But only if Alex comes, too."

"Alex?" Faith asked. She glanced at him. "Uh, sure. But why do you—"

"Hey, as great as it sounds being in a threesome with you and your cousin, it's not really my style," Caleb said.

"Don't think you can handle it?" Faith asked. She couldn't help but get in another dig at Alex.

"More like, not up for testing that theory," Caleb said. "Besides, it would do Alex some good. Meet a new girl, have a few drinks."

Alex scowled at him, and Faith turned red. *Is that what this is about? Caleb trying to set up Alex with some girl none of us have even met? Who knows how old Hannah even is!*

"What makes you think I have so much free time I can just drop everything and go drinking with y'all?" Alex asked.

"Oh, c'mon," Caleb said. "You think I don't know you and your regimented schedule by now? What time you Gonna meet her, Faith?"

"Seven," Faith said.

"See? Plenty of time to get your work done for the day," Caleb said. "What's the big deal, Alex? You got somethin' against pretty girls?"

"What makes you think she's a pretty girl?" Alex asked. He slowly pulled his shirt back on.

"She's related to Faith, right?" Caleb asked.

"Well, maybe," Faith said. "That's what we're trying to figure out."

"Good enough for me," Caleb said. "C'mon, don't be such a stick-in-the-mud, Alex. You really Gonna stick me with two gossiping hens all night?"

"Hey!" Faith said. "I'm standing right here."

"You know what?" Alex asked. "Fine. Jesus, if it'll shut you up."

"Awesome," Faith said. She broke into a smile. "I'll meet you guys here at what, six?"

"Sounds like a plan," Caleb said. "And, Faith? I hope you're bringing your credit card, because I have a mind to try all those fancy tiki cocktails now that you're paying."

"Right," she said. "I'd like to see you sipping on a mai tai."

"A real man's got no shame drinkin' a neon beverage. So six o'clock. It's a date."

She heard something in the word "date," a type of longing or flirtation that went beyond the surface. However, at this point, Faith didn't care. She turned back to the inn and felt Caleb's eyes on her the entire way. A part of her wished she'd pulled on proper shorts or something that covered a little more than this wisp of pajama shorts—still, she refused to adjust them.

And a bigger part of her wished it was Alex's eyes that watched her walk away.

22

FAITH

"Careful!" Alex said.

She grasped for his hand as Caleb docked the boat, and it bumped against the old wooden planks.

"Geez!" she said as she stumbled. She scraped her hand against a roughened edge of the dock and felt a splinter slice through her skin. "Kind of a rough landing there, Captain," she said to Caleb.

"You need to work on them sea legs, ma'am," Caleb said as he secured the boat. "There's nothin' wrong with my seafaring skills."

"You all right?" Alex asked as Faith sucked on her palm. She pulled the splinter out with a wince.

"I'll live," she said. "So where is this place? I just saw it on Google Maps. What kind of restaurant doesn't have a website or Facebook page?"

"The kind of restaurant with good food and strong drinks!"

VIVIAN WOOD

Caleb said. "Don't worry, it's just 'bout a quarter mile from here. We can walk."

Faith screwed up her face and looked at her wedge heels. They were comfortable enough, but she could tell that by the end of the night the cream-colored soles would be covered in Georgia dust.

"How'd you find this girl?" Caleb asked as the three of them trudged down the deserted street.

"I'd posted on a few genealogy forums," Faith said. "She was the first, and only, reply."

"Well that's creepy," Caleb said.

"Creepy? Why? How's it any different than Tinder? Besides the fact that I'm not looking to hook up with her."

"What's firewood got to do with this?"

Faith rolled her eyes.

Soon, a strip of neon appeared in the distance. Pirate Cove clearly used to be a plantation home, but it had been kitted out in kitschy tiki decor. Brightly colored bulbs were strung across the patio, and big plastic skeletons, parrots, and treasure chests peppered the property.

"Oh, wow," Faith said. "I hope she doesn't judge me for this."

"What's she look like?" Alex asked.

"I have no idea."

Caleb held the door open for both of them. The restaurant was bustling, even with the remote location. In the distance, a crew sang happy birthday to a middle-aged man wearing a pirate's hat, while drunk college kids downed buckets of margaritas in plastic pails.

"Faith!" A slender girl with golden skin and honey-colored eyes bounded up to her. Long light-brown hair snaked down her back in the kind of beachy waves some girls spent hours to achieve.

"Hannah?" Faith asked. "How'd you know it was me?"

The girl swallowed her in a bear hug. She was shockingly strong for how petite she was.

"I admit it, I stalked you," she said. "But not till after we talked! Impressive, law school and all."

"Oh, well, yeah," Faith said with a blush. She'd forgotten she'd been naïve enough to post her full name on the forum.

"And who's *this*?" Hannah asked as she eyed Alex and Caleb. "How'd you know I was on the prowl?" she said to Faith with a smile.

"Oh! This is Alex and Caleb. They live on the island. I'm staying in their family inn while I take care of some things."

"Pleased to meet you, ma'am," Caleb said. Faith shook her head slightly. *He could really pour on the charm.*

"Ma'am!" Hannah said with a laugh. "That's what I love about doing business down here. I swear, even though I was born in the South, I never get tired of it."

"Good to meet you, ma'am," Alex said as he reached out to shake Hannah's hand.

He had the kind of blazing white smile spread across his face that Faith had rarely seen. *Maybe it's me? He's met Hannah for less than a minute, and already the girl has won him over better than I have ever managed.*

"I already got us a table but thought I'd wait for you up here,"

Hannah said. "Come on! I want to figure out if we're really related. I hope so. You're *gorgeous*," she said to Faith.

They settled into a booth. Hannah sat across from Faith. Caleb scooted in beside her, while Alex languidly slumped into the vinyl seat beside Hannah. "I wasn't expecting to be accompanied by such handsome men, but I can't complain," Hannah said. "Margaritas for all?"

"Sure," Alex said. Faith gave him a look. *Since when does he drink margaritas?*

"So," Faith said as their drinks arrived. "I was so excited when I got your reply—not just about the family connection, but you're a realtor, too!"

"Yep," Hannah said as she took a long sip of her frozen strawberry margarita. "I used to be the only realtor working the Georgia islands. But now with the tourism booming and all ..."

"Lots of competition, I bet," Caleb said.

"That's an understatement."

"Do you know anything about Lydia Capshaw's property?" Faith asked.

"Aunt Lydia's place?" Hannah asked. "Sure. I mean I lost touch with her. Let's just put it that way. Really, it was my mom's doing. The whole family kind of, well, cut ties back when I was a child. But I'd look up the estimate from time to time. I still remember playing out there as a kid."

"You . . . you knew her?" Faith asked. Suddenly her lime margarita tasted way too sweet on her tongue.

"I wouldn't say that," Hannah said with a shrug. "I barely remember her. I think the last time I saw her, I was maybe ten years old? I guess I remember her better than you do, though!"

"What?" Faith said. "I don't . . . I didn't really know her at all. I mean, I didn't remember coming out to Saint Rose at all until I heard about her passing."

"Well, I'm not surprised you don't remember her." She shrugged. "I barely do. Most of what I know comes from my mom. Honestly, she wasn't that memorable, from what I hear," Hannah said in a faux hushed tone. "But I have a picture of the three of us together. You wanna see it?"

"What?" Faith's straw fell out of her drink, but she didn't bother to pick it up.

"Yeah! Me and you as babies, and Aunt Lydia. Mighta been at her place, for all I know."

"You . . . you have this?"

"Sure. My mom was super into archiving all the family photos. Got some fancy scanner for Christmas one year. As soon as I saw your post, I started digging through her digital photos. One thing 'bout Mama, that woman didn't miss a detail when it came to archiving."

Caleb and Alex were silent. They pretended to study the menu as the information sank in for Faith.

"Hold on, let me pull it up," Hannah said as she toyed with her phone.

"I can't believe this," Faith said. "This whole time . . ."

"Here it is," Hannah said. She passed the phone across the table. "That's me. I was bald till I was, like, two. And you with that full head of hair. And Aunt Lydia and your dad. My uncle."

The photo was a typical early 1990s snapshot. Faith had a bright-pink scrunchie holding up a side ponytail. Aunt Lydia looked stoic, even in the brightly patterned sweatshirt and overly permed hair. She looked like she was playing dress up but came from a much more serious era. Still, there was a quiet beauty about her. She didn't look a thing like Faith's dad.

"I remember you," Faith said, incredulous, as Hannah tapped through a couple more photos. It was her, the little blonde from her memories. Then again, she knew it would be. "I don't remember her looking like that," Faith said softly. She ran a finger over Lydia's image.

"You're not missing out on much," Hannah said as she put her phone away. "I heard about you every now and then when I was growing up. Apparently, you loved being on that plantation."

"I did?" How could she have blocked something like that out? "Do you know how old I was when I stopped going there?"

"No idea," Hannah said with a shrug. "Pretty young, though, I'd imagine, a bit older than me. Maybe seven? I heard that Aunt Lydia suddenly got pretty hermitlike in midlife. I don't know if it was actual agoraphobia or what. But she left that farm and moved into some kind of semi-assisted-living facility."

"How old was she?" Faith asked. In the photo, Aunt Lydia couldn't have been older than thirty-five.

"Dunno," Hannah said. "But it wasn't for the elderly necessarily. It was, you know, for people who weren't mentally capable of fully caring for themselves."

"Oh," Faith said.

"Anyway, that's just a rumor. Who knows how much truth is in it? For all I know, she could have had some torrid love affair with a foreign farmhand and run off to Nicaragua. Who knows? I mean, it wouldn't be the first time she, well, never mind. I'm sure you don't want to hear about that. Sorry."

"Hear about what?" Faith asked.

"Well, you know, anything about her love life. After your dad . . ."

"You know?" Faith said sharply. She heard the accusation in her voice, and Hannah's eyes got big.

"I, um, sorry? I thought . . ."

"Does everyone know?" Faith asked. "In the family, I mean? On the whole island?"

"I don't . . . I don't know about people on the island," Hannah said slowly. "But in terms of the family? Well, yeah. It's, you know, kind of why your dad had a falling out with everyone. I mean, you know that, though. Right?"

Faith felt Caleb's hand, reassuring on her thigh, but couldn't even register how nicely foreign it felt. "No," she said bluntly. "I, well, I didn't piece it together until a few days ago."

"But how?" Hannah asked, genuinely confused. "You're the . . . you're the one who caught them. I don't remember it myself, but that's the story I've been told."

Tears threatened to spill from Faith's eyes. "There are stories?" she asked. "I . . . I don't know. I guess I blocked it out. But going back into that house, it brought it all back," she said. Faith took a long drink from her water glass to buy time.

"Oh my God," Hannah said. "I'm so sorry." She reached across the table and took Faith's hand. "I—I mean I never blamed you, of course," she said. "My mom absolutely flipped. Refused to ever talk to your dad or Aunt Lydia again. Wouldn't even tell me your *name* for years, and I was so little I forgot, so I couldn't look you up." Hannah's voice started to tremble, too.

"It's fucked up," Faith said. She sniffed and the tears subsided. "I mean, for my dad to do that? With his own sister? It's just—"

"Well," Hannah interrupted. "I mean, it's not so bad."

"Not so bad?" Faith and the guys all gaped at Hannah at once.

"What? It's not like Lydia was a *blood relative* or anything," Hannah said. "She wasn't even formally adopted! She was, like, fifteen and was just taken in by our grandparents so they could be her legal guardians and help her out for a few years."

"Wait, what? She wasn't their biological sister?"

"Ew, gross, no! Is that—is that what you thought? This whole time?"

"Well, not this *whole* time," Faith said. She started to breathe easier. "I mean, I just remembered what I saw last week."

"Oh God, I'm sorry!" Hannah said. "I thought—I thought you knew all that."

"So who was she then? I mean, why did our grandparents take her in?"

"She was a local girl, helped them out during the harvest. Her mom was a single mom, had her when she was a teenager or something. Just up and left her on the island! Ran off to

Vegas. From what I heard, our grandparents just helped her out until she started college."

"That's . . . God, that's so nice to hear," Faith said. "So then, wow, my poor dad. I mean, first my mom. Then the whole mess with Lydia and the argument with his family."

"Honestly? My mom and the family totally overreacted," Hannah said. "I mean, who cares? I don't know if it's because Lydia ended up making bank and owning a whole freaking island and they were jealous, or they thought your dad should mourn *forever* or something, I don't know. Small-town drama," she said with an eye roll.

"When she died, it was somewhere on the mainland. I forget the name," Faith said. She was ashamed to admit that she hadn't really cared or bothered to look into it. Aunt Lydia was a stranger when she'd found out about the inheritance. Hannah's picture made her real. The story, the *real* story, made her—and her dad—people.

"Yeah, how'd you find out she passed away, anyway?" Hannah asked.

"She, uh, she left me her property. The plantation." Faith wasn't about to tell Hannah about the lump sum of money.

"Are you serious?" Hannah asked. "That's . . . that's amazing! What are you going to do with it? Do you need a realtor?"

Faith smiled at her. She wasn't ready to trust Hannah, not just yet. But the girl seemed wholly honest and transparent. There wasn't a flicker of jealousy in her eyes. *Maybe this is what having real family is like.* "Not yet!" she said with a laugh.

"That totally makes sense, though."

"What?"

"That she left it to you! I mean, who knows how long your dad and her were together? After your mom, of course. Spending the summers there . . . God, they must have really been in love. And you being his daughter, I mean that's the closest she ever got to a daughter. You look like your dad," she said, and she examined Faith closely. "From the photos I've seen of him, at least. Aunt Lydia must have totally adored you."

Faith blushed. "I don't know. So besides her mom, she didn't have any family? I mean, blood family, of her own?"

Hannah wrinkled her nose. "Some disgusting creeps of cousins or something," she said. "Super locals, like back-woods. She never wanted anything to do with them, though."

"Yeah," Faith said. *The rednecks.* "I can see why."

"So tell me more about your plans for the property! Ideas?"

"I'm not totally sure yet."

"You better be sure," Alex broke in. "After you made me spend how many hours at Home Depot."

Hannah looked at Alex in confusion. "Don't mind him," Faith said.

"Is this your boyfriend?" Hannah asked. She tried to make sense of everyone's relationship. "Do you want to switch seats?"

"No!" Faith and Alex said at the same time. "I mean," Faith said, "no, he's not. But he's done a lot to help me with the property."

"What do you mean?"

"Well, I'm thinking of renovating it. I am renovating it," she corrected herself.

"Seriously? That's great! That property could be a stunner with the right touch," Hannah said.

Faith sighed. "Here's to hoping."

"And then what? Are you . . . are you going to move to Saint Rose?"

"I really don't know yet." She hadn't thought about it aloud yet, but was it so crazy? "I guess it just feels good, to own property. Land. Very solid."

"Very adult," Hannah agreed.

The food arrived, and Hannah started to assemble her sizzling fajitas while Faith cut into the blue corn enchiladas. "Wow," Caleb said as he dug into the carne adovada. "Santa Fe-style. Nice."

They ate largely in silence, and Alex piped up that was a good sign. "Means the food is good." Faith was thankful for the quiet. She stole glances at Hannah and could still see the little girl in her, in the upturn of her nose and extreme cupid's bow of her lip.

All four of them turned down dessert, though it took Caleb a minute to truly say no to the tres leches. "Gwen tries, but that's the one dessert she can't do," he said with a sigh.

"You can always take it to go," Hannah said.

"Nah. Gotta watch my figure," he told her.

They were one of the last tables to leave the restaurant, and they lingered in the parking lot. Hannah jumped on Faith with another one of her tight squeezes. "Promise me we'll see each other again," she said.

Faith laughed. "You act like one of us is going off to war! Of course we will. You know where to find me for the rest of the summer."

"That I do," Hannah said. "Right where it all started."

The guys gave Hannah brief hugs before the trio headed back toward Caleb's boat. The full moon lit up the dirt road as good as any streetlamp. Faith stole glances at Alex. *Why can't he smile at me like he did at Hannah?*

Alex must be around the same age her father had been when that photo was snapped of her, Hannah, and Lydia. *Was life so different on Saint Rose all those years ago? Having a little girl, a dead wife . . .*

Faith shook her head. That photo of her with Aunt Lydia couldn't have been taken long after her mother passed away. Her father hadn't hated Georgia at all. Just hated the circumstances. And the stories, filtered through Hannah, who knew how much of it was true? *And now there is nobody left to ask.*

But her dad and Lydia? That she knew was honest love. *How different could it have been? For him, me, her, all of us? If they'd only given it a real shot, not given a damn what the family thought.*

I shouldn't judge Dad, she told herself. *Or Alex—especially just for not knowing what he wants. Poor Alex*, she thought. *He's probably just trying to make it through the day.*

23

ALEX

"*H*ere." Alex held out his hand to Faith as Caleb docked the boat back on the island.

"Thanks," she said. She smiled up at him openly. Alex looked at her curiously. Somehow, in the boat ride back, those walls she'd built up seemed to have crumbled.

Caleb muttered something under his breath.

"What was that?" Alex asked.

"Nothing," Caleb said. He reached for the pull rope of the engine again. "I got some stuff to take care of. Y'all go on."

"It's almost midnight," Alex said.

"Yeah, so? Some things are better done at night," Caleb said.

Faith widened her eyes at Alex. They stood and watched as Caleb left in the boat. "What's with him?" she asked.

"Who knows? Maybe the night didn't turn out as he would have liked."

A wave of exhaustion washed over him. It had been a long day, a grueling day. Chopping firewood always took it out of him, and those margaritas at Pirate Cove had been strong. Even though Faith seemed a little more open than she had in the past few days, he knew he was nowhere near being in her good graces.

"God, what a night," she said. "It's neat, though. Finding out you have family. I mean, my cousins and all, I know they care about me. But it's in that required familial way. Hannah's different, though."

"That's one way to put it," Alex said. The girl had slightly annoyed him. That bubbly personality and lack of boundaries? It put him on edge. *Sure, she seemed to be a sweet girl, but I couldn't handle being around that for long.*

Faith didn't respond, and he regretted the words. After all, who was he to put a damper on Faith's excitement? He was spoiled for company when it came to family.

At the fork, he turned left toward the cabin. He could see the lights from Greystone and didn't have it in him to be gentlemanly to walk Faith to the door. *Besides, I'm sure she's happy to be rid of me*, he thought.

"Hey! Alex!" He turned and saw Faith as she jogged toward him. "I'm all, I don't know, wired from tonight, I guess. Are you up for a walk?"

He almost said no, but it had been so long since he'd seen such openness on her face that he couldn't resist. "Sure," he said.

"Want to head down to the beach?" she asked.

His chest tightened at the thought. A full moon, the white

beach, it was a recipe for romance, and he wasn't sure if he could manage it. "Sounds great," he said.

They walked side by side in silence until the sand began to creep into their shoes. Alex pulled off his sneakers, and Faith put her arm on his shoulder for balance while she slipped out of her wedges.

He expected her to bombard him with questions. Or start to interrogate him about what they were and what the other night meant. As much as he tried, he couldn't put together a reasonable answer for that. *What were they, anyway? Did the other night mean anything? Of course she still gets me excited, she was hot as hell. Is there something more than that?* But she surprised him.

After ten minutes, Faith directed them to the shore, and they let the saltwater lick at their ankles. "It's warm," she said.

"Surprised?"

"I'm used to the so-called beaches near San Francisco," she said. "And even the water in Southern California where I grew up, they weren't like this."

"I wouldn't know," he said.

"You've never been to another beach?"

"Never been in the water of another beach. Before, well, let's just say I've never been with anyone outside of Georgia that had any interest in getting in the water."

Faith stopped and picked up a sand dollar. She rinsed it in the frothy water and tucked it into her pocket. "Tell me about Rebecca," she said.

"What?"

"Tell me about her," she said simply. "I mean, if you want to."

He sucked in his breath. Alex readied himself to tell her he certainly didn't want to talk about his ex-wife. But when he opened his mouth, he realized that was a lie. Maybe it was time to talk about her. Maybe Faith was the right person. "When Rebecca died, everyone said I should talk to someone. That's how they all put it. Like saying the word therapist or shrink would have been too extreme."

"Did you?" Faith asked.

"No," he said and turned to continue to walk. Faith stayed by his side. "I mean, I tried actually. I went to two therapists, but just once each."

"Why?" she asked. "Didn't like it?"

"I don't know. At the time I thought it was all bullshit. In reality, either I just wasn't ready or maybe they weren't the right ones for me."

"I hear you have to try a lot of therapists before you find the right fit," she said.

"Hell, who has time for that when your wife just died?"

Faith was quiet, but it was a comfortable quiet. The kind that made him want to talk more. "Rebecca and I," he said with a sigh. "We did it all too soon. Met too soon, got married too soon. Looking back now, I know she wasn't the one. Even if we'd met later, dated more before we got married, it still wouldn't have been right. Pretty sure she knew it, too."

"How'd you meet?" Faith asked.

"College," he said with a laugh. "I went to UGA, no surprise there. It wasn't so different than what I was used to. But she was totally out of her element. This loud New York Jewish girl with wild black hair and a tendency to get into trouble with that mouth."

"She sounds fun," Faith said.

"She was," Alex admitted. "And that was exactly what drew me to her. Hell, we were nineteen when we met. Engaged before we graduated. She hated that. How all her friends teased her about going to college in the South and ending up with her MRS degree. But me, I didn't care."

"When did you get married?"

"Not long after graduation," he said. "It was a whirlwind of a summer. She and I, I think we both just rode on the excitement of it. We were both still kids. Neither one of us had ever lived outside our parents' places or a dorm room. She had a trust fund, but just for college, and I had a few scholarships and some money from work-study and summer jobs. Felt like we could do anything."

"I remember that feeling," Faith said. "Doesn't last long enough."

"You know what's funny? I don't even remember the wedding," he said with a little laugh. "When I think about it, it's like I'm watching or remembering a movie about someone else. I remember her sister going berserk over everyone callin' her ma'am. Thought it meant she looked old."

Faith laughed. "Well, those are New Yorkers for you."

"I told her sister, y'all better get used to it. That southern charm's bound to trickle down to the kids. And Rebecca. She gave me this look when I said that. Even in that wedding dress that cost more than my car at the time. Like the thought sickened her."

"That . . . that must have been hard," Faith said. They stepped over a beached piece of driftwood in sync.

"I dunno. I tried, you know, to pretend that it was just the stress of the wedding. Or the drinking, or maybe I imagined it all. But I saw it. And that . . . I don't think that was the first red flag. It was just the first one that smacked me in the face."

"What were the others?"

He sighed. "Well, the little indiscretions. Ones I should've spotted as huge red flags way back."

"She cheated on you? Like, before you were even married?"

"Wasn't that simple," he said with a shake of his head. "In college, there were all these times with gray areas. We'd be off at times, or it would all be under the guise of some stupid game."

He saw Faith stumble a bit with the "stupid game" comment and rushed to cover it up.

"I mean, I told her I didn't care. That spring break was a free-for-all, long as it was everything but. And I let it slide when she'd make out with her sorority sisters. Knew she didn't go that way, and it was all for attention. But, hell, I don't know. Maybe I should have just walked away. I should have," he repeated. "I should have just walked away."

"We all make mistakes," Faith said gently. "And love makes us stupid."

"That's the thing, though," Alex said. "I don't . . . I don't know if it was love. I mean, hell, she was my first."

"Your first?"

"My first everything," he said.

"Oh. So in high school? You didn't—"

He let out a laugh. "I'm not trying to be rude, but you never saw the girls that went to my high school," he said. "First of all, there're so few kids on the island, my graduating class was a whoppin' twelve people. And three of 'em still live at the inn."

"Whoa, seriously?" Faith said.

"Good amount of home schoolin' round here," he said. "But yeah, the island's tight. The few girls that were around, well they were more like sisters. We all experimented, but it was innocent. A kiss here or there."

"And in college?"

He shrugged. "I made out with a few girls. But I met Rebecca freshman year. We were official by sophomore year. What can I say? I was faithful to her."

"That's hard," Faith said.

"Yeah, well. Like I said. Lookin' back? I don't think it was love. Not full love, the real deal. Puppy lust or infatuation, maybe. But after college? I'd figured she gotten any flirtin' outta her system."

"And she didn't?"

"Turns out, no," he said as he let out a breath of air. "I . . . I don't know how many times. Maybe it really was just the once. Or the one guy. That's what we fought about the night she died."

"Jesus," Faith said. "How did you—"

"Find out?" he asked. "Wasn't hard. Not like she hid it. Hell, for all I know, she wanted to flaunt it."

227

"Why would she do that?"

"I reckon because she was unhappy," he said simply. He'd never said it before, but it sounded right. "We both were. She just was the one who acted out 'cause of it."

"And you didn't suspect anything before? Even with her flirting with George?"

"Not really," he said, and mulled it over. "At least, not as much as I should have. And not in the right way. Earlier, I'd catch her flirting and drag her away. Felt like a caveman. And then we'd get into this whole circus act. We got pretty good at it, I have to admit."

"That doesn't sound healthy," she said.

"Far from it!" he said with a laugh. "But it was familiar. You know? And comfortable. We both knew our roles. Though, I gotta admit, I wasn't totally innocent in all of it."

"Oh?"

"I mean, I never cheated on her. Never even flirted with anyone else. That's just not me. But I buried myself away. I ignored it, unless it was just so damn obvious I couldn't. Tucked myself into work, kept myself busy. Just lookin' for a distraction."

"That's no excuse for someone to cheat. Especially when they're married," Faith said.

"I know, but still. I coulda handled it better. Even after we were married, I was just so scared of admitting it was a mistake. To anyone, myself included. I just . . . I just wanted it to work."

"I think that's common," Faith said. "A lot of people get stuck in bad marriages because of that."

"Yeah, well. Count me among 'em," Alex said.

"Alex." Faith put her hand on his arm to stop him. "Just so you know, I'm not her."

He looked down at her, with those big green eyes framed by lush lashes. Her face shone in the moonlight. Before he could question himself, he leaned down and kissed her. She responded as if no time had passed since they'd been in his bed.

Alex wound his arms around her waist and felt the heat from her body in his palms. She opened her mouth to him and his tongue found hers. Faith's hands wrapped around his neck, and he could hear her breath quicken. He started to kiss his way down her neck. The scent of her perfume was addictive.

Suddenly, Faith broke free and took a step back. "We have to stop," she panted.

"But why?" he asked, though he knew the answer.

"You need to figure yourself out," she said quietly, though it wasn't cruel.

He nodded and looked to the waves. After a moment, he heard her soft feet in the sand as she headed back to the trail alone.

You need to figure yourself out, he repeated the words to himself. Maybe so. And maybe, if and when he did, something greater than he ever fathomed would be on the other side.

24

FAITH

*I*t was impossible to sit at that breakfast table and pretend like the conversation on the beach hadn't happened. But apparently, that was exactly what Alex expected.

"Another flapjack, dear?" Mama asked.

"I'm stuffed," Faith said as she refilled her mug of coffee. "Thank you, though, Mama. They were delicious."

"Uh huh," Mama said. "Not too stuffed to pour more of that slick oil down your throat, I see."

"Mama!" Caleb said with a laugh. He happily piled another stack of flapjacks onto his plate and drowned them in syrup.

"What?" Mama asked. "I just tell y'all things for your own good. That stuff's addictive," she said. She picked up her own cup of morning tea. "Tea's good for you."

"Not with all that sugar you put in it," Caleb said.

"Hush, now," Mama said. "There's nothin' wrong with sugar."

Alex seemed morose and picked at the dry squares of protein bread coated with a thin layer of sugarless jam. He'd already torn through the bacon and egg whites Gwen had cooked up. "How you gonna call all that fat healthy?" Mama had asked.

"Protein," Caleb had said at the same time as Alex. Alex had just given him a look of warning.

Once Mama and Caleb finished breakfast, Faith still worked on her coffee. It didn't look like Alex was going to move, either. *What kind of standoff is this?*

Faith snatched up a stack of design magazines she'd picked up in Savannah and started to flip through them. "That's nice," Mama said as she wiped up the table. "That house needs a womanly touch."

"Well, design is still a long ways off," Faith said. "But I like getting ideas."

"What style you like?" Mama asked.

"I'm thinking French country. A touch of shabby chic, you know, but balanced with a little midcentury modern. Some living edge pieces, maybe."

"I don't have a clue what you just said. But I'm sure it'll be real nice."

Caleb busied himself in front of the fridge, where he packed up some of the berries from the U-Pick farm up the road. "Hey, Caleb?" she asked. "You busy today?"

Alex glanced up at her but looked away.

So that got him curious.

"Not much," Caleb said. "Why, what's up?"

"I was wondering, maybe we could go for a ride around the island today? It seems like good weather for it."

"A ride?" Caleb asked. He popped one of the blackberries into his mouth. "Sure, we can do that. On the boat, you mean?"

"Yeah," Faith said with a smile. Alex finished his toast in two bites.

Caleb looked at Alex, opened his mouth but snapped it back shut. The last thing Alex looked like he wanted to do was get on a boat.

"You ready?" Faith asked.

"Now? You wanna go now?" Caleb asked.

"Why not? Looks like you're packing a boat-friendly picnic anyway."

"Well. Yes, ma'am," Caleb said. He tipped an imaginary cowboy hat at her.

"Cool, I'll meet you out front. I just want to get my sunblock." She winced at the memory of the sunblock on Alex's sandbar. But that seemed like so long ago. *And as if it were with a different person, too.*

Caleb was still in the kitchen when she traipsed down the stairs.

"Come on," she said.

"Guess we're goin'," Caleb said.

"Y'all have a real good time," Alex said. His tone was like ice. *Why do you care?* Faith wanted to ask.

Caleb held the truck door open for her, and she climbed inside. "I've never been in—"

Caleb flipped the ignition and the truck roared to life. "You're gonna have to wait till we get to the dock," he called to her. "Can't hear nothin' till then."

It was the first time she'd sat in silence with Caleb. *It's nice*, she thought. Faith watched him maneuver the big truck Mama kept around for island errands with ease. The hair on his arms had gone white from the summer sun. The blond on his head had lightened dramatically, too, offset with the natural Georgia tan.

Caleb pulled up to the boat dock and killed the engine. The sudden silence was overwhelming. As she climbed out of the truck, the sounds of birds chirping and fish splashing in the water could be heard.

"There're no sharks, right?" she teased Caleb with a grin.

He just raised his brow at her and untethered the boat. Caleb held his arm out to her to help her in.

"Thank you kindly," she said in a terrible southern accent. "What's wrong?" she asked Caleb when she got no response.

He sat across from her in the boat and pushed off. "You wanna tell me what's goin' on?" he asked. Any flirtatious act was gone, and he fixed those blue eyes squarely on hers.

"What do you mean?" she asked. She was thankful for the sunglasses perched on her nose. Caleb kept his tucked into his shirt.

"You know what I mean," he said. "Y'all been acting off for days."

"Who has?" she asked.

"Playin' dumb don't work on you," he said. "You and Alex, who else?"

"Oh," she said. Faith looked at her hands cupped in her lap. "You noticed that, huh?"

"Helen Keller would notice that."

"Caleb! I think that's wrong."

"Don't change the subject," he said. Caleb picked up the vintage oars from their storage bin. They were kept perfectly polished but were rarely used. Most of the time, he fired up the engine.

Clearly, this is going to be a long—and serious—discussion. "Sorry," she said softly. "I don't know. I mean, how much do you know?"

Caleb shrugged.

"Alex and I, we . . . it's that obvious, huh?"

"Nah," Caleb said. "I was exaggeratin' a bit. It's not obvious to everyone, but it is to me. Lee and Matt, I think they're oblivious."

She noticed he didn't say one way or another about Mama. "So if you know that he and I are . . . were . . . *whatever.* Why have you been so flirty with me?" It was awkward to get that question out. There, on that still water where she could still see all the way to the bottom, it was all cards on the table.

Caleb grinned at her. "'Cause it drives Alex nuts when I do. It was fun to watch, for a while." Caleb looked into the distance. "But now? It's gettin' painful. It's not a game no more."

Games. Always back to games. She wished she could have taken back that night at the bar with the stupid pool table. *Or do I? Maybe it wouldn't have started otherwise.*

"So what gives?" Caleb's voice broke into her thoughts.

"Well, since *you* don't want to tell me how much you know, we were intimate. Okay?" She blushed as she said it, but surely Caleb had figured out that much.

"Wait. Y'all had sex? I thought . . ."

"You thought what?" she demanded. *Shit. He hadn't known.*

"I mean, I thought all this was over a kiss."

She turned bright red. "A kiss?" she asked.

"Well, yeah. That night at the bar."

"Yeah, no," she said. Faith tucked her hair back behind her ears. She didn't know what to do with her hands.

"Man," Caleb said. He shook his head in wonder and stared into the water. "He must be really gone on you, then."

"What? Why?" she asked. "I mean, not that I'm the most experienced person in the world, but this isn't normal behavior. How he's acting."

Caleb chuckled. "Maybe not for most. But it is for Alex. I swear, I heard him say at least a hundred times, he wasn't never gonna get as strung out over a woman as he did with Rebecca."

Rebecca? Was Caleb really comparing her to Rebecca? "I don't—"

"Now, hold on. I'm not comparin' you to her," he said. "I'm just . . . I haven't seen him like this since then. Since those years."

"Oh," she said. Faith nibbled at her lip. "Is that good? Bad?"

235

"Guess it depends who you ask, ma'am," he said. That glint in his eye was back, and she was grateful. She could only take Serious Caleb for so long.

"Look, I don't want to get up in y'all's business. Or tell you what to do, but—"

"Tell me!" she said. "Please. God, I could use some direction."

"If direction's what you're after, I'm afraid I can't help you."

"Oh," she said sadly. "Then what? What were you going to tell me?"

"Just don't hurt my brother."

"*Hurt* him?" She was shocked. First Mama, now Caleb. *Do they think I'm some kind of heartless bitch?*

"He's done been hurt enough. Had plenty o' heartbreak in his life. And, well, he just doesn't deserve anymore," Caleb said. He shrugged and put his sunglasses on. "That's all."

Faith was silent. They'd drifted farther from Saint Rose than she'd realized. From here, it looked so peaceful. *You'd never imagine it is some kind of sex trafficking hub. Is?*

"Don't think on it too much," Caleb said quietly.

She smiled at him. *He is worried about his brother, that's all. Same goes for Mama. But is that what's happening? Am I causing Alex heartache?* That was the last thing she wanted.

"And just so you know, I know you aren't like Rebecca." Caleb shivered when he said her name. "Not that that says much. There's *nobody* like her. Thank the Lord," he said.

She gave a soft laugh. "You disliked her that much, huh?"

"Hated her. Don't look so surprised! Southern boys can hate," he said. "And it wasn't just after the first time I heard about the affairs, neither."

"The first time?"

"Who knows how many times she did. Or how many times it got out or Alex told me. But way before then? I knew she wasn't no good," he said.

"Really? How could you tell? Why didn't you say something to him?"

Caleb let out a belly laugh. "Say somethin'? To Alex? You think anyone could change his mind or even get him to listen more than a second once he's got his mind on somethin'? I might as well have been talking to the moon."

"Okay, you got me," she said. "He certainly comes off as stubborn."

"That's a light way a puttin' it," he said. "But you asked how I could tell? Now, if I'm honest, I didn't even meet her in person till their senior year. Right before they got engaged—"

"Really? No holidays or anything?"

He shook his head. "I went to Ole Miss," he said. "I was young, wild, stupid an' selfish. Holiday breaks were the best times to party," he said. Caleb leaned forward and stage whispered to her. "Not much faculty or staff round to keep us outta the girls' dorms."

"Yeah, yeah," she said. "I get it. So tell me."

"Well," Caleb began. He pursed his lips and gazed to the sky. "I got a glimpse of it. You know? In the photos I saw of her? Alex, he always had this big shit-eatin' grin on his face in those pictures. And his arm was always on hers real tight.

But she . . . she always looked like she'd practiced that smile a long time in the mirror. Like one of them girls that has a gummy smile and has to practice to hide it?"

"Nice," Faith said with an eye roll.

"Hey, I wasn't talkin' 'bout you! You don't have that."

"Go on," she said before he could distract himself again.

"And, well, in the photos, she was always leanin' away from him. And rarely lookin' right at the camera. Like she wanted to seem single in case someone that caught her fancy was lookin'."

"Huh," Faith said. "You got all that from pictures?"

"I notice more than you think," he said. "But you? Anyone can tell just by looking at you that you give a shit."

"Nice," she said with a laugh.

"It's true! Might not be too eloquent, but it is. And I just wouldn't feel right about not taking the opportunity to tell you not to mess Alex round."

Faith squinted as she thought of a response. Behind Caleb's head, in the distance, a plume of smoke appeared. "Oh my God," she whispered.

"Huh? What?"

"There's . . . there's smoke," she said and pointed. "On the property. My property."

"Jesus," he said. Caleb reached for the engine pull.

Faith did the calculations. *Where is the dock? How far are they from the house?*

"It's the house," she said. "The house is burning!"

The last word was drowned out as Caleb brought the boat to life. For however long they were on the water, it seemed to take a year to reach a dock, but eventually reached one near Faith's property.

They jumped into a golf cart that was sitting by the dock and Caleb started to barrel toward Lydia's old property. "Do you think—God—maybe it's another cross? Maybe someone sneaked onto the island for a campfire? Maybe—"

"It's the house, Faith," Caleb said. It was with such certainty that she didn't even bother coming up with more excuses.

Of course it was the house. She'd known as soon as she saw the smoke. *Please let it be okay,* she thought. Faith was a little surprised at how much the thought of the house being gone pulled at her heart.

Just let it be okay. She would will it into reality.

25

ALEX

*A*lex sighed as he pulled off his thin T-shirt and wiped the sheen from his face. Faith trudged along beside him. All morning they'd assessed the damage as best they could.

"It'll take us a while to get out there," the Saint Rose fire department had told him over the phone yesterday afternoon.

"A while?" Alex had asked. "What does that mean? What else are y'all doin' over there?"

"Alex, you know we're almost all volunteers," the fire chief had said softly.

He did know. He'd volunteered with them himself the summer before college. Fires on Saint Rose were rare. Even during dry seasons, most locals knew well enough how to prevent them. It was one of the first things he remembered Mama teaching him and Caleb as kids.

"I don't know what to tell Craig," Faith had said that morning as they boarded his plane for the island. The phone was cradled in her lap. "He's going to, I don't know. I don't want to let him down if the project can't move forward."

"Don't tell him nothin' yet," Alex said. "We don't even know what we're up against. Besides, worrying about disappointing Craig should be the last thing on your mind."

Thank God she'd had the water turned back on at the property so Craig and his crew would have access. It hadn't been easy to put out the flames with Caleb. When the two of them had returned to the inn, they looked like they'd been to war.

"Faith! Caleb!" Mama had cried. "Y'all had us worried bein' gone so long. What . . . what happened?"

Caleb had sat down, dazed. "Sorry, ma'am," he'd said quietly. Slowly, he began to tell the story. Faith sat at the far end of the table, soothed by a cup of tea from Gwen.

"Y'all could see the smoke from the boat?" Mama asked. "And you *went* to it, instead of getting your behinds to the mainland and calling the fire department?"

"Like the fire department could do anything!" Caleb said. "Hell yeah, I went to the fire. Sorry, ma'am," he said. Caleb was always quick to correct himself when he cursed in front of Mama.

"Why didn't you call?" Alex demanded.

"No reception. Remember?"

"What about the radio?"

"I . . . I forgot it," Caleb said. "Fucking stupid."

Mama sighed. "So? How bad was it? Was it same as here?" she asked under her breath.

"It was pretty rough," Caleb admitted. "There were, yeah, there were similarities to here. But the whole house was ablaze."

"Was anyone there?" Alex asked. "Did you see anyone? Jesus, you could have put Faith in danger."

He noticed the look she shot him when he said that, but he was too fired up to care.

"No! There wasn't nobody," Caleb said. "Dang, Alex, you really think I'd put her in a situation like that?"

"Well, it certainly sounds like it! Bolting over there, not even having a clue what was going on."

"Yeah, okay, that was dumb," Caleb admitted. "But it was instinct! You woulda done the same."

Alex didn't respond. He couldn't. *Who knows what I would have done.*

"But it's out now?" Mama asked.

"Good enough," Caleb said. Mama gave him a look. "Trust me," he said. "We cleared the area, and it was dying down fast when we left. But I reckon it's gonna take overnight to fully go out."

Mama sat down with a thump, a fresh cup of hot tea in her hands. "My word," she said. "I just, I just can't believe this. Who would do this?"

"No idea, Mama," Caleb said.

"And to you!" Mama said as she turned to Faith. "Such a sweet girl. There's no way you deserve this. What kinda enemies you made, baby?"

Faith pinched her brows together. "I don't know," she said quietly. "There were these guys. Some kind of hillbillies—"

Mama snorted. "Honey, you're Gonna have to be more specific than that. You're in the South."

Faith blushed. "They said they were my cousins," she said.

"Cousins?" Mama asked. "Caleb, Alex, you know 'bout this?"

"We were there," Alex said.

"When?"

"Couple of weeks ago. At the ferry dock on the mainland."

"You know 'em?" Mama asked.

"Nah," Alex said. "Never seen 'em before. But they were local. Real *local* locals."

"An' what they want?" Mama asked.

"Don't know for certain," Caleb broke in. "To scare her. Maybe let her know they thought Lydia's place shoulda gone to them."

Mama frowned. "Lydia didn't have no closer living relatives," she said. "Sorry, baby," she told Faith.

"You sure 'bout that, Mama?" Alex asked. "They seemed real certain."

"And mad as a cat in a bag," Caleb added.

"Well, I'm not positive, no," Mama sniffed. "I don't know everyone's business. But then again, this island is pretty good at keepin' its secrets, and if they thought the property shoulda gone to them..."

"Exactly," Caleb said.

"And, Faith? You didn't know anything about them?"

Faith shook her head. "No, but that doesn't mean much. I didn't even know about Hannah until a couple of days ago. And, turns out, we used to play together at Lydia's as babies."

"Huh," Mama said. "Like I said, this island is real good at keepin' secrets, then lettin' 'em slip out at the worst of times. Well, the important thing is you two are safe. And the fire's under control."

"Yeah, and I'm gonna feel this in the mornin'," Caleb said. "Spent an hour puttin' out those flames."

"You still shoulda figured out a way to call us. Or the fire department," Alex said. He wasn't so much worried about the property and island as he was the two of them.

"I did the best I could, big brother," Caleb said. "Trust me, when that adrenaline's goin', you're kinda on autopilot."

"He did good," Faith said. Caleb gave her a smile that drove a stake through Alex's chest.

"Yeah, I'm sure he did," Alex said.

"Look, y'all, what's done is done," Mama said. "Fire crew said they couldn't have done nothin' different, right?"

"Right, Mama," Caleb said.

"Well, then. Let's just put it outta our heads till tomorrow."

"I wanna go back," Faith said. "First thing in the morning."

"I'm sure Alex can take you." For the first time, Mama volunteered him, and he didn't mind.

"Sure," he said. "I wanna get a look at it myself anyway."

"Y'all knock yourselves out," Caleb said. "I'm gonna smell like smoke for a week."

"What time did the fire crew say they were coming?" Faith asked Alex. She examined some of the charred siding, a deep frown carved into her face.

"They didn't," Alex said. "When they can, I s'pose." The radio he'd slid into his jeans crackled, and they both paused. But nothing came through.

"This is bad," Faith said. "Isn't it?"

He didn't know what to say. *It is bad, that's for sure.* He'd thought maybe it was the shock yesterday that made it look so burned up to her. How she and Caleb described it, the property sounded like it had exploded. He had hoped that it wasn't as bad as they said. But it was. He wasn't positive, but it looked like the house might not be salvageable.

"It's not that bad," he told her. She smiled at him. They both knew it was a lie.

She let out a gust of breath. "At least Caleb was right," she said. "It burned itself out in the night. And a good chunk of the house with it."

Alex crossed his arms and took in the house. *A smoking ruin, that is what it looks like. Then again, it was no great beauty to begin with,* he thought.

Faith let out a whimper as she touched one of the window frames and it crumbled in her hand. Seeing her like this, so frustrated and hurt, and him not being able to do anything was hard. What was even harder is that the fire was no accident.

"Bastards," he said softly.

245

"What?"

He shook his head. "It's the dry season. They coulda easily made it look like an accident. Or at least tried."

"Yeah, well, those aren't exactly meant to be subtle." She nodded toward the series of charred crosses staked in the front yard. They were even bigger than the one put on Mama's property. "God, it got some of the trees, too," she said.

Some of the oaks and magnolia trees that skirted the property were burned to nothing. Others were covered in soot and largely blackened.

"Do you, uh . . . do you want to show me? Where the . . . the thing is?" he asked.

"Might as well," she said. "Not like you can miss it."

She led Alex to the start of the old overgrown drive. "Is it that?" he asked, incredulous. "That big?"

"Yep," she said. "It was quite impressive when it was all lit up." She pointed to the outline of the message burned into the ground. Without the fire, it was a little tougher to read. However, the black message that bore into the otherwise green landscape looked fierce and deadly. "Ur Next."

He shook his head. "I thought I saw it when we were landing," he admitted. "But, Jesus, it was so big, I thought I was imagining things."

Faith furrowed her brow and approached one of the crosses next to the X. With her beside it, the full seven feet of the cross looked even more imposing.

"Hey," he said. "Don't . . . don't take this so personally."

"Don't take it personal?" She whipped around to face him. "How else am I supposed to take it? I mean, God, they came all the way out here? And for what?"

"It's not your fault," Alex said gently. He approached her and wanted to put a reassuring arm around her. But all he could manage was to close the distance.

Faith shivered, even in the Georgia heat. "No? Whose, then?"

"Whoever set this place on fire!"

Faith made a face. "We should go," she said. "I don't want it getting dark on us."

He thought about telling her it was far from dusk but stopped himself. Still, he couldn't figure out why she seemed to be taking this so much to heart. Sure, she'd gotten excited about the idea of renovating the property, but that was easy when you just got a windfall of money. *Since when does she actually care about the land?* Not that he could blame her. Hell, she hadn't even known her roots were here.

For the first time, Alex opened the passenger door of the plane for her. She paused briefly before she crawled in. It took him two attempts to slam the door shut.

On the now familiar flight back, he racked his brain for something—anything—to talk about. To take her mind off the property and the threat. Alex came up short, instead grateful for the rumble of the engine.

As soon as they landed, Faith hopped out of the plane and started to walk back to Greystone. "Shit," Alex said under his breath as he rushed through his postlanding checks. He caught up to her when she was halfway there.

"I'm going to find out who did this," she said coldly. Faith stared at the ground. "And they're going to pay. Starting with my *cousins*."

"Hey, slow down," Alex said. "Why do you think they'd do something like that? Sounded to me like they wanted the house."

Faith sighed in exasperation. "I don't know! But do you have any better ideas of who was behind it? Maybe . . . maybe it's not the house they want."

"What do you mean?" Alex stopped her where the trail turned to asphalt. He was aware of his hand on her waist but didn't want to move it. She gazed toward the inn, but Mama wasn't in her familiar spot on the porch.

"Maybe there's something about the land, or the water around there, or, God, I don't know."

He had a feeling there were things she wasn't telling him, but it wasn't the time to dig. "You have to be careful," he said.

"Why?" She looked up at him with defiance. "Those guys think they can scare me; they're wrong."

"Faith." He cupped her face in his hand. It brought her stillness, but her eyes filled with questions. He wanted to comfort her but didn't know how. "Whoever they are, they've shown they can and will come after you."

Faith looked at him with a strange cocktail of longing and confusion. Finally, she pulled away from him with a step back. "I'll be fine. I can look after myself."

"Faith . . ."

She looked at him with a jolt of anger but shook her head and looked back at the inn. "I need to go inside."

As she stormed away from him, he felt a surge of protective-
ness move through him. *What the hell is wrong with her? Or
me?* Finally, though he hated himself for it, he followed her
into the house.

Like a goddamned puppy, he thought.

26

FAITH

"Thank you anyway, ma'am," Faith said into the phone. "Oh my God," she groaned as she set it down. She rested her head on the kitchen table.

"Anything?" Alex asked. He pushed a fresh mug of coffee toward her.

She shook her head. He'd been sticking close to the property —and to her—ever since the fire. *It is nice*, she had to admit. Ever since she and Caleb had walked into the house reeking of smoke, covered in ashes, something had shifted in Alex.

Faith took a long sip of the coffee and scrunched her nose at him.

"Too strong?" he asked.

"That's an understatement."

"Sorry. So what'd the geologist say?"

"Ugh, the same thing as the last one," she said. "She said the arsonists aren't after oil or precious metals or anything like that." She cringed inwardly at the word "arsonists," but that's what they were. A part of her had hoped the land was oil rich, full of hidden diamonds, or something. That would make sense. *And make it not about me.*

Alex nodded thoughtfully.

"You really should let me go talk to those guys. My, uh, cousins," she said. "They couldn't be too hard to find."

"No. No way," Alex said firmly.

Faith made a face at him. "I know you know how to find them," she said.

"It's not like I have their address hidden in my diary."

"You know what I mean. You could find them. I,. well, I can't." Faith sighed. "If it's not oil or mineral, maybe it's access."

"Access?" Alex asked. "What do you mean?"

"Didn't you say there's a natural cove that pirates used on the island?"

"Yeah, sure," Alex said. "Smuggler's Cove. But what could they possibly be bringing to the United States?" he asked. "Drugs? They don't exactly strike me as international drug lords. Maybe cooking up some meth in their trailer, sure. But they don't seem like the million-dollar cocaine type of operation."

"Drugs, yeah," Faith said. "Or, you know, people."

"*People?*" Alex asked. He put down his mug. "What are you talking about?"

"I'm just saying!" Faith said. She regretted mentioning it. The whole thing did sound kind of insane out loud. However, all those news articles she'd read had wormed into her brain. "Whatever they're after, it was worth burning down a house for. That's serious arson. Not to mention the threats."

"Faith," Alex said. "We don't even know that they're smuggling anything at all. A lot of those stories, they're just that. I mean, Smuggler's Cove? A nickname like that just begs for urban legends."

"But it was real, right? The pirates, back in the day?"

"I think so, but that was a long time ago. And I highly doubt it was all *Pirates of the Caribbean*-like anyway."

"We should do a stakeout," Faith said suddenly.

Alex widened his eyes. "A stakeout," he repeated.

"Yes! We can hide out on the island near Smuggler's Cove. That's got to be where they come in."

"No." Alex was firm. "No way. This is crazy, Faith!" he said. "I don't know what these guys want, but I'm not about to let you go all Nancy Drew on them."

"What's with all the fictional references today?" she asked. "And besides, it's this or I go talk to my cousins. Your call."

Alex sighed, aggravated. "No," he said. "You're not going to talk to them. And I know how stubborn you can be. You'll figure out a way to track them down with or without me."

"So a stakeout it is," Faith said with a smile.

"Fine. You're absolutely insane, though."

"I'm thinking that we probably need to start with three days."

She grabbed a notebook buried in the stack of design magazines and started writing down plans.

"What?" Alex leaned over to see what she'd scribbled down.

"On the island, camping," she said. "You camp, don't you? I'm sure you do. Probably got great camping gear out in storage. Could you—"

"Are you crazy?" Alex interrupted her. "There's no way. No way in hell I, or you, are gonna—"

"My cousins are starting to look pretty approachable, aren't they? Almost friendly." She put down the pen and stared into his eyes. It was a showdown across the table, complete with steaming coffee and two abandoned waffles from breakfast.

"No," Alex said begrudgingly.

"It's your choice," Faith said with a shrug. "I'll pack the food. You just bring yourself, whatever camping gear you think we need, and the boat."

"Oh, is that all?" Alex asked.

"That's all," Faith said. "Get your stuff together. I want to leave before dusk."

Alex stared at her another beat then stood up and stomped out of the house.

Faith smiled after him.

"Alex!" Mama hollered. "Don't slam the door. What y'all plannin'?" Mama asked Faith as she breezed into the kitchen. Her hair had been recently rinsed with a toner, and it made the platinum hair shine silver.

"Oh nothing much, Mama," Faith said. "We're thinking of

camping out a few days. You know, get away from it all. Put this whole mess behind me for a bit."

"That sounds like a mighty good idea," Mama said. She sat down in Alex's seat and tsked at the empty mug he'd left behind. "No point in dwellin' on it. Still nothin' from the fire department? Police?"

Faith sighed. "Nope. All they can say for sure is what kind of starter was used for the fire. Other than that, no leads. So many boats dock there, either kids sneaking away to drink or fishermen docking for a minute, there's no way to trace them."

"What a shame, what our tax dollars go for," Mama said. "So. Is it just you and Alex camping?" There was a twinkle in her eye.

"Um, yeah. I think so." Faith blushed.

"Hmm," Mama said. "He tell you he was a Boy Scout? Eagle Scout, actually."

"No!" Faith said. She couldn't imagine Alex dutifully taking orders from a scoutmaster in a little brown uniform emblazoned with patches. "But I guess that's good for me. The only time I've gone camping, it was no less than fifty feet away from full restroom facilities."

Mama wrinkled her nose. "Restroom facilities or not, camping's just not for me. Why would I want to sleep on the hard, cold ground when I have a perfectly good feather bed in my own house?"

"You never want to just get away?"

"Baby, when you live your whole life on an island, how much farther away can you get?"

"Well, I better go start packing. We're thinking three days," she said.

Mama whistled. "That's a mighty long time. That long in solitude, just the two of you, well that can change things."

"What do you mean?"

"Wait three days," Mama said. "Then you won't have to ask me."

Faith shook her head and pondered what Mama hinted at as she climbed the stairs.

"Morning, ma'am," Lee said. They met on the landing midway. "Where you off to?"

"Hi, Lee. Actually, I'm going camping for a couple of days."

"Camping? While all this is goin' on?" he asked. "I thought you and that phone had become permanently stuck together."

She laughed. "Yeah, well, I could use a break."

"Alone?" he asked. "I dunno if that's such a good idea—"

"Oh no. Alex is taking me," she said.

"Really."

She couldn't gauge the tone of his voice. It sounded a little knowing but a little cautious.

"Yeah," she said. "Is that weird? Mama said he camped a lot."

"Well, that's true," he said. She thought he would ask to join, but Lee kept quiet.

"Got any tips?" she asked.

"Tips?"

"You know. For camping. Or dealing with Alex camping," she added with a smile.

Lee grinned. "Don't poke the bear."

"What?"

"That's just good advice all round," he said.

"Thanks?" she said questioningly as Lee turned away and continued downstairs.

"He and I were Boy Scouts together," Lee called over his shoulder. "Y'all will be just fine."

Faith shoved three days' worth of clothes in the backpack she'd bought for her last trip to Europe to use as her carry-on. She'd thought it would save her some trouble, only having one wheeled suitcase to drag through the airports, but she never ended up using it. *Might as well make use of it somehow.*

But what to pack for a three-day stakeout? She dug through the dresser and pulled out a pair of denim shorts, khaki shorts, two tank tops and a zip-up Nike hoodie. Three pairs of underwear, three pairs of socks. *What else?*

She had no idea what Alex would bring for camping equipment. Tents? Or just sleeping bags under the stars? Was she supposed to pack something separate to sleep in? *Maybe I should have thought more about this.* However, she wasn't about to back out now.

Faith shoved a pair of yoga shorts and a long tank top into the backpack just in case. She'd spend most of the days in her hiking boots but slid some flip-flops into the side pocket of the backpack as well. *Baby wipes*, she thought. And a swimsuit for a makeshift bath in the water. There was a freshwater creek on the island, but it wasn't very deep.

By the time she'd finished thinking about three full days away, the backpack bulged. Her packs of vitamins, a hairbrush and ties, dry shampoo, plenty of sunblock, and travel-size bottles of her face-care regimen. *God, I really am a city girl*, she thought.

She ran her hands up her legs and felt a smattering of stubble from not having shaved in two days. *Might as well. This will be my last chance for a proper shower for a while.*

Underneath the warm fall of water, Faith closed her eyes and let her head fall back. She tried to pretend the careful shaving of her legs, thighs, and bikini area were so she'd feel as fresh and clean as possible for three days on the island. But she knew that wasn't it. If something happened between her and Alex, she wanted to be as prepared as possible.

Faith blushed while she thought about it and ran conditioner through her hair. *Will he think this is all a ploy to get him alone?*

She wrapped herself in one of the big white towels that smelled of bleach and stepped out of the steamy bathroom. Alex lingered in the doorway to her bedroom, his broad shoulder against her doorframe.

"Oh my God!" she screamed. "Alex? What are you—"

"Your door was open," he said. "I thought you were in a hurry to get goin'."

"I am," she said awkwardly and pulled the towel tighter around her chest. "I just figured I would have the chance to shower first."

Alex scanned her, and his eyes lingered at her legs. She

cleared her throat, uncomfortable, and it seemed to bring him out of his stupor.

"You packin' for a month or three days?" he asked, and nodded to the pregnant backpack.

"I need clothes, don't I?" she asked.

"I dunno. It's three days," he said with a shrug. "What else you got in there?"

"Not that it's any of your business, but some vitamins, my hairbrush. You know, women stuff."

"Women stuff," he repeated. His eyes never left her.

"Now, if you don't mind?" she asked with raised brows.

"What?"

"I'd like to get dressed. I'll meet you down in the kitchen. I still need to pack the food."

"Oh. All right," he said.

He closed the door slowly. Faith waited until she heard the click and the sound of his footsteps on the stairs before she removed the towel. *What is his deal?*

She caught a glimpse of herself in the vanity mirror and paused. The hourglass figure she was so used to had bronzed during the summer. And were her hips wider? She couldn't tell, but her nipped-in waist looked the same. *It's Mama's cooking*, she told herself.

Faith pretended it was a coincidence that the underwear and bra she pulled on matched. Both were bright red with a lace trim. *Yeah, this is exactly what everyone wears on a stakeout*, she thought.

She ran a wide-toothed comb through her hair and wove it into a loose braid. After she slathered sunblock onto her limbs, she hoisted the backpack on and headed downstairs.

"It's a Sherpa!" Caleb said when he spotted her from the wingback chair in the sitting room.

"Ha ha," she said and dropped the backpack onto the bench by the front door.

Alex had already rooted through the kitchen and pulled out his camping snacks. Boxes and boxes of strange-looking items with "High Protein" and "No Sugar" printed on the sides. "I take it I'm packing those?" she asked.

"You guessed right," he said. She swore he gave her a wink, but it was so surprising she couldn't be sure. He sat at the table and watched her carefully assemble two coolers of food.

"Looks like you're catering the fanciest camping trip ever," he said.

"Y'all going camping? That's what Mama said." Caleb poked his head into the kitchen.

"Yeah," Alex said quickly. "Faith just wants to zone out everything for a bit."

"Wish I could go," Caleb said. "But duty calls. And by duty, I mean a group of Canadian tourists who booked a two-day rafting trip."

"Too bad," Alex said. Even with her back to the boys, Faith could hear the relief in his voice. *Too bad because Caleb annoys him or because he wants to be alone with me?*

"Too bad, nothin'," Caleb said. "I checked the ages of 'em.

Three girls, ages nineteen, twenty-two, and twenty-four are comin'."

"Lucky them," Alex said. "And stuck on a raft with you for two days, where their only escape option is whitewater rapids and certain death."

27

ALEX

*H*e put down his own framed backpack and looked around the island. Faith had given him shit, rightfully so, at the size of his own pack. "One of us had to bring all the camping gear, ma'am," he'd said. She'd clamped shut those thick lips.

It had been years since he'd docked at Smuggler's Cove instead of the updated and better maintained dock near Lydia's old plantation. He could see evidence that Smuggler's Cove was far from abandoned. Old beer cans were stuck against the bank along with plastic chip bags and cigarette butts. A bottle of Olde English and a travel pack of Jack Daniels were full of seawater and tossed onto the grass.

"Ew," Faith said as she jumped onto the grassy knoll.

"Yeah," Alex said. He shook his head in disappointment. *What is wrong with people coming all the way out here just to trash the place? They are probably mostly kids, but still. Mama woulda whooped him and Caleb straight had they ever done that.*

"Help me hide this," he said.

Faith dropped her backpack next to a towering oak tree and helped him push the boat around the bend to a smaller cove. This one really was abandoned. It was tiny and treacherously slippery. When he was a teenager, he'd tried stupidly to dock here but gave up after he fell in for the third time.

"Gross," Faith said as she slipped in the mud and dropped to one knee.

"Good thing you're not wearing them fancy big-city clothes," he said. She wrinkled her nose at him.

"C'mon," Alex said. "It's a bit of a hike to the lookout."

"The lookout?" she asked. "Now who's into Nancy Drew?"

"That's actually what it's called," Alex said. He raised a brow at her. "Only one spot on this island where you can get a clear view of any vessels comin' in."

"Oh, I like the pirate talk," she said.

Alex didn't have time for her teasing. He hitched up his pack and took off. Faith's footsteps trailed right behind him. "Can you slow down?" she asked. "Some of us don't run five miles a day."

"Not if you wanna get there before dark," he said over his shoulder. She'd twisted the damp braid on top of her head and her face was flushed from the heat and the hike. New freckles sprayed across her nose, much more than what she'd arrived with. She was more muscular, too. *Healthier*, Alex thought. He tried not to notice the swell of her thighs or the way her collarbone glistened.

"Is this it?" Faith asked. She was slightly out of breath.

"This is it," Alex said. From the water, it didn't look like the island had much elevation to it, but that was deceptive. At the eastern tip, there was a small cliff absolutely covered in giant oaks. Moss and clover covered much of the ground, but tall, wild grass framed the edge of the cliff. It was like it was made to be a rendezvous point.

"This is awesome," Faith said. It was one of those evenings when the moon and sun were equal in the sky, though the moon looked humongous. "Blue moon," Faith said.

"I'm surprised you knew that," Alex said as he started to pull the tent out of his bag.

"We have the same moon in California, you know."

"Nah," he said as he slid the poles into their sleeves. "It's not the same."

"Maybe you're right. Can I help?" she asked.

"Probably not." He gave her a smile to let her know he was joking. "How 'bout you start unpacking for dinner?"

He listened to the rustle as she went through the cooler. "Just one tent?" she asked.

"Sorry it's not more," he said as he hammered the stakes into the ground. "Boss gave me kinda short notice."

"Sorry," she said. "I know, I'm impulsive."

"Got two sleeping bags, though," he said. He felt her eyes on him as he strung up the overhead tarps.

"Your mama told me you were a Boy Scout," she said. "Now I can see it."

Alex laughed. "Doesn't take a Boy Scout to throw up a pop-up tent," he said. Alex detached the camping chairs from the side of his backpack and unfolded them. He took extra time dusting them off, a lot more than he would have bothered if it had just been him and one of the guys.

He heard the sound of wood being dumped behind him and whipped around. "No fire," he said.

"But—"

"The fire, the smoke, anyone could see it."

"You're right," she sighed. "Dang. And I brought stuff for s'mores, too."

"They taste just as good cold," he said.

"You're wrong about that." Faith started to assemble a cold dinner while Alex got to hitching the food over a strong limb. "What, are there bears on the island now?" she asked.

"Who knows what's on this island." At that, she got quiet. He could have kicked himself. *As if they both weren't on edge enough.*

"I'm guessing your cardboard square things will be okay in the cooler," she said.

"Yeah. Probably."

"God, I'm exhausted," she said as she finished arranging a dinner of smoked salmon, prepacked salads, and fruit from the local farms. "I think the past few days are just now catching up to me."

"Don't be chickening out on me now," Alex said.

"I'm not," Faith replied quickly. "It's just when everything happens so fast, it's kind of hard to digest."

"Yeah, I get that," he said. He pulled at the strung-up food to make sure it would hold, then sat down in the chair beside her and reached for his plate of salmon.

"Cheers," Faith said. She held up a plastic Nalgene bottle of sweet tea. "I have some gin to go with it if you want."

"Best stay clearheaded," Alex said, though he had to admit, a cocktail sounded good. However, it wasn't just needing to stay sharp that kept him dry. Out here, alone with Faith, the last thing he needed was lowered inhibitions.

She sighed as she dug into her plate. He could watch her eat forever, those incredible lips and the high cheekbones. "What?" she asked suddenly. Alex realized he actually had been staring at her.

"Nothin'," he said. "I think I'm just a bit out of it, too."

They ate in comfortable silence. The chorus of crickets got louder each minute. "Hey," Faith said. "Is that them?" She pointed to a boat in the distance.

Alex sat up straighter. "Nah," he said. "That's the Stewart twins from the other end of the island. Night fishin'."

"Oh." She sounded disappointed.

Alex crumpled up what was left of their dinner, sorted it for recycling, and strung it up the tree.

"Now what?" she asked as he sat beside her.

"Now we wait. What else you think we were Gonna do out here?"

"I don't know. Stakeouts sounded a lot more exciting than this."

The two of them stared into the distance. He realized he was in a prime position for another barrage of questions about Rebecca, but Faith didn't seem interested in it. For once, she acted like the silence was all right. She slipped out of her hiking shoes and into flip-flops. Those long legs stretched out forever, propped up on a root that had shot out of the ground.

Alex sipped his sweet tea and watched the water. The moon grew higher and smaller. "What time is it?" Faith asked. Her voice, sudden in the night, was like thunder.

He glanced at his watch. "Nearly midnight."

"They're not coming," she said.

"Doesn't seem like it. Not tonight."

"I'm tired. Are you tired?" she asked.

"I could sleep. Ready for bed?"

"I guess so."

Alex crawled into the tent while she "did her face regimen."

"Alex?" she called.

"Yeah?" He'd just gotten into Caleb's old sleeping bag.

"You in there for the night?"

"Yeah, why?"

"I'm going to change into my pajamas out here."

"Pajamas? Just sleep in what you got on."

"No! I packed them, and I want to be comfortable."

"Are you serious? Actually, go for it," he said. "And bring the clothes you got on in here for a pillow."

"You didn't bring pillows?"

"This isn't glamping."

She laughed. "I can't believe you know what glamping is."

When she finally crawled into the tent, he turned on the solar-powered flashlight so she could find her way. "What are you wearin'?"

"Hot yoga shorts," she said.

"Looks like underwear."

"Underwear? What kind of women's underwear have you seen that are this big?"

"I dunno."

"You need to get out more."

"I don't need to be goin' to no yoga places if that's how y'all dress." He watched her slide into his old sleeping bag and fuss at her bundle of clothes for a makeshift pillow.

"This isn't so bad," she said. "But I wish I'd known. I wouldn't have packed clothes with so many buttons and zippers."

"Sleep always comes easy in a tent," he assured her.

He wished it were true for him. It was awkward sleeping next to another person. The same as the night they'd spent together. She rolled away from him and fell asleep almost instantly. Her hair had uncoiled and fanned out wildly, and Alex watched the even rise and fall of her body with every deep breath.

The moonlight shone with ferocity through the thin summer camping tent and lit it up like an intimate bar. He'd forgotten that small birthmark on her left shoulder. The night they'd been together, he'd lingered over it with the tip of his tongue.

Shit. Just thinking of that night got him hard. *She's right there. And already asleep.* Apparently, Faith didn't share his discomfort.

Alex closed his eyes and willed himself to be still. *Get some sleep. I need some sleep if I'm gonna be out here three days.*

He counted breaths, just as one of those therapists had taught him to do. Even count in, even count out. He was hyperaware of his stiffness. *Would it be so bad just to brush myself? There is a good foot of distance between them. No, stop it.*

*A*t some point, he must have fallen asleep. The tent was roasting hot. When he opened his eyes, it was still dark out, but Faith was curled up against him. She'd pulled herself out of the sleeping bag and was spooned next to him, one leg thrown across him. Even through the thickness of his own sleeping bag, he could feel her heat as it burned into him.

In the night, his own sleeping bag had become partially unzipped. *How the hell did it get so hot in here?* He felt a flicker on his stomach and glanced down. His T-shirt was halfway up his torso, and Faith's hand rested on his stomach. He was hard again, or still hard from earlier, he couldn't tell. Her fingers were just inches away.

He looked at her closed eyes with those thick lashes that fluttered in sleep. A small smile played at the corner of her lips. Whatever she was dreaming about, she seemed miles away. *Would it be so bad to just kiss her? Wake her up with my lips on hers?*

Alex wanted so badly to just take her right there. Rip those little shorts off and bury himself deep inside her. And he knew she'd be wet fast, just like the first time. He craved those little moans she gave when he fingered her, how her breath caught when he licked her clit.

Faith stirred and murmured something in her sleep. Her hand went an inch lower and hovered at the top of his shorts.

Shit. Carefully, he took her hand and moved it away. She tucked it under her head and sighed in her sleep.

Alex unzipped more of his sleeping bag as quietly as he could. It took him a good three minutes to get out of the tent. He had to unzip the opening one inch at a time, otherwise it would squeal and she'd surely wake up.

He crawled outside and slid on his shoes. As he zipped Faith back up in the tent, he saw that she'd rolled onto her back. Her tank top was so loose, it had fallen to the side. One of her breasts threatened to spill out completely. He could see the outline of one of her nipples, which made the hardness in his shorts almost unbearable.

Alex stood up, grabbed the flashlight, and sat in the chair. The moon had lowered again in the sky. *Why the hell am I even resisting anymore?* He dug through the cooler for one of his protein bars, anything to distract himself.

It's not like she's not into me. Most guys would kill for a girl like that for the summer.

But that was the kicker. It was just for the summer. *Why feel so deeply for someone who's just going to leave?* And this time, it was for certain. Anything he and Faith might have came with an expiration date. That was something he just couldn't handle.

28

FAITH

When she'd woken up, Alex's sleeping bag was rumpled, and he wasn't in the tent . Outside, she found him with the thermos of cold brew and mussed up hair. "Couldn't sleep?" she asked.

"I slept enough," he replied, though his face betrayed him. He looked exhausted.

For most of the day, Faith perched herself on a smooth rock to soak up the sun. She hitched up her shorts and rolled up the sleeves of her T-shirt in hopes of an even tan. Although she'd wanted to catnap, sure nobody would be brazen enough to sail onto the island in broad daylight, she couldn't sleep.

Faith spent the day with her eyes on Alex. Mostly, he stuck close to their camp immersed in busywork. "What are you doing?" she'd ask occasionally. He was full of endless excuses about why particular small jobs needed attention. She wanted to ask him to relax but knew that would be pointless.

It wasn't one-sided. Numerous times she caught his eyes on

her. By the afternoon, she was restless. The way he looked at her, with no sunglasses to hide his expression, it was clear he wanted her. She relished the attention, the hungry glances.

Is it wrong to want to push him, see if he will break? Faith let out an audible sigh to get his attention. She sat up and pulled off the T-shirt to reveal the triangle bikini top beneath. As she rolled down the waistband of her shorts to create makeshift denim briefs, she was aware of her every movement.

Her arched back and pushed-out chest caught his attention. She flipped onto her stomach, sprawled across the single towel he'd packed, and poked her ass into the air. "You just Gonna lay around all day?" Alex asked.

Faith pushed herself onto her forearms. Her breasts were dangerously close to spilling out. "You have a better idea?"

"If you wanna get in some kind of shower before dark, might wanna get to it."

She pushed herself up and stretched overhead. "The creek?"

"You got a better idea, ma'am?" he asked.

"I'm ready," she said.

She followed him down the small hill to the cool creek that snaked through the island. At the bank, Alex pulled off his shirt and tossed it aside. He pushed down his cargo shorts to reveal black boxer briefs. Faith sucked in her breath as he hitched up the boxer briefs. *Is he going to leave them on?* She felt a rush of disappointment run through her when he waded into the crystal-clear water with the boxer briefs still on. "Comin'?" he asked over his shoulder.

She toyed with the idea of making use of the potential double entendre, but thought better of it. Instead, she pulled off her own shorts and followed him into the water in just her bikini.

"God, it's freezing!" she said as Alex shot up from his dip under the water.

He laughed. "It's not so bad," he said.

She crossed her arms over her chest and felt her nipples as they poked through the material. His eyes went to her breasts, and she dropped her arms.

After she'd tied her hair on top of her head, she held her breath and forced herself into the water to her shoulders. Alex started to swim lazy laps back and forth from one bank to the other. "You don't swim?" he asked her on his return.

"Not in water this cold," she said. She shivered below the calm surface.

"Swimmin'll warm you up," he told her.

"I'm good."

She covertly ran her hands beneath her breasts and between her legs whenever he turned his back to her, an attempt to get as clean as possible.

"I'm getting out," she said.

"All right. Gonna be dark soon, anyway." She heard him splash out behind her, and could feel his eyes on her ass.

Faith did her best to towel off, but kicked herself for bringing no clean clothes. She pulled on the little shorts while Alex stepped into jeans and a new T-shirt.

"Cold?" he asked, his eyes firm on her erect nipples.

"Kind of," she muttered.

"Can I interest you in a fleece, ma'am?" he asked. He pulled a navy-blue fleece zip-up out of his backpack.

"Don't you . . . don't you want it?" she asked.

"I'm not cold," he said with a shrug. "'Sides, I brought it down here for you."

She smiled and took the warm, soft material from him. Once she'd pulled it on and zipped it up, the sleeves hung nearly to her knees, and the hem brushed the top of her thighs. Faith felt like it was a game of dress up. She glanced down and saw nothing but her long legs and the tips of her fingers. "I look like I'm naked," she said.

She saw Alex stand straighter at the remark. Slowly, she raised her eyes to meet his. His breath had quickened. There was a desire in his eyes stronger than anything she'd seen before. He was *this close* to snapping, she knew it. "Let's go," he finally said and started up the trail back to camp.

Frustrated, she stomped after him. The sun had nearly set when they arrived at the tent. "What do you want for dinner?" she asked him as she started to look through the cooler. "Your choices are basically ham or chicken breast sandwiches." Once again, she felt his eyes on her and leaned over farther while she straightened her back. From this angle, he'd just barely get a glimpse at where her thighs kissed slightly at the top. It would really look like she had nothing on below his fleece.

"Not hungry," he said finally. "Actually, I'm goin' to bed early."

"You're going to bed *now*?" she asked in disbelief. Faith turned around to face him, one of each sandwich in her hands.

"Some of us only got a couple hours of sleep," he said pointedly, though he hesitated at the tent and looked at her. *Is she supposed to join me?*

She watched, incredulous, as he unzipped the tent. "You just put on fresh jeans to go to bed?" she asked. "How is that comfortable? Who sleeps in jeans?"

"No," he said slowly. "I put on jeans so the nettles and blackberry shrubs wouldn't scratch me up on the walk."

Faith looked down at her own unmarred legs. When she glanced back up, Alex had pulled off the jeans and set them aside. The boxer briefs clung tight to his toned legs.

Once he'd zipped himself into the tent, she looked around their little campsite with a sigh. Faith shoved the sandwiches back into the cooler and dutifully strung it back up the tree. "Goddamn it," she said as she struggled with Alex's complicated knot system.

By the time she'd figured it out, it was nearly dark. *What, are we not even going to keep a lookout tonight?*

In the tent, she could make out a tiny light. Alex's phone. He'd let it charge all day with a solar-powered charge kit, though they were far from reception. *What the hell is he doing?*

Faith shivered and walked to the tent. She unzipped it just as he put down the phone. "What are you doing?"

"Setting the alarm for a few hours." She could barely make out his shape in the sleeping bag.

"A few hours?"

"We're on a stakeout, aren't we? Figured you were taking the first shift."

She mewled in frustration. Faith could tell he watched her but couldn't make out anything distinct in the dark tent. *It is now or never*, she thought. *Enough of this cat and mouse game.*

Faith stood up, aware that the circular opening of the tent would frame her perfectly. Slowly, she reached under the hem of the fleece and unbuttoned her shorts. Straight backed with locks of hair that reached toward the ground, she pulled the shorts down and tossed them aside.

She stepped out of her flip-flops and crawled into the tent. "I'm cold," she said, with the most pitiful voice she could manage. She unzipped his fleece and pushed it to the edge of the tent. Immediately, her nipples responded again to the cold. The tiny bikini was still slightly damp from the creek. Faith bit her lip. "Can I share your sleeping bag?"

Her eyes adjusted to the darkness, and the moonlight streamed through the tent opening. Alex had watched her over his shoulder, and now he rolled to face her. She delighted in his eyes as they traveled across her body.

Just as she thought he'd offer up a snarky remark, he bolted out of his sleeping bag and was on top of her. Faith sucked in her breath as she felt his mouth on her neck. He sucked with ferocity, the heat of his bare chest on hers. As she started to pant, his mouth found hers, and his tongue delved deep.

She felt his hardness pressed into her center, just thin material between them. Faith spread her legs wide, her nails dug into his lower back and she pressed herself closer against him. Even through his briefs and her bikini bottom, he was partially inside her.

Faith tried to topple him, to climb on top, but he wove one hand through the hair near her scalp and firmly stopped her.

He was possessive, dominant. It made her flood through the slip of a bikini bottom.

With his other hand, Alex reached down. With a single pull, he untied one side of her string bikini. He bit her lower lip lightly as he dipped a finger into her. "You're so fucking wet," he whispered.

Quickly, he pulled down his boxer briefs and buried himself deep inside her. She cried out and whipped her head to the side. But he didn't move. Faith wiggled and squirmed, desperate for him to fuck her, to feel his length slide firm against her G-spot.

"Stop it," he said. His voice was domineering, but she heard the playfulness deep inside.

He tightened his grip on her hair and kissed her softly. His hand traveled to her breasts. A thumb ran across her rock-hard nipples. Alex released them from the triangle of spandex, the material bunched at her rib cage. He kissed his way along her jaw, down to the hollow of her throat and finally—with pleasure so intense it bordered on pain—he flicked a tongue across her nipple.

Faith felt a new surge of wetness, a trickle of juices that made its way down her legs. Alex took a nipple between his lips and sucked. She let out a cry, and finally he started to fuck her.

With every thrust, she felt herself get wetter. Alex released her hair and brought his mouth back to hers.

When she started to get close, he gripped her waist and rolled onto his back to pull her on top of him. Faith straddled him in the little tent that now felt hot as a sauna. The bikini bottoms were still loosely tied to one of her thighs, and her breasts bounced above the pulled-down top. She braced her hands on his chest, let her head fall back, and rode him with a wildness she'd never felt before.

Alex grasped her hips and slowed her down. "Not yet," he said. "You don't get to come yet."

As she began to match the rhythm he commanded, he circled her clit with his thumb.

"Alex," she groaned.

He spanked her smartly on the ass. "Quiet," he told her. "We're on a stakeout, remember?"

She leaned over him and pressed down on his hand that worked her clit expertly. Every time she bore down on his cock, she delighted in the pressure against her G-spot. Faith teased him, her nipples inches from his mouth. When he licked at them, pulled a nipple into his mouth as she rode him, she felt the first waves of an orgasm start.

"I'm going to come," she whispered. "You're making me come."

"Yes," he said lowly. With his permission, the tremors began at her center. "Come for me, Faith," he urged her.

"Now," she groaned. "I'm coming now."

"I fucking love you," he said.

Her eyes shot open, and she felt him release into her at the peak of her climax. As she felt his hot juices shoot into her, it brought on a fresh wave of orgasm. He held her hips firmly with fingers that dug into the crest of her ass. As his grip loosened, she pushed against his hardness a few more times. The aftershocks of her orgasm spread through her entire body.

Finally, she dismounted and fell beside him. His eyes were closed, and his breath had just started to return to normal. Faith rolled onto her side and ran her fingers across his chest. A thin layer of sweat stuck to her palm.

Their combined juices began to leak from her and spread onto Caleb's sleeping bag. She didn't care, enjoyed knowing she carried a part of him with her.

She opened her mouth to say something, but couldn't find the right thing to say. Wordlessly, Alex shifted and welcomed her into the crook of his arm.

Faith fell into him, happy. His last words to her rang in her head.

29

ALEX

*T*he pastel morning light had started to pour into the tent. Alex opened his eyes and saw that neither of them had bothered to close the opening.

Faith let out a sigh in her sleep. As he turned toward her, he drew in a breath. She was covered in little bruises, marks of their long night together. When he reached out an arm toward her, he felt stings down his back. Her scratch marks. They must have scattered from his shoulder to the small of his back.

This, right here, is why enough is enough. That brooding possessiveness that had overpowered him last night, the dominance. It was exactly why they couldn't be.

But now? Now feelings had started to take hold of him. She was an obsession, an addiction. *Or maybe just old-fashioned infatuation*, he told himself. *No. It is more than that.* He knew better, knew himself better.

There was no escaping what he'd felt last night. Alex pressed the heels of his hands into his closed eyes until the pressure created patterns of light. *I can't believe I said that.*

He could have kicked himself for what he'd blurted out. Faith had looked surprised, shocked, but maybe she'd written it off as the heat of the moment. *Or maybe she hadn't heard him, right? No, of course she had. And it wasn't a coincidence that she didn't say it back.*

Alex had tucked that mishap away and kept his feelings to himself while they'd fucked all night and into the early morning. Now, as he felt busted and worn out, he finally had time to mull everything over. Alex turned onto his side, aware of the stings that peppered his back, and scrutinized her.

Even with the marks, his marks, all over her body, she was perfect. The kind of beautiful that hurt to look at. It wasn't the first time he'd felt something like this.

Rebecca. He'd felt this way once about Rebecca. Not that she'd been anywhere near as exquisite as Faith, but she'd been his first. Rebecca had been the first girl to ever really look twice at him. In the early days, as freshmen, she'd pursued him. It hadn't just felt good, it had been easy. He just had to sit back and let things unfold as they would.

However, as he watched Faith's deep breathing, he felt the last of his ties to Rebecca slough away. Anything like this that he'd felt for his ex-wife was a shadow of the real thing. Like the last dregs he'd clung to for way too long. *Maybe it had never really felt like this with Rebecca at all. Clearly, the early days with Rebecca really had been infatuation—and the thrill of something brand new. Who didn't get crazy over their first?*

Alex slid his hand over Faith's curves, from the softness of her shoulder to the steep inward slope of her waist. She murmured in her sleep, and her eyelashes fluttered. As he curled his hand around the curve of her ass, an incredible sense of possessiveness came over him. *But what if she doesn't feel the same way? What if she, like Rebecca, likes to spread her love around?*

Alex sighed. What would he do if Faith ended up just like Rebecca? *Worse, what if she just up and leaves one day?* It would destroy him, he knew. Faith's hand was spread palm up beside her face. He traced the lines of that softness, thinking how those small delicate hands cradled his entire heart. *And they could crush it just as easily if she wanted.*

"Hmm," Faith said as she started to stir. Slowly, her eyes opened, and she offered up a sleepy smile. "Hey," she whispered, her voice thick with sleep.

"Mornin', ma'am," he said, which made her giggle.

She tilted her head for a morning kiss, and he was happy to escape those treacherous thoughts for something that was easier. Natural. And it felt so goddamned good.

His lips consumed hers. He could taste the salt from their bodies on her tongue. When Faith slipped her hands around him, he straightened. "What's wrong?" she asked.

"You're Gonna have to give the back a break," he whispered.

She flushed. "Sorry," she said.

What does she have to be sorry for? With a little growl, he pounced on top of her and held her hands over her head. "Think I'll just have to make sure you behave, ma'am," he said into her ear. She faked a struggle, but as he worked his way down her naked body, he felt the resistance in her arms fade away.

Alex lowered her bound hands to her chest as he made his way to her navel. "You Gonna be good?" he asked.

"Yes," she said. Her breath caught in her throat as she widened her legs and pushed her wet mound against his chest.

"Turn over," he commanded as he raised himself to his knees.

"What—"

"Get on all fours." Faith did as he told her, though she looked at him uncertainly from over her shoulder as she settled into position.

It was a tight fit in the little two-person tent, but the forced closeness turned him on even more. He could see that already her juices had started to flow in anticipation.

"On your forearms," he instructed, and she lowered immediately. Her perfect round ass poked into the air, presented just for him.

Alex took one of her cheeks in each hand and spread them apart with his thumbs. His cock ached, the tip slick with precum. *How am I always ready to give her more?*

He slid a finger through her folds, always shocked at her heat and wetness. She let out a cry as he flicked across her clit, and let out a gasp of frustration as he moved across her opening without a dive into her.

Finally, he came to her ass and circled her rim lightly. Her own intense wetness was the ideal limitless lubricant.

He'd expected her to flinch, to move away or look back at him in worry. Instead, he heard her let out a moan while her head dropped onto her forearms.

Alex leaned forward to kiss and nip lightly at one of her cheeks. He kept rimming her with his finger, the pressure firm and steady. As he kissed his way closer, her panting increased to the point her whole body shook.

He worked his tongue along her rim and slipped two fingers inside her. Faith started to call out his name and pressed into him. "More," she begged while she reached between her legs and started to rub her clit.

He slid a third finger into her, incredulous at how wet she could get. Alex could tell she was getting close. He removed his fingers from her, though she let out a cry of frustration. Quickly, he reached around her to grab her wrist and force her hand from her clit. "Please," she said, though she kept her hand at bay.

Alex gave her rim one final flick of his tongue and a kiss. The hand that had been inside her dripped with her juices. He licked the excess from his forefinger, hardening even more at her flavor.

On his knees, he towered over her. Alex leaned forward and traced one wet finger along her lush lips. "Taste yourself," he demanded, and she greedily started to suck at his fingers.

The feel of her lips, her tongue, on his hand was irresistible. He stroked himself, spreading the precum up his shaft. Alex slid into her with ease. Faith moaned heavily and sucked wildly at his fingers.

He took hold of one of her shoulders to control the rhythm. His fingers slipped from her mouth, reached underneath her, and pinched a hard nipple. As he straightened up onto his knees, he grazed once again across her clit. It was swollen, incredibly large, and slick with her juices.

"Play with yourself," he told her as he grabbed her hips and started to fuck her faster. Faith reached for her clit and started to buck against him as her orgasm built. He could feel her fingertips against his length every time he slid out of her.

Alex closed his eyes and listened to the wet slap of their bodies together. Her ass slammed into his torso, and a fresh flood of wetness poured out of her. Faith started to cry out his name. Each time he pounded into her, he held her there, deep inside her, for an extra beat.

"I'm coming," she said.

He reached for her hair and wrapped it around his fist. With a smooth, hard motion, he pulled. Faith let out a yelp as her head snapped back. She rose up to her palms.

"You want to come?" he asked. He bore into her slower, deeper.

"Yes," she said, nearly out of breath. "Please, I'm so close."

"You're going to come all over my cock?" He twisted her hair even tighter and leaned back to bring her with him. Faith sat on his lap. The sweat of their bodies glued her back to his chest. He released her hair and wrapped an arm around her chest to pull at her nipples. His other hand brushed her hand from her clit. Alex lightly flicked at her swollen center.

Faith's entire body shook. She tried to ride his cock harder, faster, to press herself more firmly against the finger that teased her clit. "I want to," she said.

"You want to what?" he asked. Alex pulled at one of her nipples.

"I want to come on your cock," she whispered. Faith turned her face to the side to search for his lips.

He obliged and kissed her deeply while his length pressed against her G-spot. "Are you going to?" he asked between kisses. He slightly released his grip on her, and Faith hungrily started to ride him. She glided along his stiffness and he felt her breasts start to bounce in his hand.

"Yes," she said. "Fuck, yes."

"Say it," he said. Alex's finger pressed firmly on her clit.

"I'm going to come on your cock," she said.

He worked her clit harder and delighted in the cries she let out into his mouth, all in between their kisses. "Louder," he said.

"I'm, fuck." Faith panted. He squeezed a nipple. "I'm coming," she cried out loudly. "Alex, fuck!" she shouted. "Fuck me! I'm coming on your cock."

He felt her orgasm, unbelievably powerful, and willed himself not to let go inside her.

Not yet, he told himself. Faith mewled and shook violently. He felt her wetness pour down his thighs. Inside her, he couldn't believe how hard he was. "You didn't . . . you didn't come," she said, exasperated. Or disappointed.

"Not yet," he said and kissed her deeply. He was still inside her, and she didn't make any movements to leave.

"Why not?" she asked.

"You didn't tell me where you wanted me to," he said.

"Alex!" she said. "Come on."

"Where?" he asked. "Where do you want me to come?"

She bit her lip and searched his eyes. "I want to taste you," she said finally.

As she dismounted, he could see how shaky and weak her legs were. She turned to face him. "Oh my God," she said when she looked down at him. "It's so wet."

"That's all you," he said. She smiled up at him as he pulled her hair into a ponytail in his fist. "You wanna tell me how you taste?"

She took his tip into her mouth. "Mmm," she said.

"Well?" he asked.

"Good," she said as she released him from her lips. "But I think you'll taste sweeter."

Faith gripped his base and began to take him into her mouth. He gasped as she took him inch by inch to the back of her mouth. She released her grip and he felt his tip slide into her throat.

"Jesus," he said.

For a moment, she held him there while her tongue pressed and explored his shaft. It took all his willpower not to fuck her face, but he resisted. She looked up at him, and he twisted her hair around his fist tighter.

Slowly, Faith released him. He felt the tip of her tongue flick across his tip and glide down his length. With her in control like this, her teases and licks, she brought him immediately to the edge of orgasm.

"You're gonna make me come," he said lowly. Alex pushed a stray lock of hair away from her cheek.

"Ma'am," she said, and smiled up at him while she stroked his cock with her hand.

"Huh?"

"You're supposed to say, 'You're going to make me come, ma'am,'" she corrected. Before he could respond, she took his length back in her mouth and all the way down her throat.

"Jesus," he choked.

She reached up and pressed his hand against the back of her head—gave permission.

As he cradled her head in his hand and started to fuck her face, he glanced down and saw that she once again played with herself while she got him off.

He felt the tightening and gritted his teeth. "You're gonna make me come, ma'am," he said, though he could barely get the words out before he released himself to the back of her throat.

FAITH

aith rolled onto her back with a cry, fresh off an orgasm. She'd lost track of how many times they'd fucked and had long stopped caring about the streaks of white stains that covered Alex's and Caleb's sleeping bags.

Her body was sore, overworked and absolutely covered in Alex's marks. By now, the sun had set again. They'd spent the entire day exploring each other's bodies and trading orgasms. Most were simultaneous. She couldn't help it. Every time he came inside her, it made her come again, too.

Even with the tent's opening unzipped, the heat from the day had turned their little fuck nest into a hot pot. The night breezes hadn't started yet.

Alex reached for her, and she trembled. She was almost to the point of telling him, "My God, no more," but couldn't. Her body craved him, and it was insatiable.

But instead of going for another round, Alex simply traced her rib cage lazily. *It is the great kind of sore*, she told herself. Faith propped herself up on Alex's fleece and gazed down at her body. There was barely any part of her that wasn't covered in bite marks or bruises, and she loved it. Alex's entire torso was covered in tiny scratch marks, bruises, and her bite marks.

"I like this," she said.

"Like what?" he asked, though he didn't open his eyes. One of his forearms was splayed across his face.

"*This*," she said. "Being marked by you."

"I like it, too," he said with a grin. "Though we might have some explainin' to do when we get back, ma'am."

She giggled. "I have a feeling we'll be okay."

"How come?"

She shrugged. "I think maybe we weren't as covert as we thought."

"You mean Mama? Hell, she always knows everything."

Faith was lightheaded just looking at Alex. This amazing man, with his incredible smile that could light up an entire island. Even as she was, feeling pleasurably exhausted from hours in bed with him, she was filled with lust whenever he smiled at her. *Not just lust*, she told herself. *Gratitude.* She was grateful that he'd chosen her, that she'd been filled to the brim with him.

Still, she couldn't help but mull over what he'd said. *Does he really love me?* Of course, it had been said in the middle of sex. That could certainly make it null and void, right? She didn't know. Faith wove her fingers through his hair and felt a spark rush through her as one of his fingers grazed her thigh, dangerously close to her mound.

She wanted to ask him if he'd meant it. *Maybe he doesn't even realize he said it*, she cautioned herself. *But if he did? Did he mean it?* She looked down at him. Alex didn't seem like the type of guy who would just say things like that carelessly.

And what if he did mean it? Where does that leave me? The idea of actually being in love with him felt absurd. They'd only known each other a few weeks! But then again, what did time have to do with anything? She'd dated some men exclusively for months and never felt anything close to love. *Who says there has to be a time frame we all stick to?*

No, she told herself. *I can't possibly love Alex. Lust, sure. Maybe I'm even on the road to love—if I had the luxury of time.* Time. That was the real bitch. Soon enough, she'd have to go back to San Francisco. Taking the summer off was a big enough risk, but there was no way she could extend her vacation into autumn.

But the thought of going back to the West Coast without Alex? That hurt. That incredible physically painful kind of hurt. *Jesus. What the hell is up with me?*

Faith had no idea how to broach the subject with Alex. If she did it back at the inn, when he'd had time to strap on that "who gives a shit" attitude again, he'd just brush it off. *If I really want to talk about it with him, do it now.*

She opened her mouth, but the words didn't come. What could she say, or ask, anyway? *Come to California with me?* That was childish, selfish, and stupid. *But what if I don't even try?*

"Alex—"

"Shh," he said harshly and put a finger to his lips.

She wrinkled her brow, but then she heard it, too. There was a rustle in the distance. *Christ, get it together!* she thought. *We're here on a stakeout.* Suddenly, she was acutely aware of being completely naked in broad daylight. They could clearly see the end of the trail from their position in the open tent.

Faith wanted to search for her clothes, but they were nowhere in sight. When she even lifted herself onto her elbows, pain from their hours of sex seared her body. *I'm a fucking idiot.*

"We need to get dressed," Alex said quietly. The unusual sound had stopped.

Maybe it's a bear, Faith thought. The idea was ridiculous—what kind of bear would be on this tiny island? And since when did anybody hope for a bear, anyway?

Alex miraculously had some jersey shorts in hand and pulled them up. He tossed her bikini bottom at her. "Where are the rest of your clothes?" he hissed.

She pointed, wordlessly, outside and pulled on the fleece. It made the heat immediately worse, but what other option did she have?

"Jesus," he said and started to crawl toward the opening. He looked both ways and exited the tent. One minute later, he'd tossed her backpack full of clothes inside. "Get dressed," he said. "Fast."

She saw him swap the shorts for jeans outside the tent, and a wave of embarrassment came over her. As Faith dug through the backpack for shorts and a tank top, she knew the moment to talk about the future had passed. *I had, what, like eighteen hours to talk about that? Just couldn't pass up another orgasm, though, could I?*

"Ready?" Alex asked as he popped his head into the tent.

She nodded and followed him outside to lace up her hiking boots. "Fuck," she muttered as she struggled with the laces.

"Shh," Alex whispered from the cliff's edge. "Come here."

She rolled her eyes at him but made her way beside him. "Oh my God," she said quietly.

In the bright moonlight, the boat was easy to see. It was the size of a small yacht, though far from a luxury vessel. It hugged the shore perilously and didn't have any lights ablaze. Still, thanks to the full moon, she could make out a little rowboat dropped onto the bank.

Alex pulled out a pair of binoculars from his pack. "Hey," she whispered. "Do you—"

He handed her another, smaller pair. *And I thought coming prepared meant cute bikinis, sandwiches, and sunblock*, she thought. *I really am stupid.*

Several men crowded onto the rowboat, and half of them jumped onto the muddy bank. Clearly well practiced, they began to unload tightly packed bricks. "Is that cocaine?" she whispered.

"I'm guessin'," he said. "It's not weed," he added and squinted into his binoculars. "Stay here."

"Alex!" she hissed, but he'd already scrambled to the tent. She looked back down at the men. *How much do they have?*

"Here," Alex said suddenly. She jumped at his voice. He held two small handguns and pushed one toward her.

"Oh," she said. "No. No way in hell—"

"Hopefully you won't have to use it," he said as he cut her off. "But just in case. Do you know how?"

She shook her head, wide-eyed. This shit had become way too real.

Alex tucked both the guns into his waistband and picked up his binoculars. She waited for him to make some kind of comment on her being a city girl, but he was silent. She picked up her binoculars , too, and watched the men below. They made several trips between the shore and the bigger boat. The size of the bricks grew impressively large. Three men stayed on the bank to guard the coke.

"God, how much do they have?" she whispered.

The rowboat made another return to the vessel, but this time it lingered. The men in the rowboat deboarded and went below deck. *Is this what we came out here for?* Faith thought. *To watch a bunch of rednecks transport cocaine?*

She scanned the boats for any identifying information but saw nothing. Even the men were largely nondescript. Most wore baseball caps, and they all had on dark jackets and jeans. *What am I supposed to do, anyway? Go report to the police that "a boat and men in baseball caps" are transporting drugs? Not that there's any cell phone reception out here anyway...*

"Oh, fuck," Alex said suddenly.

Faith squinted into the binoculars. The men dragged two teenage girls onto the rowboat. The girls moved sluggishly, as if drugged, their waist-length black hair obscuring their faces. Both were barefoot and in jeans. One wore a Mickey Mouse T-shirt and the other a men's plaid button-up shirt.

"Oh my God," Faith whispered. She'd been right, though she hadn't realized how much she'd wanted to be wrong until now.

The men made one more trip to the boat and this time

brought three Latina girls on board. They didn't seem quite as drugged as the last and looked around wildly, clearly terrified. However, none of them dared to make a sound. The smallest one looked as if she couldn't have been older than twelve.

Alex was on his hands and knees. *Don't go*, she wanted to say. Faith wanted to beg, plead, do whatever it took to keep him beside her. But she knew he'd go before he even said it. "Alex," she said quietly. "You can't."

She reached for his arm, but he gently brushed her hand away.

"*Please*," she said. Faith blushed, ashamed at how much her begs now sounded like her pleas in the tent. "You can't stop them, not right now," she said. "It's dangerous. There are tons of them—"

"And those girls?" he asked.

She let out her breath. He was right. "Then let me go with you," she said. Faith scrambled to her feet and followed him. "You can't go alone. And maybe with me, they won't be as quick to, you know . . ."

"You're not going," he said firmly. "It's way too dangerous."

"If it's so dangerous, you shouldn't go, either!"

"Keep your voice down," he said. "Are you tryin' to get 'em killed?"

Her mouth snapped shut and tears sprung to her eyes. "At least tell me what you're going to do," she said. "You can't just leave me up here wondering, not knowing . . ."

"I'm gonna wait till that boat leaves," he said. Alex tested a flashlight and put it in his pocket. "That way, there will only be a few of 'em. And given they gotta control those girls, that'll stack the odds in my favor."

"In your favor? Your favor to do what?" She felt hot tears spill down her cheeks but didn't care.

"To make my move," he said simply.

Together, they returned to the bank to watch the boats. It looked like the bricks and the girls were all set. *What are they doing down there?* Faith wondered. All she and Alex could do was sit and wait.

Through the binoculars, Faith tried to make note of any unique details of the girls or their captors. One of the men seemed to be wearing a massive gold ring on his finger. A high school ring? An NFL-type ring? She couldn't tell.

The girls mostly kept their heads down, their faces hidden. All had thick black hair that was perfect for obscuring features. However, one, the only one with shoes—cheap plastic flip-flops—gazed around. She seemed to want to take in where she was, though from where she was crammed onto the muddy bank it had to all look the same.

Suddenly, the girl looked up. Faith could swear she looked right at her. "Alex," she said as she lowered the binoculars.

"I see," he said. The girl had huge doll-like eyes. If she saw them, her expression didn't change.

Faith opened her hand without raising it higher. She hoped if the girl saw it, it would offer some kind of solace. But the girl's face didn't shift at all.

"She's looking at the moon," Alex said.

Finally, the larger boat began to depart. Faith's heart sunk.

"That's my cue," Alex said.

He stood up as the men began to lead the girls away. One of the men hoisted the bricks onto a portable cargo wagon. Faith jumped up and walked with Alex to the start of the trail. "Please don't go," she whispered, though she knew it was pointless.

Alex kissed her on the top of the head. She wrapped her arms around him and pulled him tight.

When he left, she watched him until he was swallowed by the darkness. *It might be the last time I see him*, she thought. That idea hit her hard and made her fall to her knees in tears.

31

ALEX

His heart hammered in his chest. Alex hoped Faith couldn't tell how terrified he was, though the adrenaline had started to overpower the fear. When he'd agreed to this so-called stakeout, he'd thought the worst they would find would be a bunch of kids drinking, smoking, and vandalizing the island. Sure, the KKK arsonists and vandals were off-putting, but this is the South. He could see how such overt racism would shock somebody like Faith, but unfortunately for Alex it hadn't been surprising.

Seeing millions of dollars of cocaine being unloaded, though? Worse, human trafficking—likely sex trafficking? That he hadn't been prepared for. When he'd packed the pistols, it had almost been an afterthought. More for peace of mind than anything else.

He willed his breath to steady as he made his way down the path. This trail wasn't burned into his psyche like the trails near Greystone. Roots reached for his feet, and he stumbled. Alex didn't have a plan. There was a small part of him, a part he was ashamed of, that hoped he wouldn't be able to find them.

"*Vámanos!*" The grizzly voice with the wretched Spanish accent was just around the corner. The traffickers didn't seem to be using flashlights. The moon was enough for them.

Alex had a feeling this particular crew wasn't the same as those who had lit the house on fire. *Nah. They probably hired some low-level thugs for that*, he thought. This was a professional ring.

He pressed himself against a massive oak and listened to the sounds on the other side.

"*Ten cuidado,*" one of the traffickers said.

He heard the sound of a boot hitting flesh and a low cry from one of the girls.

"Fuckin' spics," one of the men said. "Lazy as hell. Rodney, you Gonna have to help 'em."

"Y'all ain't doin' shit," a man said. It must have been Rodney. "Y'all can't help, too?"

"Me?" one of the men laughed. "Shit, one of us gotta supervise."

"I think this coke's gettin' heavier," Rodney said with a grunt.

A smattering of Spanish broke out. Alex heard a slap. "*Cállate. Volver a trabajo,*" one of the men said.

Alex peeked around the tree and saw the girls as they were forced to pick up and carry the bricks. They transferred the bricks from the trolley used to get the cocaine from the bank to a bigger cart that was easier to navigate. *Where the hell did they have that hidden?*

When he saw the men up close, he realized there were four of them. Three of them he recognized from trips on the ferry or markets on the mainland. All but Rodney, who worked among the girls, were stationed in a lazy cluster toward the rear of the group. Each of the three men cradled a few bricks in their big hands but seemed to leisurely enjoy the show before them.

That's one advantage, at least, Alex thought. The men seemed at ease, completely sure of their anonymity out here. *How many times have they done this?* Alex thought.

One of the girls paused to yank her hair into a ponytail. However, one of the three men was faster. He rested a cigarette between his lips, reached into his back pocket and pulled out a small whip. It was black, leather, likely from a sex shop rather than a grange or feed shop. Still, she cried out when he whipped her across the back of her legs.

"Damn, Frank," one of the men said. "Not on the legs. These bitches gotta ways to walk, and customers want 'em lookin' pretty."

"Pretty?" Frank asked with a laugh. "They as pretty as any wetback Gonna get. She Gonna walk it off just fine. Ain't that right, *mamacita*?" he said.

The girl could tell she was expected to smile, and she shot a grimace toward Frank as she picked up another brick to transfer.

Alex took in the three men and ignored Rodney. He was obviously at the bottom of the totem pole. The other three had their hands full of cigarettes and bricks, which they tucked like children into their arms. He scanned their bodies for firearms. Surely they had them, but they were either in ankle holsters or behind their backs.

He'd have to pick them off one by one as best he could.

"I gotta take a piss," one of the men said.

"You need one of these bitches to hold yo' hand or somethin'?" Frank asked. "Y'all don't need permission. Go on."

The man bristled slightly at Frank's tone. As he stalked off into the woods, Alex scanned his body. He didn't see a gun in the back waistband, but that didn't mean the man wasn't packing.

Alex backtracked slightly and moved through the trees. The one who searched out a place to piss whistled as he walked. *Thanks for the cover*, Alex thought. A few yards away from everyone else, the man stopped in front of a magnolia tree with his back to Alex.

"*You need one of these bitches to hold yo' hand?*" the man mimicked. "Fuckin' Frank."

Alex waited for the sound of a zipper, of urine to hit the tree. It didn't happen. Instead, he watched the man pull a pocketknife out and cut into the brick. Even just with moonlight, he could see how snowy white the powder was.

The man dipped a finger into it and brought it to his mouth to test. "That's the shit," he said to himself.

Alex glanced behind him, toward the rest of the group, but they seemed to be hard at work. He heard the snort of the man in front of him, gripped his handgun, and rushed the large man.

When he was a foot away from him, the man turned. His eyes were wide with surprise, and the powder had streaked from his nose to his lip. "What the—"

Before he could finish, Alex pistol-whipped him in the head.

He'd thought he'd get the back of his head, maybe the neck, but the butt of the gun landed squarely between the eyes. A burst of blood exploded into the air and sprayed across Alex's shirt. The man hit the ground with a thud while the brick fell from his hands.

"Joe?" one of the men called out. "You taking a shit out there or what?"

Alex steadied his breathing and waited. "Joe? Motherfucker," he heard one of the men say. "That bastard took one o' the bricks with 'im. I'mma be right back."

Alex looked around wildly, but there was no way to hide Joe's massive body sprawled across the ground. Instead, he raced to a tree between Joe and the man who approached. At least he could take him by surprise.

"Joe?" The man who came through the woods wasn't Frank—and, fortunately, he didn't have a gun pulled. "What you doin'—goddamn it." The man stopped three feet away from Alex and bent down to tie his shoelace.

The timing couldn't have been more perfect. Alex jumped him. This time, he got the back of the head. He was grateful he didn't have to look this monster in the eye. Like Joe, this one also went down nearly in silence, just a small grunt.

Now what? It was just Frank and Rodney left, and he had a feeling Rodney wouldn't be a major threat. But Frank, the boss? He was surely locked and loaded. And it wouldn't be long before he came in search of his minions.

Alex leaned back against the tree and tried to anticipate the next best move. *Should he wait it out here or take the offensive?*

He listened for any clues from the trail but only heard the shuffle of feet and the occasional drop of a brick onto a stack. Frank and Rodney were silent. Alex knew that couldn't be a good sign.

He started to make his way back to the trail, giving it a wide berth. Alex hoped they couldn't hear his footsteps. *Maybe if I come up the trail the way they're headed, it'll catch them by surprise.* He knew it wouldn't be long until one of them found the unconscious bodies in the woods. *Damn, I should have taken their pictures,* Alex thought. He didn't know if he'd make it out of this alive. But at least he could have left behind some type of evidence of who was behind all this.

Finally, he came to the overgrown path they would soon be headed down. It couldn't be much longer before all the bricks were stacked. Alex hugged the edge of the trail and started to sneak toward the crew. Suddenly, the girls came into view. He saw Rodney alongside them, but Frank was nowhere to be seen. *Shit.*

Alex sneaked into the bushes that skirted the trail. Then he saw Frank. The man frowned at the girls and surveyed the area. He had deep crevices in his face, bushy brows, and a mean slit of a mouth. Without warning, he walked toward the wagon and placed his brick on it. He looked at Rodney and jerked his head.

Rodney stopped in his tracks, shoved a brick into one of the girls' hands, and bounded to Frank's side.

What the hell?

He watched Frank drop his head and whisper something to Rodney, who nodded eagerly.

Just as Alex started to recede farther into the bush, Frank and Rodney turned with inhuman speed toward him and opened fire. *Fuck.* The bullets missed, though two whizzed through the bushes and shook the leaves.

Alex tumbled backward to an oak tree and waited for the hail of bullets to stop. He could hear the girls screaming between the shots. As soon as there was a break, he leaned out from behind the tree and took aim.

Frank was no stupid southern redneck. He stood behind the girls and used them as a shield. Rodney was another story. He stood stubbornly in the middle of the trail. Alex took aim, but even as he fired the shot, he knew it was way off.

He'd never been much for hunting, and clay pigeons or the shooting range were nothing like this. Alex was a decent aim, but he couldn't bring himself to fire anywhere close to the girls. Even though Rodney was eight feet from them, it was too close for Alex's comfort.

Still, just the sight of Alex taking shots at them was enough to make Rodney panic. He screamed, high pitched, and fired wildly into the night.

And Frank smiled. In that moment, Alex realized Rodney had probably always been on the crew as a distraction. Frank raised his pistol and took aim at Alex, even as Rodney hollered into the night. *Move*, Alex told himself. *Move!*

He barely made it back behind the tree in time. Pieces of bark flew off the trunk as Frank's shots came as close as they could. *What does he have, anyway? A Colt?* Whatever it was, it couldn't hold that many bullets. Then again, neither could Alex's. He only had four left in the chamber. *Fuck. I should have checked the other guys' bodies for firearms.*

Rodney's screeches stopped, and Alex could just make out quiet whimpers and cries from the girls.

Frank let out a low wolf whistle, like he'd just spotted a gorgeous woman on the street. "Come out, come out," Frank called in a singsongy voice.

Alex heard the chamber of Frank's gun snap closed. He'd just reloaded.

Frank fired another shot into the tree. It shook the entire trunk. "Wherever you are," Frank called. Another shot hit the tree and bark flew.

As soon as the shot stopped, Alex peered out from behind the tree again. Rodney now stood next to Frank behind the girls.

Four of them were curled up and rested on their haunches with their arms over their heads. One of them started to keen, a feral cry, and Frank didn't even bother to stop her.

Rodney held one girl in front of them, though most of her body protected Frank. She clawed at his forearm, but it was locked tight across her chest. Her bare feet dug into the dirt, and even from fifty feet away, Alex could see the whites of her eyes. "*Por favor*, please, *no quiero morir*," she begged. When that failed, she started to pray. Her Hail Mary rang through the night. "*Dios te salve, Maria, llena eres de gracia . . .*"

"I see you!" Frank called out, his voice full of cheer.

"*Bendita tú eres entre todas las mujeres . . .*" the girl in Rodney's arms cried. Alex raised his pistol to take a shot, but he knew he wouldn't. There was no way he could guarantee he'd miss the girls. With a groan of frustration, he went back behind the tree.

" . . . *Santa Maria, Madre de Dios, ruega por nosotros pecadores . . .*"

"I don't think he wants to play with us," Frank said to either Rodney or the girls.

Alex's heart began to race. He was stuck. At this point, he hadn't heard Frank reload. Everyone probably had the same number of bullets left—four at the most. *And what happens when we all run out?*

" . . . *ahora y en la hora de nuestra muerte.*"

"Amen!" Rodney shouted.

"Ready or not." Frank's voice lilted in melody. "Here I come."

32

FAITH

Faith pressed her lips together and held the rifle against her chest. She'd trailed behind Alex all the way to where the traffickers were transferring the cocaine. But when she'd heard a shot ring out, she'd raced to Alex's boat to search for something—anything—to help.

Buried underneath what she'd thought was tackle gear was a heavy rifle wrapped with a worn leather strap. Faith had tried, without success, to figure out whether it was loaded. Too scared to tamper much with where she thought the bullets were, she'd grabbed it and hoped for the best. If nothing else, the traffickers didn't know she couldn't shoot.

As soon as Frank had sung to Alex, "Here I come," something deep inside her took over. Faith stepped out from between the trees and came face-to-face with the two men.

"What the hell?" Frank said. He was just five feet from her. His gun still pointed toward Alex, and there were no girls on his right side for protection. "Who're you?"

"Put down the gun," she said. Her voice didn't sound like her own. It sounded like some bad Hollywood script.

Rodney started to giggle, and her finger found the trigger. Stories about how rifles could kick so hard into a grown man's shoulder it could break his collarbone rushed through her head. *Don't think about that.*

"Fuckin' Yank," Frank said. "Shoot her," he said over his shoulder to Rodney.

Faith braced the rifle against her hip and squeezed the trigger. She aimed for the sky and prayed it was loaded.

The shot was so loud that the pain in her hip barely registered.

"Jesus Christ!" Frank shouted.

Rodney dropped the gun and released his grip on the girl. She fell to the ground, but her prayers got louder.

"They're Gonna hear!" Rodney yelled at Frank. "Fuckin' rifle, ya know the feds are all up about illegal huntin' this time a year. They're Gonna hear—"

"I fuckin' know, goddamn it," Frank said.

Faith was charged with adrenaline. The girls started to crawl away toward the cover of trees. She braced the rifle against her hip again, away from the bruise she was sure had started to spread, and shot into the air again.

"We gotta go!" Rodney said. He sounded like a little boy afraid he was about to get spanked.

"Alex," she said under her breath. She saw him race through the trees on the other side of the trail. With the girls out of the way, he fired straight through Frank's hand.

"Shit," Frank said in a tight voice. He dropped his own pistol and grabbed his bloodied hand. "Get goin'," he said to Rodney. "Take what you can." Rodney glanced around for the girls, but Frank gave him a kick in the shins. "Forget them bitches. The coke! Go!" Rodney grabbed a few of the bricks and took off alongside Frank.

"Are you . . . are you going after them?" Faith said. They stood side by side and watched the two men run toward the rowboat.

"Nah," Alex said. "They won't get far. 'Sides, they left two of their own back in the woods."

"You didn't . . . you didn't kill them?" she asked.

He gave a short laugh. "Nah. Just knocked 'em out."

She let out a breath of relief. No matter who they were, what they were, she didn't want Alex to bear the burden of having killed them.

"Gimme that," Alex said and reached out for the shotgun. She happily handed it over. "Nice shootin', ma'am," he said. "Thought you didn't know how to fire a gun."

"I don't," she admitted. "I just pulled the trigger and prayed."

"Yeah, I could tell," he said. "Thank God they couldn't."

The girls had settled into a cacophony of quiet sobs. Faith made her way toward them, while Alex trailed behind. "Let me," she said to him softly. "You'll probably scare them."

"*Está bien,*" she said to the girls. She approached them with her hands open and squatted down to them. "*Estas seguro. La ayuda viene. Mi nombre es Faith. ¿lo que es tuyo?*"

"Sofia," said the one who looked youngest. One by one they wiped their eyes and said their names.

"What did you tell them?" Alex asked.

"Just that it's okay, they're safe," she said over her shoulder.

"I didn't know you spoke Spanish."

"I'm from California," she reminded him. "Besides . . . there's probably a lot you still don't know about me."

"I'm starting to see that," he said. She heard the smile in his voice. "Let's head to the boat. Y'all will be safe there."

"Where are you going?" Faith asked, worried. She glanced around but saw no sign of the bad guys.

"I need to tie those guys up in the woods," Alex said quietly. He saw the dark eyes of the girls watch his lips, but they didn't seem to understand. "Then I'm gonna grab just the essentials from the campsite. Don't worry," he said. "We'll have to pass by where they'd docked anyway. I promise you, they're far gone."

Faith explained it to the girls as best she could, her Spanish not nearly as good as it had been when she'd worked tirelessly with a client based in Mexico City.

"*Parco?*" one of the girls asked, and wrinkled her nose in confusion.

"*Barco,*" Faith said, embarrassed as she corrected herself. "Boat. We're going to our boat."

"Ah," the girl said. She smiled up shyly at Faith.

"Bring down my flip-flops for them," Faith said.

Alex nodded as he helped the girls up. All but one pulled away from him as if his touch stung.

"I think it might be better if I'm the only one who touches them," she said to him gently.

Alex jogged into the woods to check on the two men. He returned quickly and nodded to her. "They're still out cold," he said. "I'll still tie 'em up once I get y'all to the beach, though."

The youngest girl, Mercedes, held tightly to Faith's hand as they walked toward the beach. It was slow. Even though the girl with flip-flops had given one to the youngest girl, they still winced at the stones and pebbles below their feet. Mercedes stiffened as they passed the area where the boat had docked.

"Nobody's here," Alex said, slow and loud. "They're gone."

The girl nodded, but pulled tighter at Faith's arm. Footsteps were still evident in the mud.

It was just a five-minute walk to Caleb's boat. "Y'all stay right here," Alex said. "Here." He pulled one of the walkie-talkies out of the boat and handed one to her. "Just push this button if you need me. I'll be twenty minutes, max."

"Alex," she started but didn't know what to say. *Don't leave me alone? I don't know what to do with these girls? What happens if they come back?* She searched his face, which was calm and stoic.

"It'll be okay," he said. "You want to keep your rifle?" he asked with a smile. "Or should I put it back in the boat?"

She rubbed at her hip. There was already a goose egg that had emerged from its kick. "The boat," she said.

"I'm going to leave you with this handgun just in case," he said. "It'll make you feel safer, at least."

The girls winced when he pulled out the gun. "*Está bien*," she told them, but it wasn't enough to soothe their anxiety. It wasn't until she'd tucked it into her shorts that they breathed again.

"*¿A dónde va?*" Mercedes asked as Alex walked away.

Faith did her best to explain, leaving out the part about Alex's plan to tie up the men in the woods.

"*Novio?*" Mercedes asked. "Your boyfriend?"

"Um," Faith said with a blush. "I don't know," she said finally. "*No se*," she added with a shrug. It made Mercedes giggle, and she covered her laugh with a small hand.

Faith looked at the young, curious eyes that probed her face. She tried to ask them how they'd stumbled into this situation but wasn't sure how much they understood one another. The oldest, at sixteen years old, said she'd found an ad on Craigslist for a "professional cuddler."

"I've heard of that," Faith said in Spanish. "I have a friend who thought about doing it in California."

"California?" Mercedes asked. Her ears perked up.

"I live in California," she explained. "I'm here on business."

"*Y Alex?*" Mercedes asked.

"It's a long story," Faith said with a sigh.

Another girl had responded to a similar ad, though it was supposedly for stripping in Miami. She shrugged and said it hadn't sounded too bad. She'd been promised a lot of money and had a cousin who used to do it legitimately in Texas.

For Mercedes, her parents had been approached by a man who'd been looking for young girls to work as au pairs, housekeepers, and cooks. All she'd packed had been a backpack nearly as big as her full of spices and cooking utensils her parents thought wouldn't be available in the United States. It hadn't taken long for her to figure out she wouldn't be cooking. The traffickers had tossed her entire backpack in a dumpster as soon as they'd cleared the border.

Part of her wanted to ask how much abuse they'd already faced, but part of her didn't want to know. *What difference does it make to me?* She started to think about who to call for help. *Natalie,* she thought. Natalie's firm had worked with human trafficking victims before, though Natalie had never been on any of those cases. Still, these girls would need someone beyond ICE on their side.

"Do you know your parents' numbers?" she asked the girls. "In Mexico? Or family here?"

They looked at each other, unsure whether they should tell her or not. "I can help you call them," she said. "As soon as we get off this island. You should talk to them before we have to tell the police."

"No police," Sofia said firmly. "No police, no police. *La migra,*" she said to the rest of the girls.

Faith let out a sigh but didn't want to argue at the moment. "Do you want to talk to your parents?" she asked again in Spanish.

"Yes," Mercedes said vehemently.

"Okay," Faith said, grateful that she had at least one ally among them. "We can do that. I'll help you do that."

"Y'all all right?" Alex called suddenly. Faith's heart leaped when she saw him round the corner of the trail, her backpack slung over his shoulder.

If she'd had any doubts before, they vanished in that moment. *I love you.* She wanted to yell it but kept it together in front of the girls. "Yeah," she said warmly. She felt a stupid smile spread across her face but couldn't help it.

"*Su novio,*" Mercedes told the other girls and giggled again.

Alex looked at Mercedes, aware that she was talking about him. "Huh?" he asked.

"Nothing," Faith said quickly.

"*Alex es su novio,*" Mercedes said, a knowing tone in her voice.

Faith groaned. "Did you bring my shoes?" she asked.

"Oh, yeah, here," he said. "I have one of my extra pairs, too. It'll be too big, but good enough till we get to Greystone."

The girls dug through the backpack and pulled on shoes along with Alex's extra T-shirts.

Alex straddled himself between the boat and the dock. "After you, ma'am," he told Sofia. He'd learned not to reach his arm out to her, but she grabbed his arm as she stepped onto the boat. Mercedes happily took his hand and leaped onto the boat.

"Comin'?" Alex asked Faith once the girls were on board. She took his hand and saw Mercedes cover her mouth with a smile once more.

"*Nada de ti,*" she said to Mercedes with a smile. It made the little girl laugh.

"What y'all gossipin' about?" Alex asked as he started the boat.

313

"Oh, you know," Faith said. "You."

She sat by the girls while Alex directed the boat toward Greystone. The girls chattered in Spanish and wrapped themselves in Alex's too-big shirts.

As she watched him at the helm, his broad shoulders lit by the moonlight, emotion overwhelmed her. *God. I really do love him,* she thought. This . . . this she hadn't expected. None of it. Not that she'd really been right about what had been going on with the trafficking, not the hours of endless sex on a cliff, and certainly not that she'd end up falling so hard for him. Faith looked into the distance and blinked back tears.

"*Que está mal?*" Mercedes asked. She scooted close to Faith, reached up, and wiped at Faith's eyes.

Faith laughed. "Nothing's wrong," she said.

Mercedes nodded as if she'd figured out the whole story. The girls all held their long hair in their hands as the wind whipped across them, but Mercedes let hers fly wild like a wedding veil.

"Almost there," Alex called over his shoulder.

"Mama? Papa?" Mercedes asked. Her eyes bore into Faith's. "*Llamada?* Call now?"

"Yeah," Faith said. "We're going to call them right now."

33

ALEX

As soon as they got reception, with the dock near Greystone in sight, Faith called the inn. He couldn't hear what she said because of the wind, but he knew whatever happened, Mama would be on their side.

He docked the boat and jumped out. "C'mon, y'all," he said and offered his hand to Sofia. Already the girls were more comfortable with him. He took in Sofia's wide hips and the swell of her thighs and winced, unable to imagine what the girl had been through.

Faith emerged last, and as she gripped his hand, he saw Mama and the boys up the path. Mama was in front and looked impeccable as ever. However, Alex knew she'd really pulled on something fast in the middle of the night. The navy-blue slacks and cream-colored blouse looked well thought-out, but Mama's staple matching jewelry was nowhere in sight.

"My word," Mama said as she looked at the girls.

"They don't speak English," Alex said. "Faith's been translating."

She blushed as Mama looked at her. "I'm not fluent," she said quickly. "But I promised they could call their families before we got anyone involved."

"Of course, of course," Mama said. "I don't know anything 'bout calling Mexico, but you take as long as you need."

The girls were wide-eyed as they approached the inn. "*Su casa?*" Mercedes asked her. "Home?"

"Mama's," Alex said. He pointed to each of the boys and said their names. Mercedes was quick to offer her own, but the older girls hung back. Alex suddenly realized what this must look like—him bringing them to a big, fancy house full of young American men.

"Everything okay?" Alex asked as they entered the foyer. He could sense the trepidation in the group.

"I think it might be better if they come with me to make the call," Faith said. "Having a bunch of men around, it's making them nervous."

"Will one man be okay?" Alex asked.

Faith nodded, and led the way upstairs. The girls followed her upstairs to her room, with Alex trailing behind. "*Mi dormitorio*," she explained as they entered.

He watched as she bought a digital calling card to Mexico, one that offered both English and Spanish audio instructions.

"Call home?" she asked them. Sofia cocked her head. "Uh, *quieres llamar a tus padres?*"

"Mama," Mercedes said with a smile.

Faith showed the calling card instructions on the screen to Sofia, who nodded as she read the Spanish portion. When Faith handed her the phone, Sofia grinned and said "iPhone."

Faith laughed. "Yeah."

The volume was loud enough that Alex could hear the robotic calling card as it barked instructions in Spanish followed by the unfamiliar Mexican ringtone. "Papa?" Sofia asked as tears filled her eyes.

Alex felt a pull in his gut. *I shouldn't be here*, he thought. "I'll be downstairs," he said, and Faith nodded.

Alex, Mama, and the guys were seated at the formal dining room table with mugs of tea in hand when Faith came downstairs alone. She looked exhausted, but he could hear the happy smattering of Spanish upstairs.

"I just can't believe it," Mama said when she saw her. "I mean, I'd heard stories about drug smuggling on the islands. But I thought they were just stories. This . . ."

"Nobody could have known," Faith said. She sat beside Mama and squeezed her hand.

"You did," Mama said.

"No," Faith said. She shook her head. "I just suspected."

Mama sighed. "I shoulda never let y'all go to that island alone."

"Well . . . you didn't really *know*," Faith reminded her.

Alex gave her a look, but Mama laughed. "Isn't that the truth! I s'pose I should have asked for details beyond 'going camping.' To be honest, I though y'all were just taking up an excuse to get away and be all romantic."

Caleb, Lee, and Matt stared with intensity at their tea. "What're they doin' up there?" Caleb asked to break the silence.

"Calling home," Faith said. "But now . . . we need to call the police," she said. "Especially with those guys, you know, tied up on the island."

"What now?" Mama asked.

Alex and Faith went into the kitchen to make the call. "How do you even report human trafficking?" she asked.

He shrugged. "I reckon you just call the local police and they take it from there."

Of course, Alex knew the dispatcher and the Saint Rose chief. He'd gone to high school with both of them, though the chief had been a senior when Alex was a freshman. "You shittin' me, Caldwell?" the chief asked.

"I wish I was, ma'am," Alex said. He'd put it on speakerphone.

"And you're telling me you left two men tied up out there, and what was it? Couple dozen bricks o' cocaine?"

"Something like that," Alex said.

"Jesus Christ. Get Child protective Services out to Greystone!" the chief barked at someone. "The feds? Yeah, yeah. Look, Alex," the chief said. "In all honesty? I've never dealt with nothin' like this. CPS is on their way, but comin' from Savannah. It'll take a while. You sure those girls aren't goin' nowhere?"

Alex looked at Faith, and she shook her head. "They're good," he said.

"All right. What? There's nobody at CPS on call who speaks Spanish? What the hell?" The chief groaned into the phone. "Might be a beat longer," she said.

By the time he hung up, it was clear both CPS and the FBI were en route, but there was no telling when they'd arrive.

"You should try and get some sleep," Alex said. "It's going to be a long day once they get here."

"I don't think I can," she said.

Mercedes stepped into the kitchen and held out the phone to Faith. "Die," she said.

"What?"

"Phone *es* die."

"Oh!" She took the phone and looked at Alex. "I'll be upstairs," she said.

Alex stepped onto the porch to watch for the lights to come up the driveway. When the screen door creaked open, he glanced up and expected to see Mama or Faith, but it was Lee, two beers in hand.

"Olive branch?" Lee asked as he handed him one.

"For what?" Alex asked.

Lee settled into the chair next to him. "Oh, I'd say for the past four years or so."

Alex let out a chuckle. "Think that'll cost more than a beer."

"Beer's all I got," Lee said. "And an apology."

"For?"

"For gettin' all googly-eyed over Rebecca," Lee said. He stared into the darkness beside Alex. "It was stupid, you know. Just some crush. She and I . . . we never did anything. You know that, right? I'd never do that to you."

"Yeah," Alex said. He took a slow sip of the beer. "I do know."

"Then why you so mad for so long?" Lee asked. "I never even, you know, flirted with her or nothin'. I just thought she was interesting was all."

"Interesting. That's a way to put it."

"Well, hell, you know. Different from round here. Y'all went to big colleges, I didn't. I'd never met anyone like her before."

"Count your blessings," Alex said.

"And now, with Faith . . ."

"What about her?" Alex asked, his throat tight.

"Well, I dunno what you think," Lee said. "When she arrived? 'Course I thought she was pretty. I'm not blind. But you know, as soon as I saw you two had eyes for each other, I never even thought 'bout her like that again."

"And when did you see that?" Alex asked.

"Shit, Alex. I dunno. Day two?"

Alex felt embarrassment wash over him. *Had it been that obvious?* "Thank you," he said softly.

"For what?"

"I dunno. Saying sorry. Putting up with me holding this goddamned stupid grudge for so long. Honestly, Lee, I don't know why I clung to it so tight."

"Sure you do," Lee said. "You needed somethin' to hold to. 'Specially after Rebecca was gone."

"Maybe you're right," Alex said. The beer had started to sweat the label off. "I'm sorry, too. For taking it out on you. Hell, I knew it was just a crush. I knew y'all didn't do nothin'."

"No problem," Lee said.

"It is a problem. Was," Alex said. "I knew her for, what, six years? And you were like my brother since we were kids. But once it started, me snubbin' you and all, I couldn't stop. And it's stupid, but it made her bein' gone easier."

"It's not stupid," Lee said. "I get it. I got it then, too."

"You're a good man," Alex said. He turned to look at Lee. "A good brother. Sorry I was a prick for so long."

Lee shrugged. "Happens to the best of us."

CPS arrived before the FBI, although it took eight hours. Nobody at Greystone slept besides the girls. Each of the boys gave up their beds, and Gwen and Jessie came early to help change the sheets.

"*Es* too much!" Mercedes said.

Faith was firm. "Sleep," she said. The girls passed out fast, though Sofia and Mercedes managed a shower beforehand.

"You did a good thing," Gwen told Alex as she put together a lavish breakfast. She patted his head like she used to when he was a child.

The girls stumbled downstairs around nine, sleepy eyed with stomachs that rumbled. CPS showed up right as they finished stacks of waffles, piles of fluffy and cheesy omelets, and endless slices of toast. One officer still had a trace of his Mexican Spanish accent; the other was a slight blonde with an unmistakable Boston dialect.

As soon as the male officer sat down and started to speak, a flood of Spanish started to pour out of the girls. They spoke so fast, Faith threw up her hands at Alex. "No idea," she confessed.

"I'll talk to you in the other room," the blonde said with a nod to her and Alex.

They were both sleep deprived and had pounding headaches but recounted the events over and over for the blonde officer.

"A rifle?" the woman asked Faith. "And you never fired a gun before?"

"No," Faith said quietly.

"Care to show me the bruises?"

Faith stood up and hiked up her shorts.

Alex gasped when he saw the welts. He'd assumed it had hurt but didn't expect that.

"Looks like a rifle bruise to me," the woman said as she made a note.

"What . . . what's going to happen to them?" Faith asked. "To the girls."

"Hard to say at this point," the officer said. "I don't know, but I'm guessin' they're here illegally. Most seem underage. If they have family in Mexico, I'd say they'll be sent back."

"Will they be okay, though?" Faith asked.

The officer stopped her notetaking and looked up. "I dunno," she said. "Why are you so concerned?"

"Why aren't you?" Faith snapped back. "Sorry," she said as the woman bristled. "It's . . . it's been a long night."

The officer finally offered up a smile, though it looked strange on her hard face. "That's probably putting it lightly."

When they were finally released, the girls were all smiles. They chattered away with the male officer. Mercedes caught his eye and laughed.

Who would do something like this to these girls? "Any . . . any leads?" Alex asked the male officer. "I mean, on who did this?"

"That's something for the FBI or police," he said. "We're just taking care of the kids."

"Oh."

"*Listo?*" the officer asked the girls. "Ready?"

They nodded happily.

"Wait! You're taking them? Already?" Faith asked. "We just—"

"We drove separately," he said gently. "I've handled cases all over Georgia. Unfortunately, this kind of situation isn't exactly unique."

"But where are you taking them? I mean right now? Are they going to—"

"It's okay, ma'am," he said. "They're safe. From what I gathered, they all have families and stable homes in Mexico. I'll need to confirm that, *claro*, but I'm pretty good at figuring out when people are telling the truth."

"But what about until then?" she asked. "Can't they stay here?" Alex looked at her in surprise but realized he felt the same way.

The officer smiled at her kindly. "I'm afraid not. They'll be well taken care of, I promise you. There are facilities, kind of like a hotel or a dorm, where they'll stay in the interim."

"Bye!" Mercedes said, and jumped on Faith with a bear hug. Sofia gave her a hug, too, though it was softer and more reserved. The other girls waved their hands shyly at Alex.

Mama put her arm around Faith as they stood on the porch and watched the officer help the girls into a black SUV. "They'll be okay," Mama consoled her. Caleb, Matt, and Lee watched silently from the porch chairs.

"I hope so."

By the time the blonde officer emerged from the house, she looked satisfied as she tucked away her notepad. "Y'all done in there?" Mama asked. She put a protective hand on Alex's arm.

"Yes, ma'am, thank you," the officer said. "I might be in contact with you two," she said. "But I think I got all I need. You bein' able to identify two of those men is very helpful," she said to Alex.

"We're done?" Faith asked.

"With CPS, for now," the officer said. "But don't be surprised if the FBI or police come knocking soon."

Faith groaned. "I can't," she said. "I need to sleep."

"Then I suggest you get some while you can," the officer said. Her steps were heavy on the wooden porch as she walked toward her Ford Taurus.

"Y'all do as the officer said, and get some sleep," Mama said.

Alex took Faith's hand without thinking. From over Mama's shoulder, Caleb grinned and tipped an imaginary hat at him.

"Think maybe we'll take a walk first," Alex said. "Could use some fresh air."

"Y'all didn't get enough *fresh air* the past couple of days?" Mama asked. She sounded tough, but he could tease out the playfulness in her voice.

"Not the right kind," he said. He saw Faith blush.

The questioning from that officer, the detailed recount of what had happened, it had made Alex think about how well he knew Faith. He knew he loved her. *That was certain*, he thought. But he'd just barely found out she spoke Spanish. What else didn't he know? Her middle name, her favorite flower, or even her favorite ice cream. As they'd sat being interrogated by the blonde officer, he'd realized for the first time he wanted to know those things. Alex wanted more of her, period.

He led her to the trail, her hand tucked snugly into his. They walked in silence toward the beach. He wanted to quiz her now, find out everything, but the look of exhaustion on her face stopped him. *There's time*, he told himself. *Plenty of time.*

Or is there?

When they'd circled back and were at the fork that separated the inn and his cabin, Faith smiled at him and dropped his hand. She started to walk toward the inn and left Alex to his cabin. Alex reached out and took her hand once again. He pulled it gently.

"What about if the police come?" she asked.

"Don't worry 'bout it," he said. "Mama will let us know. C'mon."

She chewed her bottom lip and let him pull her toward his cabin. Inside, they both headed directly to the bed. Faith collapsed onto the thick down bedding. She looked completely spent.

"Alex," she started, "we need to—"

"Later," he said. "The police will be here soon, and I'm guessin' they'll be askin' us to the station on the mainland by tomorrow at the latest."

"But we need to talk—"

"I know," he said. "We will. But right now, we sleep."

She sighed, unable to put up any more of a fight. Alex crouched down and pulled off her shoes. Faith groaned in delight.

He pulled back the comforter and tucked her in. By the time he'd circled to the other side of the bed, pulled off his shirt, and climbed in beside her, her breath was already steady.

Alex wrapped an arm around her, pulled her tight, and spooned her as he drifted off.

34

FAITH

*F*aith woke up and squinted at the clock. It had only been a few hours and there had been no call from Mama. She rolled over and looked behind her to an empty bed. Sadness and disappointment flooded her. *Again? After all this?*

Suddenly, Alex appeared in the doorway. He'd slipped on pajama bottoms in a plaid print and was shirtless. She was still exhausted, but the sight of him with mussed up hair and that perfectly toned torso instantly turned her on. *How can I still want him this badly, even after what we've just been through?*

With him, it will never be enough, she realized.

Alex smiled and brought two cups of coffee to her bedside table.

"Mmm," she said as he leaned down to kiss her. He sat beside her while she propped herself up on the pillows and took a long swallow of coffee.

He watched her closely as she got her caffeine fix. "What?" she laughed, nervous.

"I . . . I think it's time we talked," he said.

"About what?" she asked, in hopes of putting it off.

"About us," he said.

She sucked in her breath. "Are you breaking up with me?" she asked. Her voice squeaked. She'd heard about this, about trauma and tragedies that tore apart even decades-long marriages. What could it possibly do to her and Alex, who hadn't even got a real relationship off the ground yet.

"Breaking up with you?" Alex asked, incredulous. "No! God, no, the opposite. I mean, I'm not going anywhere," he said. "You're the question mark in all this."

"Me?" she asked.

"Yes, ma'am. You. Yeah, I . . . Listen. I've never been good at talking about this stuff."

"Why doesn't that surprise me?" she asked with a laugh.

"Faith, I . . . I care about you. A lot. Hell, I love you."

She felt her eyes widen in surprise. Alex had told her he loved her before when they were having sex, but she had chalked it up to the heat of the moment. He hadn't mentioned it after, and neither had she. Looking at him now, she could see lines of tension running through Alex's body. He was nervous!

"You love me?" she asked, challenging him to look into her eyes.

Alex met her stare. "I said I did. I just...I didn't trust myself with just anyone. You know?"

That was all she'd ever wanted. To hear those words, she felt the last of the walls between them fall down.

Faith put down her coffee mug and kissed him long and deep.

"I love you too," she said, and she could feel the relief surge through his body. His hand went to her waist, and she felt the wetness start to spread between her legs. "Alex," she whispered and pulled back. She searched his eyes and saw nothing but transparency.

"I don't know what to do," he said. "I mean, your whole life's in California. And me . . ."

"Yes?" she asked. "We, uh, we never talked about that," she said. "What are your plans? What do you want to do? Are you going to stay here—"

He held up a hand. "Slow down on the questioning," he said with a laugh. "Your law school is showing."

"Sorry," she said.

"But to answer one of your questions, I don't know what my plans are. I know you're not s'posed to say that, not when you're almost thirty years old, but it's the truth."

"Yeah, well, I'm not one to talk," she said with a sigh. "I spent my whole adult life preparing for a law career, and now I dread the thought of going back."

"To California?"

She thought she heard some hope in his voice. "I don't know," she said honestly. "To my firm, that's for sure. But as far as leaving law entirely, I just don't know."

"You could always stay here," he said with a shrug.

"Here?" she asked. "You mean—"

"You still got the property," he said. "And I'm sure Craig or another contractor could do somethin' with the house. Even if it was just to use the foundation."

"I . . . you know, I guess you're right," she said. "There are all kinds of law specialties I never really fully considered. And if I can pass the bar in California, I'm sure I can here. Maybe, I don't know, environmental law," she said as she remembered his suggestions for the property. "Or immigration law," she added. She'd never forget Mercedes's smile, or the way Sofia had looked at her with those trusting eyes.

"I don't want you to change your whole life, not for me," Alex said. "I was just, you know, sayin'. You do own a whole island in Georgia."

"Yeah," she said with a laugh. "God, that sounds weird."

"And, hell, I could always go to California," he said. "Not much keepin' me here. 'Sides the family, but that's what planes are for, right?"

"You'd . . . you'd go to California?" she asked. "For me?"

"Not for anybody else," he said with a grin.

"Ugh," she said. "You'd hate it. I hate it a lot of the time, now that I think about it."

He gave her a strange look. "You aren't s'posed to say that 'bout your hometown," he said.

"I don't mean California as a whole," she said. "Just, I don't know, maybe the crowd I ran with back in San Francisco. But some sleepy little beach town, like where I grew up? I could see you there."

"You mean us," he corrected.

"Huh?"

"You could see us there."

"Oh," she said and looked down.

"That is, if you'd have me," he added.

"Of course!" she said. "Don't be weird. So what is it? Georgia or California?"

"Heads Carolina, tails California," he said.

"What's Carolina got to do with this?"

He laughed. "It's a song! A country song, so I'm not surprised you don't know it. All y'all Californians don't care much for the good stuff."

"Hey!" she said. "I have fantastic taste in music."

"Yeah, I bet you got some Kesha on your playlists and everything."

"Okay, the fact that you even know who Kesha is says more about you than me."

"All I'm sayin' is, we don't have to make any hard decisions right now. And if it comes right down to it and we can't decide? Hell, we can just flip a coin."

"How romantic," she said.

"That's me—can't help myself."

She bit her lip and looked at him. When she'd arrived on Saint Rose, the last thing she'd expected was to stumble right into her future. Faith remembered that first day, when she'd walked in on the argument between Alex and Caleb. Lee had tried to soothe her with promises that Alex was just that way.

He'd scared her that day—and many days after. So brooding and moody. She never would have guessed what was underneath it all. And now he was all hers.

"You know," she said, "I'm sure the police will be here any moment. Maybe we should . . ."

"You sure know how to sweet-talk a guy," he said.

Faith started to protest, but his lips were already on hers. He bit her lower lip playfully, and she let out a yelp.

Alex grabbed her waist and pulled her on top of him. Even through the khaki shorts she'd fallen asleep in, she could feel his hardness as it pressed into her. "I should shower," she said between kisses.

"Nah," he said. "I wanna taste you. Just how you are."

He ripped open her button-up blouse, and Faith didn't care about the buttons that flew around the cabin. Underneath, she wore nothing. Alex's fingers caressed her bare breasts. "Naughty," he said. He spanked her smartly, and she cried out into his mouth. "Take 'em off," he said.

She pressed herself up and started to pull at her shorts.

"No, stand up," he said.

Faith did as he said and balanced precariously on the soft mattress. She watched him pull off his pajama bottoms as she stepped out of her shorts and thong.

"Sit," he said and gestured to his face.

Faith smiled, straddled his face, and lowered herself onto his mouth. She groaned in pleasure as soon as his tongue slid across her clit and started to explore her depths.

With her hands braced on his toned stomach, she watched his cock grow even harder as he lapped at her juices. She reached for him and ran a thumb over his tip. The touch made him flick his tongue harder against her clit.

On all fours, Faith lowered herself and took him in her mouth. His tongue licked at her clit as he slid a finger into her. She called out as she trailed her tongue along his length.

He knew her body expertly, how each touch would make her respond. Alex brought her close to orgasm before he backed off. With every tease, it made her suck his cock with more vigor.

"Are you gonna come on my face?" he asked her. He'd taken his mouth from her center and bit her inner thigh.

"I want you to come inside me," she said.

He slapped her ass, and she pushed herself up. Faith moved down and grasped his shaft. As she lowered herself down, she faced away from him and felt his hands as they gripped her thighs. The angle hit her G-spot perfectly, and she had to pause to keep from coming immediately.

Alex squeezed her ass and pulled her cheeks apart with his thumbs. Faith traced her hands across her nipples and down to her clit while she started to ride him in reverse.

As she worked toward her climax, he twisted her hair in his hand and pulled lightly. Faith called out his name as she came.

"Fuck," she heard him say through gritted teeth as he spilled himself into her. Eyes closed in ecstasy, she thrilled at the throb of him inside her. She kept him inside her until she couldn't any longer. Their juices spilled out of her as she fell backward into his arms.

Alex kissed her forehead and pulled her close to him.

"I don't know what it is," he whispered to her, "but I just can't get enough of you."

She giggled. "The feeling is mutual."

"Even though," he said in mock seriousness, "I'm gonna have some serious explainin' to do to Caleb about his stained sleeping bag."

"Hey!" she said. "It's not my fault you do that to me."

"Do what?"

"You know," she said, suddenly shy. "Get me so wet."

"All right, all right. I'll take the blame, ma'am," he said. "But I have a real good excuse, I hope you know."

"Yeah?" she sighed. "And what's that?" Faith draped a leg over him.

"I'm no expert," he said, "but I reckon it's 'cause I'm crazy in love with you."

"Sounds like a good reason to me," she said. "Especially since I'm madly in love with you, too."

ABOUT VIVIAN WOOD

Vivian likes to write about troubled, deeply flawed alpha males and the fiery, kick-ass women who bring them to their knees.

Vivian's lasting motto in romance is a quote from a favorite song: "Soulmates never die."

Be sure to follow Vivian through her Vivian's Vixens mailing list (http://vivian-wood.com/get-news) or Facebook page (https://www.facebook.com/VivianKWood/) to keep up with all the awesome giveaways, author videos, ARC opportunities, and more!

VIVIAN'S WORKS

For more information....
vivian-wood.com
info@vivian-wood.com